Destiny Restored

Felicia Jedlicka

Book 4

For those who keep their promises, even when no one else does.

More titles by FELICIA JEDLICKA

DESTINY REJECTED
DESTINY RECLAIMED
DESTINY RAZED
DESTINY RESTORED

DÉJÀ VU

SAVE THE HUMANS

THE NECROMANCER'S CHILD

SISTER WITCHES
THE DEVIL'S SHADOW
THE DEVIL'S SOUL

THE NEBRASKA APOCALYPSE NOVELS
CORN COWS AND THE APOCALYPSE
COW TIPPING AFTER THE APOCALYPSE
CORN HUSKING AFTER THE APOCALYPSE

THE WARDEN SERIES
SUCCESSORS
RIVALS
LOVERS AND LIARS
BAD BLOOD
TENANTS AND TYRANTS
THE RING BEARER
GODS AND MONSTERS
BEASTS AND BURDENS
MAGIC AND MAYHEM
FORK IN THE ROAD
DETAILS AND DEADLINES

Destiny Restored

Felicia Jedlicka

All Aboard?

"What do you mean you couldn't retrieve his escape pod?" I asked as the ship rocked from an impact. The medical base I had recently escaped from had been destroyed, but there were still a hundred jetships attacking Captain Reynard's vessel. The biomechanoid soldiers of the Coalition's army would not give up or fall back. Surrender was not in their programming.

"I mean that it was programmed to go to the nearest habitable planet and Rey couldn't override it," Ayil yelled over the rumble of weapons' fire outside. "He was a little busy with other stuff." He pressed his face to the clear vinyl wall of my biohazard tent. "Don't worry, Terrin will be fine. This is the least danger he has been in for months.

I was about to explain that Terrin was not the one I was concerned about. My premature daughter was in the pod with him and would not survive long without medical attention. However, Dr. Kessler shoved a breathing apparatus into my mouth before I could clarify.

Since returning from the Coalition's laboratory, Kessler had put me through a vigorous decontamination process. Besides the concoctions the space station had exposed me to, my child had been shedding viruses that should have remained dormant in her body. Though I was immune to disease, everyone else on board was susceptible, so precautions had to be taken. After a full body exfoliation treatment, he drenched me, head to toe, in a chemical spray that stung like a bitch and made me smell like a farm animal.

I put my conversation on hold while Kessler checked my temperature, heart rate, and blood pressure. I was grateful Ayil hadn't been present for the earlier, more probing examinations. As it was, my tolerance for humiliation was reaching its limit. I was only wearing a pair of medical-grade granny panties and in place of a bra; I was hugging myself. This was the part of being a medical anomaly I had never gotten used to. Doctors poking and prodding me without regard for my privacy.

I dreamed of a day when people would no longer covet my DNA, but fleeing my home planets hadn't done me any favors. Mercenary lab geeks and hitmen had hunted me, and now my father's government—the Coalition—was coming after me with military force.

Contrary to the expectations of my people, my genetically engineered DNA could not cure humanity. Quite the opposite. My DNA allowed me to be the carrier of a viral weapon. One that would decimate every primate-based species in the galaxy if released.

The Coalition hatched this decades-long plot to incapacitate the empire, starting with my mother—the queen. Once the leaders were out of the way and nearly a third of the human population was dead, the Coalition planned to devise a cure miraculously. That cure would give them the leverage to take control of every planet under my mother's rule. Making them the largest and most powerful planetary alliance in the universe. They would be unstoppable.

Fortunately, the medical base where they had created this deadly virus was now space dust. The only proof it even existed was in my and my daughter's DNA.

"We 'eed 'o 'ind 'at 'od," I mumbled over my mouthpiece.

"We need to get the Coalition's zombies off our backs first," Ayil stated back to me like I was too stupid to notice the barrage of gunfire still pounding against the hull.

Dr. Kessler shifted me to look at him. Fully garbed in his hazmat suit, I could barely see his eyes. He shifted his pen light in and out of my eyes—checking my pupil dilation.

"Was she there?" Ayil asked somberly.

I glimpsed his indifferent expression before Kessler pulled me back to face him. Ayil no doubt knew the answer to his question already. He just had to hear the answer so he could begin to process his pain.

My eyes bloomed with tears as I thought about my friend. I had underestimated her and taken her for granted, but now, in the wake of her death, I wondered how many times she might have saved me from peril when I wasn't looking. I had seen the empire's tattoo on her chest. Was she loyal to me as a friend, or something more?

I turned to Ayil, since Kessler seemed to be through with my eyeballs, and pulled the plastic device from my mouth. "She saved us," I whispered. "Again." I chuckled. I pressed my hand up to the plastic tent, wanting so much to embrace my friend in this moment. He raised his hand and pressed it to mine from the other side of the plastic.

Ayil looked calm, but I knew Aresties' death tormented him. He never made a monogamous commitment to her, but he loved her. His past of forced prostitution had skewed his views of male-female relationships, as well as male-male relationships. While I was just screwed up enough in that department to earn his friendship, others did not fare as well.

The downside to that devotion meant we were on this dodgy escapade together. Besides losing Aresties, his son Edric was still missing. At least, I prayed he was only missing. If the Coalition picked up his escape pod, then he may have died on the base with Aresties.

"What about Edric?" Ayil asked, as if reading my thoughts.

I shook my head. "He wasn't there," I stated with enough certainty to qualify it as a lie. I refused to let him lose two people he loved in one day. He looked me over, checking me for the lie.

He must have been preparing himself for the worst news. "We will find him. I pro—"

An explosion rocked the ship, and a gust of air ripped Ayil from my view.

Suckered

"Ayil!" I screamed as his body slid down across the room toward a crack in the hull.

He arrived at the opening just as the capillary-like piping in the hull released its amber sealant. The fluid hardened almost instantly, preventing air from leaking out of the ship. Unfortunately, Ayil's foot had gotten caught in the flow before it had finished hardening and he was stuck. "Doc, you need to be done now," I told Kessler.

He nodded, but still injected me with something before I peeled away the plastic barrier. As cold air hit me, I realized I was still naked and grabbed a medical gown. I threw it on as I raced over to Ayil.

I skidded to a stop by his foot and examined his predicament. My hope that I could simply unbuckle his boot and pull his foot out vanished when I saw the amber clot had covered his entire calf.

Ayil looked back from his face-down position. "How bad is it?"

"Do you use this foot?" I asked.

"Ha, ha, just find something to cut me out."

I looked around the room for anything useful. Kessler had some medical tools, but scalpels, while sharp enough to cut the amber, would do little to remove it. I considered the option of brute strength and moved to search for a hammer and chisel instead. Ayil grabbed my ankle. "I'll be right back," I said, misinterpreting the reason for his clinginess.

"No, look." He pointed to the adjoining room.

I looked into the dark, empty room and saw a flicker of light that should have belonged to a candle. Instead, it was the red glow of super-heated metal being penetrated by a laser cutter. Even before my frustrated cuss words could leave my mouth, the laser pierced the hull, showering the room with sparks.

"Not this again," I grumbled and leaned down to Ayil's head and pushed the com device he had wrapped around his ear. "Rey, we got a suckerfish down here."

"I know, dear. Don't worry about it," Rey said cheerfully on the other end of the device. Ayil and I looked at each other.

"Ayil is stuck. I need to get him out of here before they breach the hull and start shooting."

"We're a little busy with the other forty jetships out here," Rayne said over the coms. "Can you figure something out?" I was about to ask him where I could find a sledgehammer, but I caught sight of something within the plastic maze of isolation tents. "Kit?"

"Yeah, I got it." I weaved and peeled my way through the plastic and retrieved a device that looked like a fire hose connected to a vacuum cleaner. Kessler had recently used the dermabrasion device to exfoliate my skin. With the click of a few buttons and a slew of safety warnings, I raised it to the level of rock erosion.

It wasn't the fastest process, and I was still risking taking off Ayil's skin if I didn't aim just right, but it would be safer than trying to crack the amber and certainly much faster than cutting him out.

I monitored the sparks in the other room to make sure they were still there. The moment they weren't, we would be in trouble. After several seconds, Ayil gained some room to shift since I had exposed his calf.

As I shifted my aim toward his shoe, the sparks in the other room subsided. I held my breath as I stared at the bright orange circle on the wall. It shifted and fell to the floor with an echoing *thunk.*

We were about to be boarded, but Ayil was still stuck.

Ayil tapped his earcom. "Gonna need some help down here. The bios are coming on board."

"Not to worry," Rey assured him.

"Not to worry?" Ayil mumbled and widened his eyes at me. "How is he a genius?"

The soldiers poured from the hole like black ants and lined up in formation. The clank of their heavy boots was almost rhythmic as they landed and repositioned. They scanned the area and immediately noticed Ayil and me on the floor in front of them. I swallowed hard as they raised their pulse pistols at us and marched forward to apprehend us.

I released the trigger on the abrasion gun and slowly twisted the nozzle to shrink the spray into a tight beam. The machine twittered an alarm warning me that what I was about to do was against the parameters of the machine and extremely dangerous.

I pulled the trigger and slashed the beam across the invaders at the midsection of their bodies. To my surprise and relief, the focused beam cut the soldiers in half. Their slightly bleeding torsos toppled to the floor.

"Holy shit!" Ayil looked back at me. "That was awesome. And kind of gross." He shifted away from the mixture of oil and blood that was oozing out of one of the downed corpses.

Another group of biomechanoids poured from the hole in the hull, replenishing the threat against us. I aimed my weapon again, but it beeped in objection. Whatever I had done had wasted the energy of the device.

The biomechanoids raised their pistols again and moved forward. Ayil groaned with effort, trying to yank his foot out by force. I slammed my foot down on the remaining amber formation and cracked it. Ayil yanked again, pulling his foot free from his boot. We scrambled away from the amber just as the biomechanoids opened fire. Narrowly missing death twice, we dove into the hallway and raced to a safer location.

Despite having multiple rooms to choose from, none of them would hide us well enough to give up our flight. We reached the central corridor of the ship and turned toward the cockpit where Rey and the others would likely be.

We reached the door, finding it locked. Ayil pounded on the door, demanding that someone open it. The screen next to it turned on and Rey peered at us. "Sorry, everything auto-locks during battles. You'll have to wait for the all-clear."

"We are being chased down by bios. Help us," Ayil insisted.

"Yes, I know. I am monitoring the situation. I need a few more minutes. Just don't get shot."

"Rey!" Ayil and I both yelled at him.

"Run now, please. Hurry!" Rey pointed behind us where the soldiers were coming into the hall.

"Shit!" I hissed as Ayil shoved me into motion. We barely rounded the next bend in the hallway before a torrent of charring shots hit the wall just inches behind us.

After another turn, we arrived at the interior freight zone—a slightly smaller cargo bay designed for more temperature-sensitive cargo like food. Just as we entered, a new group of soldiers entered from the other side. I wasn't sure if they were from the same ship or a second one, but they had already gotten the message that we were hostile and raised their guns to fire.

"Down!" Ayil leaped on my back, shoving me to the floor between a pallet of fruit and a stack of crated liquor. We landed as a shower of orange juice and guava nectar splattered down on us.

Ayil rolled off me and leaned against the bleeding fruit. "You know, I miss the days when Rayne would save us from danger."

I scooted next to him, completely clearing myself from the path of gunfire. "Yeah, you and me both," I said bitterly.

"Now what?" he asked as an orange peel slapped him in the face.

"Now we drink." I pulled a bottle of hard liquor out of the crate in front of us and twisted the lid off it. I took a big swig from it and handed it to Ayil. He looked at me strangely. Since I wasn't a heavy drinker, he probably assumed I was thoroughly yielding to my inevitable death. However, this was far from the worst situation we had ever been in and I would not let a bunch of militarized zombies take me out.

I winked at Ayil to let him know I was only being dramatic. He smiled and took a swig of the liquor before handing it back to me. I put the lid back on and shifted to peer over our barrier of fruit.

"Bottoms up!" I yelled as I tossed the bottle into the melee of pulse fire. The soldiers instinctively fired at the incoming projectile. Glass shrapnel scattered as the liquor ignited, sending fluid fire in all directions.

The biomechanoid uniforms were mostly fireproof, but the alcohol fed the fire, allowing it to burn longer. This caused damage to their face shields, which inevitably interfered with their detection scans.

Ayil followed my lead and threw a few more bottles. Since the soldiers had very hard and fast rules for the battlefield, they couldn't choose to not shoot the liquor bombs. The fire continued to rain down on them. The smell of burned plastic and whiskey permeated the room.

Soon the bottles started breaking on the floor because the soldiers could no longer aim accurately enough to break them. Ayil and I laughed as they searched the room, trying to get their bearings through their charred face shields.

"Cheers," I said, unable to resist adding one more cliché line to our battle.

Ayil laughed, but his levity died as he looked behind me. "Kit, look out!"

A hand gripped my neck, lifting me like a mother cat carrying her kitten. It dragged me back even as Ayil tried to hold on to me. I hung from the mechanical grip and stared at my terrified reflection in the glossy black face shield before me.

Ayil tried to barrel into the soldier, but another one captured him. He stared at me wide-eyed as he swayed like a slab of beef in the biomechanoid's grip. The bios programming included various murder methods. They didn't frequently break an opponent's neck, but they certainly could.

"Kit," Ayil whispered, fear overriding his instinct to kick and scream.

I waited for the soldier's hands to twist, but our spines remained intact. A moment later, they both let out a descending trill and slumped over.

Ayil and I dropped to the floor and squirmed away from the machines. We looked around for more assailants, but all the bios were inactive. They couldn't technically die, but apparently they had an offline mode.

Bitten

"Are you telling me you could do that the whole time?" I screamed at Rey as he waded through the bodies of the biomechanoids, pointing out body parts like he was shopping. The battle was over and everyone was safe, but Ayil and I had nearly lost our lives because Rey had failed to push a button.

"It's not that simple," Rey finally answered me.

"Since when is saving lives not that simple!" I pushed Rey back to get his attention. An action I knew I would regret, but I was too angry to think straight. "You have the power to stop wars and you just hold it in your hands like a deadly game of poker?"

"Yes!" Rey came at me, his face turning red, and he backed me into a crate of crackers. "Because it is a game of poker! And I'm the one bluffing." He was not a large man, but the psychotic break he seemed constantly to be on the verge of made him scary. "What do you think happens if the Coalition finds out I programmed a backdoor into the biomechanoid soldiers? They would shut it down—that's what? I have the power to collapse their entire army and they don't even know it. That isn't the kind of power one flaunts. I didn't use it to save the people on Trylin. I didn't use it to stop the massacre on my home planet that killed thousands of people. What makes you think I would do anything to reveal that secret for the two of you?"

I stared into Rey's distorted features and saw the source of his insanity. As the creator of the biomechanoids, he must have carried a great deal of guilt for their destructive force. However, knowing that at any moment, he could stop them must have been a constant moral debate inside of him. He had the ultimate power, but he could only use it once. When to use it was the hardest decision he would ever make.

Rayne stepped up beside us, not breaking us apart necessarily, since unlike me, he knew better than to get in Rey's way. "We had to destroy all the ships before we could shut them down. If the soldiers outside the ship suddenly went offline, it would be suspicious and encourage an investigation. This way, the Coalition will just assume Rey used a bomb, or some localized device, to take the rest of them down." Rayne rested his hand on my shoulder. I noted that Rey backed away as he did this. "I'm sorry. I thought you two could handle things out here."

"We can." Ayil came up beside me. "And we did."

"Yes, you did." Rayne glanced around the freight zone. He gave me a proud smile. "Still, I should have come down to help you. I thought it was more important I assist with the ships outside."

"It was, I'm sure," I said, relinquishing any annoyance I had for having to rescue myself. What was one more near-death experience? "I'm sorry, Rey. I didn't understand."

Rey had since left me to return to robbing the dead. He looked back at me, a quiet shame on his face. "I am glad you're okay," he said, making at least an effort to sound compassionate.

"Thank you," I murmured.

"Ayil, help us with this one." Rey waved Ayil over. With Mr. Davis's help, they pulled a prosthetic arm off one soldier.

"How's your neck?" Rayne asked, as I rolled my head around to get the kink out of it. Apparently, hanging by one's head does not constitute good chiropractic health.

"Just pinching a little."

"Here, let me." He turned me around and started massaging my shoulders. I groaned with appreciation and thanked him. The gentle pressure of his hands reminded me of why I enjoyed his company. Rayne had been my first proper relationship and lover. The only thing I knew about the pleasures of sex, he had taught me.

Since Rayne and Ayil had hijacked my wedding, I had unknowingly said my vows to Rayne. I had even signed the marriage certificate across from his name. In my mind, we were technically married, but in reality, he was just as much a stranger to me as the other sap I was going to be wed to. Not counting the years Rayne had spent in a freeze-lock coma, we had only been in a relationship for about a year.

Under normal circumstances, it might have been enough time to get to know each other, but our travels together had been anything but normal. He had spent more time rescuing me than he had talking to me. And, of course, that left us with an overabundance of thank-God-your-alive sex, which didn't readily allow for conversation.

Despite all that, we were making it work. We probably would still be together if it weren't for the fact that he was a lying bastard. Rayne's real name was Alex Turner, and Captain Reynard had employed him long before I knew him. He was Rey's personal assassin.

While I was on my home planets trying to figure out how to escape to the stars, there was a political chess game being played—mafia style. In fact, everything about Captain Reynard and his team was a little sketchy. Be it the financial maneuvers of his assistant, Mr. Davis, or Rayne's surreptitious murders, Rey had his finger on all the major players in the universe. He dictated who to help and who to hurt in order to keep the warfare to a minimum. It was an admirable endeavor, but one that came at the expense of a lot of bloodshed. And much of it landed on Rayne's hands.

Granted, I knew he was an assassin when I met him. I just didn't know he was a corporate assassin. The worst of it was if he hadn't gotten poisoned by his last target and ended up in a freeze-lock coma, he would have turned up on my doorstep to assassinate me. Which automatically downgraded our relationship status to: *it's complicated*.

Recent months revealed so many lies that I could hardly trust him, but that didn't mean I was completely immune to his charms.

Rayne's soothing grip on my shoulders halted mid-squeeze. I was about to beg him not to stop when he brushed the hair away from the back of my neck. I already knew what he saw there. I tensed, feeling his angry eyes surveying the damage left by Terrin's bite.

A love bite, by gattaw standards, but without the thick skin necessary to endure it, my neck received a rather noticeable scar. One I had been thus far hiding beneath my hair.

I turned slowly to face Rayne. The look on his face was a mixture of emotions—the strongest of which was disgust. My relationship with Terrin had put us at odds on more than one occasion. That, combined with him witnessing a rather heated bedroom scene between the two of us on the battlerunner, was only adding to his current level of emotion.

"It's not what you think," I whispered calmly.

"Hickies?" he whispered. "Bites? What's next?" He moved closer to me, eyes lit with fury. "I saw you two on that ship. How far will you let this go? You can't be with him," Rayne seethed.

It was the truth. I couldn't be with Terrin—or any gattaw. Our species were biologically incompatible.

It was a nice way of saying his penal spurs would rip me to shreds if we tried to have intercourse. The best-case scenario would be a very painful experience that could damage my reproductive system. And yet, despite that warning label, there was still an attraction between Terrin and I. So much so that we had been progressively getting bolder with our exterior pleasures.

But Rayne was right. It was a dangerous game of chicken neither of us was ever going to win.

"I didn't mean for" I considered my lie and opted for the truth instead. "I didn't mean for you to see that."

"Okay, time to go find Terrin." Ayil came up behind me and wiped his hands off on my medical gown rather than sully his own clothes.

Rayne's eyes seemed to bloom at the mere mention of Terrin's name. "The fuck it is!" he yelled and stomped away from us. "Let him rot."

"We can't leave him on an unfamiliar planet, Rayne," I yelled after him.

Rayne turned back. "We just blew up the medical base. If you think they aren't sending a battlerunner to investigate, then you're wrong. We need to get out of this system."

I looked at Rey. "I'm not leaving him behind."

Rey looked between Rayne and me as if he didn't want to choose sides. "Mr. Turner is correct about the risks, but we can return in a day or two and retrieve him."

"We can't wait that long," I insisted.

"Terrin can handle himself for a couple of days on his own." Rayne turned to leave again.

"But our daughter can't."

Rayne stopped. Everyone stopped.

"Aresties gave birth?" Rey asked.

"Yes," I said, bypassing the details of her emergency c-section, which was burned into my mind as yet another of her heroic acts.

Rayne looked back with growing shock and worry on his face. "I have a daughter?"

I couldn't help smiling at the pride on his face. He had always been more excited about this pregnancy than I had. I was glad to see he was still looking forward to fatherhood. "Yes, you do, but she is technically premature, and the birth was not exactly conventional." I turned to Rey to continue pleading my case. "I know Terrin will keep her safe, but he has no medical supplies. Nothing to feed her. I know it's a risk to stay in the area, but..." I looked at Rayne. "...our child is at risk if we don't."

Rey huffed out a breath. "I'll consult with Dr. Kessler. We'll need to get the child vaccinated before she can come on board."

"Thank you." I turned to thank Rayne as well, but he was already gone. Ayil gave me a small smile before hugging me.

"Congratulations," he said halfheartedly. I knew he was thinking about his son and I couldn't help feeling guilty that my baby would soon be home while his child was still missing.

Jungle

"I hate rainforests," I grumbled as Rayne and I trekked through the dense foliage of a planet called *Saltu*. Although it was habitable by galactic standards of temperature, air quality, and predator-to-prey ratio—it was far from hospitable. It took us hours to find a clearing to land our shuttle and even then, we had to send it into levitated orbit to prevent the ground cover from attaching to it. The planetary warnings dismissed notions of a "living forest" because researchers hadn't studied such lifeforms enough to positively identify sentient plant life. However, they noted that falling asleep without a knife or cutting tool was inadvisable.

With that in mind, Rayne and I aimed for a quick extraction without an overnight stay. Since it had taken us nearly twelve hours to locate the escape pod, we were also eager to get to Terrin before he opted to take a catnap.

Rayne pulled out the machete he had brought for just the occasion and began chopping through the vines and leaves that were preventing us from seeing more than a few feet in front of us at any time. Despite the daylight shining down on the planet, the canopy high above was keeping everything in a perpetual shadow.

I smacked another mosquito-like bug that was the size of my hand. He squashed just fine under the impact of my palm, but

I had to peel him off. The splatter of blood and guts left on my arm made me gag. I turned my head in case I needed to vomit.

Once my faculties were under control again, I observed the path created in our wake. The chopped foliage created a lovely green carpet that extended some twenty feet behind us. The rest of the path which should have extended into the clearing we landed in was not as visible as I would have preferred. Branches and leaves mostly obscured the daylight at the far end of our tunnel. The jungle seemed to close up behind us, making our trail of "bread crumbs" useless.

I reached down and checked the tracking device clamped to my hip. It was still reading the shuttle in orbit, and it was still registering the escape pod. That was all that mattered.

"Kit, keep up," Rayne yelled back at me. "We don't want to get separated in here. I don't have you on a tracker."

I ran to catch up with him and directed him to shift his movements to the right to avoid what I assumed was a giant rock coming up in the middle of our path.

After another minute, Rayne let out a frustrated huff. "So, are we ever going to talk about this?"

"Talk about what?" I asked, honestly wondering which "this" he was referring to.

"This thing with you and Terrin."

"Actually, I was going to let the topic fester for a while."

Rayne glared at me. "What can you possibly see in him?"

"Is it him that bothers you, or a gattaw in general?" I asked.

He scoffed and went back to chopping through the forest. "This isn't just a species thing—if anything, it's a culture thing. Do you know what that bite on the back of your neck means?"

I averted my eyes, not wanting to get into the specifics of Terrin's motivations.

"It's a symbol of ownership, Kit." I knew Terrin wouldn't agree with that statement, but I also knew it wasn't wrong. However, it was no different from an engagement ring or a devotion tattoo, or any other culturally recognized symbol of couplehood. Granted, Terrin and I weren't officially a couple and, at the time, he was acting on behalf of his steroid-infused territorial instincts, but...

What was my point again?

"Did you know the men make their mates walk behind them in public?" Rayne glanced back at me to see if I better understood the brutish, domineering culture that shaped Terrin. As if witnessing the dogfights firsthand wasn't proof enough for me.

"That's why they bite the back of the neck. So other men know the female is taken. Is that what you want, Kit? To be a kept woman, domineered by a man? Because I thought you were more independent than that." Rayne stopped and looked me over, searching for the woman he was describing. I didn't bother defending myself or Terrin, because he wasn't wrong. Terrin was not above his culturally mandated control issues. And I, despite my rebellious nature, was far more tolerant of his ascendancy than any other man.

"You know it won't work, right?" I could hear the pity in Rayne's voice now. "I get that you have a history with him. I know you're in love with him and there is nothing I can do to change that. I can accept I'm not your first choice." I looked away, not willing to pay credence to his suggestion that my relationship with Rayne was satisficing—just an alternative biologically sound lover to fill the void Terrin could not.

"Kit." Rayne holstered his machete and gripped my shoulders. "I know you're still mad at me and you aren't sure if you want to be with me anymore." Although I was pretty certain I had already decided not to be with him, I was willing to hear him out. He seemed to recognize this and continued. "What I saw on the battlerunner" He trailed off, his jaw clenching at the memory of my incident with Terrin. As it stood now, the interaction was so sullied by my mortification I couldn't even think about it fondly. The realization that Terrin had only indulged my unrealistic fantasies out of pity had also taken the shine off our time together.

"It wasn't... He didn't... We just" I babbled, trying to defend the event at least so far as Rayne's previous accusation.

He raised his hand and brushed my hair from my face, stilling my words and most of my thoughts. "Terrin's a good guy. I know that—dogfights aside—he would never do anything to disrespect you. And I can see how the two of you being alone there might have encouraged you both to... experiment." He pinched his lips together as if picturing this presumed relationship was forcing him to bite back a slew of cuss words. "But can you really see a future with a man who can't be with you the way a man is supposed to?" That same pity was back in his eyes. "Maybe it works for a little while, but, Kit, I'm telling you—not a man competing for your heart, but as a man—there is no way Terrin will be satisfied by a human woman."

Rayne held my face, ensuring that I looked at him. "You have to start thinking clearly. I know you know this, but I'm going to say it so you can hear it out loud, once and for all." Rayne's grip on my jaw tightened. "Regardless of how much he cares for you, Terrin needs a woman he can fuck. And you can never give him that."

An impermissible tear dripped down my cheek. I tried to nod, but Rayne had me held too tight. "I know."

"Then stop pretending you can," Rayne said through gritted teeth, as if trying to keep from yelling the words at me. "This isn't a fairytale, Kit. Terrin isn't a man cursed to be a beast. He always was a beast."

Rayne released me and pushed on through the jungle, slashing away anything that got in his way. I found it apropos that Rayne would choose the Beast as his metaphor for Terrin. However, when I considered it further, I realized there were plenty of fairytales involving one member of a couple changing to meet the needs of the other. While this martyr's intention is to prove their love, in reality, they create a foundation for bitterness.

Rayne's renewed efforts to clear a path revealed part of the rock I had warned him about. Upon seeing it in person, I gasped and nearly took off back down the path. "Rayne!"

"What?" he looked around for the danger because all he saw was a mound of green earth to his left. Seeing the horror on my face, he moved back to get a better view of the lump in our path. His mouth slowly draped open—matching my aghast expression. "Is that a skull?" he asked tentatively—in case he might have misinterpreted the moss-covered mass. "It looks humanoid."

I nodded, pointing out the jawbone that was slightly askew to the skull. It had the dentition of an herbivore, which eased my concerns of being eaten alive by a giant. However, the two puncture wounds in the dense bone of the skull alarmed me. Judging by the position of the head, a fall hadn't caused them. Unless something burrowed into the bone posthumously, they were the likely cause of this creature's demise.

What sort of creature—or creatures—could bring down prey this large?

Rayne ushered me forward, advising that we hurry, and I gladly followed.

Overgrown

After nearly an hour of chopping and several shift changes, the veil of foliage finally opened to a beautiful oasis. The sun shined bright over the crystal blue waters below. On the far side of the pond was a cascading waterfall that fed it.

I breathed in the fresh scent of life that smelled less like dirt and more like flowers.

"This way." Rayne directed me to a path that led down into the vale. When we reached the bottom, we both took a much-needed break. After a quick water test, I determined it was safe enough to wash up in, and even drink. However, rather than risk it, I used the filtered straw from Rey's emergency pocket kit to quench my thirst. "Pocket" was a rather inaccurate description since it was about the size of a fanny pack, but it was light and easy enough to strap onto my belt with the tracking device.

I checked the screen and noted that Terrin's escape pod had landed close to this location. If he had found this waterfall, I was certain he would have stayed nearby. Water was the first necessity of life, which was why the pod would have sought it out as a landing site.

"I'm going to release the beacon," I shouted over to Rayne. He had removed his shirt and was splashing water on himself, rinsing off the sweat he had worked up from chopping through the foliage. He nodded in agreement.

I pulled the beacon from my emergency pack and shot it up into the air. Unlike a flare, which only ascended and descended, this small device floated for hours, blinking and warbling at a pitch audible for miles. If Terrin heard it, he could find us.

Glancing at my tracker again, I noticed our shuttle signal was a little weaker than it had been when we arrived. I assumed the shuttle's orbit would have eliminated the dense foliage as a factor for interference. Anxiety curdled my stomach, but I ignored the feeling and turned my attention to Rayne.

He caught me staring at him and gave me a knowing smirk, but I didn't return it. I wasn't ogling his finely sculpted torso, as he likely assumed. "What about us?" I asked.

"What about us?" he asked.

"You're so certain about my fate with Terrin. What do you see in that *magic eight* for you and me?" I leaned back on my elbows to let my skin absorb some natural vitamin D for a change.

"I guess that depends on you," Rayne said. "Whether you can forgive me."

"Let's assume I do. What then?"

"What do you mean?" Rayne came over and stood in the path of my rays.

I opened my eyes and stared at him humorlessly. "My ship is destroyed. We've officially become parents. Now what?"

"Rey will let you stay on."

"And Ayil? We're a package deal, you know. And our daughter—and Edric when we find him. Rey is going to be fine with four civilian mouths to feed. Mouths that are of little use to his financial and political agendas."

The look on Rayne's face was much as I expected it to be, confusion slowly rising to worry. He hadn't thought about our future. He was hanging onto the hope of our relationship, much as I was hanging onto the hope of Terrin. Our lives may have collided in a very significant way, but that didn't mean we were going in the same direction. Quite possibly, we were going in opposite directions.

"Let's say I do stay on. How do we raise a child together? Never mind that Daddy kills people and Mommy is hunted by the Coalition. How do we educate her? How does she make friends? She'll be locked up on that ship, *protected* for as long as the Coalition knows she exists." Even as I said the words, I knew I was describing the same childhood I had experienced—only much worse. I at least had mansions to stretch my legs in. My child would have the stars, but that would be all she would have. Maybe some very monitored planetary trips, but then back home to the ship again.

"I don't know what you want me to say, Kit. Rey is the only man I trust to keep you safe."

"Yes." I chuckled to myself. "The only man."

The warbling beacon above us exploded, and the pieces fell into the pond. I looked around for the cause and saw Terrin standing on a cliff next to the waterfall—a small pulse pistol still outstretched in his grip. At some point, he had removed the arms of the biomechanoid uniform he was wearing and fashioned a sling to hold my daughter. I smiled up at him—as relieved by his safety as that of the baby in his arms. For one fleeting moment, I felt elated. Then Terrin aimed at me and fired.

Trap

Too stunned to move, I just watched him shoot at me. I waited for the incapacitating, potentially lethal hit, but he missed. "Kit, look out!" Rayne yelled just as I felt something wrap around my leg and yank me backward.

I slid across the ground back toward the treeline we had just emerged from. Rayne pulled his machete and raced after me. Unfortunately, another attacker thwarted his rescue attempt. A thick vine twisted around his leg and started dragging him back into the jungle as well.

I looked down at the green tendrils pulling on me. I tried to reach for my pulse pistol, but the vine had wrapped tightly around my leg holster, preventing me from pulling it free.

Terrin shot two vines hovering over my head. In my mind, I imagined a squeal of pain from them as their internal juices splattered all over me like blood, but the only noise around us was the waterfall and the cracking of tree branches.

Rayne cut through the vine that was tugging him away and slashed at three new ones reaching for him.

As I neared the treeline, I looked at Terrin. He was still shooting, but he wasn't hitting the primary culprit in my abduction. Sadly, he couldn't get a better shot because my body was in the path of his aim.

Rayne finally made some leeway with his attackers and pulled his pulse pistol. He shot the vine pulling me and it released, recoiling into the jungle like a wounded animal. I jumped to my feet and snatched my weapon while I was still able. I unloaded several shots at anything green moving in my direction.

As the attacks lessened, Rayne and I backed ourselves away from the trees.

"They get the hint pretty fast," Terrin called down to us. "But I would recommend you find some rocks to stand on. It seems to sense you better on the soil."

We moved back to the water's edge and found a boulder to stand on while Terrin made his way down to us. The closer he got, the more anxious I felt. My eyes settled on his chest—or, more accurately, the back of my baby's head. I was desperate to see her again. I had only held her for a moment after she was freshly born. Though exhilarating, my terror had soured the moment for me.

Rayne must have been just as anxious because he jumped off the rock and headed to meet Terrin.

"Rayne, wait!" I yelled after him.

"I want to see my child," he insisted.

"I know, but it's too dangerous for you." I moved to him and grabbed his hand. "You'll just have to keep your distance until Kessler can examine her. I'm sorry," I whispered and squeezed his hand. He didn't look at me. His mouth twisted in defiance, as if he might break free at any moment to be with her, but his body eventually went slack and he took a few steps back.

I nodded to Terrin, and he slipped off the makeshift baby sling and laid my daughter on a mossy rock for us to observe her. I gasped at her adorable face. When I had seen her last, her skin was slimy with mucus and vernix. If I'm being honest—she looked a little gross. Now her coloring was normal and her eyes were open. She stared back at me, those bright hazel eyes, trying to figure out who I was and possibly why I wasn't green like Nanny Terrin.

I wanted to hold her, but for reasons of spreading potential viruses to Rayne, I didn't. Plus, I didn't want to torture him any more than necessary. I was also a little afraid to hold her. Having lost out on carrying her in my body, I felt disconnected from the concept of motherhood. Looking at her this close, I expected to recognize her as my own, but I didn't. However, I could tell she belonged to Rayne.

I let out a barking laugh that could have easily turned into a tearful lament if I had let it. I glanced at Rayne, who was itching to touch her. "She has your eyes," I told him, hoping it might appease him a little. He paused and glanced between me and the baby. A small smile perched on his lips—pride for his part in creating a brand-new human being. That satisfaction was enough to settle him, and he took a seat on his boulder to watch her.

I dug through my emergency kit and pulled out the hypospray Kessler had created just for my baby virus factory. It effectively provided the antibodies she should have received in my womb. There was still some debate if she would require regular boosters, or if the viral production would become dormant once her body understood that they were the enemy and not part of the normal bodily process. Regardless, Kessler was prepared for every scenario. I knew that one of those scenarios was to eliminate her, but I was confident it wouldn't be necessary.

I gave the baby the injection, and she squawked with slight disapproval but didn't cry. I waited, observing her. Kessler had given me several worst-case scenarios should the baby have an adverse reaction to the vaccine. I was hoping none of them would be required. My first aid skills were rather poor and performing them on an infant appealed to me even less than an adult.

When there was no immediate reaction, I relaxed and turned to thank Terrin for his service as a babysitter. I suddenly remembered he was relying on his natural immunity, which, given his close contact with the child, may not have been enough. "Have you had any symptoms?"

Terrin shook his head. "No."

"No headaches, fever, rash—"

"I'm fine, Mallory." He smiled at my concern.

"Good." I got caught up in his eyes as he watched me. It had not been long ago that we had... Well, that I had... "I assume Aresties didn't make it," Terrin asked.

"No." I looked away.

"I'm sorry." Terrin rested his hand over mine. "I know you two were good friends."

"We were." I had known Aresties for a long time. And yet, I was wondering if I had known her at all. I could only presume she kept her status as "loyalist" away from me because she didn't want me to know. But why? What did her political views have to do with anything? "Did you know she was a loyalist?" I asked him.

"No, she never divulged her devotion to the queen to me. I only knew of her devotion to you." Terrin's thumb dragged across the back of my hand, a gentle caress. I looked down at the contact and then at him. There was sympathy in his eyes, but there was also something else. Something I wasn't used to seeing. An intensity I assumed I had inspired.

I glanced at Rayne. He was watching us, observing my reactions. I wanted and needed to talk to Terrin about what had happened before we arrived at the base. I wasn't sure I had the willpower to refuse him. Assuming he wished to repeat our experimental relations, I needed to say something before my body bypassed my brain.

The question was when. I couldn't wait until we were alone—that was just tempting fate. But I also couldn't do it right in front of Rayne—not that he wouldn't enjoy watching me snatch away that damned carrot again. It would have to wait until we were back on the ship.

Speaking of...

I drew my hand from beneath Terrin's and grabbed my tracker. "We need to get off this planet." I punched in our coordinates for the shuttle to pick us up. The device beeped, declaring that the signal was too weak to reach it. "The shuttle isn't responding."

"It's probably underground by now," Terrin said.

"No, we left it in hover-park so the vines wouldn't attach," I explained.

Terrin glanced at Rayne. "That doesn't do much good when the vines can reach out to it."

"Why would a plant want our shuttle?" Rayne asked.

"Why did it want the escape pod I landed in? Fortunately, I got all the necessary supplies out before it sank." Terrin looked around the area as if searching for an enemy. "I'm glad you both came to rescue me, but I'm afraid you've walked right into a trap."

"How is this a trap?" Rayne asked.

Terrin shifted to his left and started scraping at the dirt. Only a few inches down, he uncovered something white. Bones. "Do that anywhere in this valley and you'll find them."

Not quite questioning Terrin, but also very curious, I reached over and scraped an area behind me. Rayne moved from his rock and did the same. Within a few scrapes of the topsoil, we each found a set of bones. As small as a mouse or as big as...

I thought back to the giant in the middle of the forest with two fanglike punctures to its skull. Could a plant inflict that damage? Was it a feat of strength? Or was it proof of determination and patience?

I looked up at Rayne, suddenly anxious about our prospects for survival. He stood and scanned the jungle before looking back at me. "We'll just have to track down the shuttle and dig it out. Once we get to the door, we can do a blast burst to pop the shuttle out and disconnect the vines."

"That's an excellent plan, Rayne," Terrin said, "but I doubt you'll be able to make it back out of here."

"What do you mean?" he asked.

"You're welcome to try. I'm sure the machete is more efficient than my sword, but I don't think it will make a difference."

Rayne frowned and ran off to check our exit options. When he reached the top of the bluff, he began slashing at the foliage in his path. He made it a few feet in before one of his strikes resulted in the machete getting caught up on something. He yanked it free and moved to a new area. Each spot he moved to; he found a similar wall of thick vines. I got the sense that even if he cut through them, there would be another row waiting for him on the other side. And another, and another, that would ultimately trap him in a deadly maze.

"We're in trouble, aren't we?" I asked Terrin.

He tore his observational gaze away from Rayne and looked at me. His eyes flickered over my face as his expression morphed into the ardor I had longed for most of my life. He leaned forward and kissed me. It was a hello and a goodbye all in one. When he pulled away, he gave me a somber nod. "Yes, love, we are in trouble."

Foliage

My curses echoed through the valley as I kicked flowers and ripped leaves off plants that were potentially unaffiliated with the ones trying to kill us. Rayne had traded in his rescue efforts to ogle his baby girl. Terrin had moved closer to monitor me. At first, I thought he was going to stop my tirade, but I now suspected he was monitoring the treeline for a revenge attack.

"I will not be killed by a fucking plant!" I yelled at the top of my lungs. "Do you hear me?" I yelled upward to whatever deity might be listening to this planet.

Rayne chuckled. I looked back at him, but my annoyance only increased his laughter. He turned his amusement to Terrin. "Hitmen, slave traders, lab rats, the Coalition." Rayne rattled off my short list of challenges. "They should have just sent some poison ivy."

Terrin smiled at Rayne's dark humor and eventually joined in. Their laughter echoed through the valley.

"I'm glad you're both finding hilarity in this. I don't know why you're laughing," I said to Rayne. "You saw what that thing did to the giant. If something that big can't survive here, then we are screwed."

"You saw a giant?" Terrin tensed.

"Back a hundred yards, we found a skull," Rayne explained. "It was big."

"How big?" Terrin asked.

"As big as our shuttle. Why?"

Terrin looked around. "I've been hearing some noises just over that bluff." He pointed toward the waterfall. "Also, some fairly substantial ground vibrations. Footsteps. I've been doing my best to stay quiet and avoid drawing attention to myself. That's why I shot your beacon. I'm not interested in meeting whatever belongs to those footsteps."

I looked up toward the canopy above the waterfall and imagined the giant that might just crest the top of the treeline and peer down on us. I was still certain such a creature would be an herbivore, but that didn't make the prospect of a giant any less frightening. It could still step on me like a bug. However, that wasn't the biggest threat against us at the moment.

"Why is there no record of giants on this planet?" I activated my coms. "Rey, come in."

"The new shuttle should be there in twenty minutes," Rey responded.

"I know, put Kessler on."

A moment later, Kessler came on the line. "Yes?"

"Doc, what's your thought on plant sentience?" I looked over at the treeline, which at the moment, may as well have been a line of sentinels instead of trees.

"Well, there is evidence of communication between plants."

"Give me the short version." I stepped off my rock and Rayne shifted to stand.

"Kit."

Waving my hand at him, I continued to walk gingerly across the clearing, back to where the plant had attacked me.

"Well, the short version is plants don't have a central nervous system—no brain. Without an expanded definition of sentience, they cannot be considered aware."

"Then how did it know to attack our shuttle? How did it know to trap us here?"

"Plants can react to stimuli. Perhaps the energy coming off the shuttle drew it in."

I stopped at one of the downed vines we cut during our altercation. Nudging it with my foot, it tensed and wriggled like a snake. I leaned down to look at it closer. Rayne once again called to me, informing me of my stupidity. I brushed my finger along the vine, feeling the undulation of muscular contraction. "This isn't a plant," I said, more to myself.

Pulling out my tracker, I changed the image to a satellite view of the area. I zoomed out and noticed a similar valley several miles to the west before the view became too distant to identify the vacancies in the trees.

I adjusted the device's settings to the heat sensory mode so I could see beyond the jungle. With thoughts of a nervous system already in my mind, the image on the screen reminded me of brain neurons. Core cells that branched out and connected with one another.

However, I wasn't looking at a brain. This was the landscape of a planet. I zoomed back in on our location, noting that the *neuron* in this area matched the boundary of the tree line and craggy rocks. I looked around the beautiful oasis with fresh eyes. This wasn't a natural clearing at all. It was a barren tract of land. Trees couldn't grow because there was something beneath the soil. Something beneath the bones.

I looked down at the ground, suddenly very aware of just how much danger I was in. I turned a fearful expression to Terrin and Rayne. "Don't leave the rocks," I instructed them both forcefully.

Rayne narrowed his eyes on me, not understanding why I was suddenly standing so still.

"Kit?" Rey's voice was now in my ear. "I think I know what's happening. There is some kind of matrix covering the planet.

"Thanks, Rey, but I already figured that out. Can you tell me how we are supposed to avoid it?"

"Just south of your location is an extensive rock plateau. If you can make it there, you should be well out of the sensory range of these creatures."

I glanced at the waterfall, which was no doubt the beginning of the plateau. It was also could have been where the giants lived. Unfortunately, we didn't have a choice. It was the only haven for miles.

I turned to Rayne and Terrin. "We have to go up—" A yelp cut my words off as I dropped into a newly formed sinkhole. A hole leading to what would inevitably be a mouth.

Rooted

A spider web of roots snared me just below the surface of the ground. Dirt showered down on me as I tried to claw my way back out into the fresh air. The light above me clouded as plant tendrils filled most of the vacancy.

I coughed and spit dirt from my mouth. I looked around the hollowed-out ground, in search of a predator, but there was no open maw or gnashing teeth. This should have been a relief to me, but as the roots tightened around me, drawing my limbs apart, I found no satisfaction in avoiding a quick death. I suspected being quartered would be just as painful as being eaten alive.

I grabbed my pulse pistol while I still had some flexibility in my movements and started shooting at the plant. No matter where I hit, the roots seemed unaffected. The few I singed were replaced by others in a matter of seconds. I needed a flamethrower, not a match.

I hissed as I felt something burning me. I looked down at my arm and saw blood seeping from beneath one plant lassoed to my arm. It was feeding on me like a leech. Or perhaps it was injecting me with something. A poison? A blood thinner? Or perhaps it was a solvent so it could slurp me up like a spider feeding on a fly smoothie.

The thought of being injected with anything made my stomach twist with worry, but it reminded me I had more in my arsenal than my pulse pistol. I reached into my back pocket, retrieved the hypospray, and cycled through its alternate settings. They were all designed to save my baby, but surely one of them could negatively interact with this species.

At the very end, I found a setting that beeped, warning me it was only to be used during emergency situations. This *was* an emergency. Ignoring the recommendations of caution, I selected it and injected the largest tendril I could reach.

It took nearly a minute for anything to change, but when it did, it seemed to be unanimous across the vines. They didn't like what I had given them. Quivering and shriveling, they relinquished their grip on me. I dropped to the soft soil below and watched them retract, revealing the hole I had fallen through above. Rayne poked his head into it. "Kit!"

We reached for each other just as the ground beneath me quaked. The soft soil I had landed on was coming to life. The heat signature of the entity I had seen on the tracker's map was awakening—no doubt pissed off by the deadly cocktail I had just injected it with.

Rayne grabbed my wrist just as the ground fell away from my feet. I dared to look down, to see what I had narrowly avoided falling into. Beneath me, the last of the dirt fell into a deep, wet chasm. The mouth I had assumed was missing from this creature was now open and waiting for me to drop. Instead of gnashing teeth, it had a giant radula—a tooth-covered tongue—that was ready to drag me in.

Rayne pulled me up, keeping my legs from snagging. As my head rose above the ground, I heard Terrin's pulse pistol. He fought off the attacks of the creature's above-ground tentacles, which my poison didn't seem to affect much. With the baby strapped to his chest, he had a free hand to use his sword.

There was a hissing sound below me, not like a snake, but like air escaping a seal. I looked down just in time to see the creature's mouth pucker and spit mucus up at me. I shielded my eyes, and the secretion missed most of my upper body, but it coated my legs.

I rolled up onto solid ground, already feeling the effects of the final liquid attack. My skin was burning. "It's acid," I said, confirming my suspicions and possibly Rayne's. I wasted no time getting my pants and boots off, but some of the caustic goop had bled through the material.

"Come on!" Rayne tugged me up, and we ran toward the waterfall to rinse me off further.

I gasped as I came into contact with the coldest water I had ever felt. Rayne continued to fight off the vines with Terrin while I washed my legs. They were likely going to hurt like a bad sunburn regardless of how much I rinsed off, but I could at least reduce the severity of the burns.

When I felt recovered enough, I stepped forward instead of back and found myself in a cove behind the waterfall. Further inspection revealed it wasn't just a cove, but a cave—and a deep one at that. I poked my head back out to where the men were fighting. "Hey, in here!" I yelled at them.

They each glanced back, wary of my hiding spot, but they backed toward me. I moved away from the fall and waited for them to pop through. First Rayne, and then—hunched over to shield the baby—Terrin. They both looked around, still unsure about this option.

"Do you feel that?" I raised my hand, noting the breeze wafting through the cave, proof that it had an exit shaft somewhere down the line.

"Do you smell that?" Rayne asked with a frown.

The waterfall parted and a thick green appendage came through. Rayne shot at it, after which Terrin cut it with his sword. A nub of the vine dropped to the floor of the cave, writhing spasmodically.

Terrin nodded toward the cave. "I vote for that direction."

Rayne nodded, and we all headed deeper into the cave.

Cave

I had hoped the cave shaft would easily lead us to an exit and back into the light of day, but the further in we went, the more ragged the terrain became. In more than one area, we crawled rather than walked. I feared the exterior opening was going to be too small for us to get through. Despite our distance from the falls, the vines kept coming, circumventing the passageway easier and faster than we could. Whatever I had done to the creature, it seemed determined to reap its revenge, no matter how far we traveled from it.

"What is that smell?" Rayne complained when the noxious odor overwhelmed us. "It smells like... like" Rayne struggled to find the words.

"A toilet," Terrin submitted flatly.

"Yeah, like—" Rayne noticed Terrin was staring ahead of us. He followed his gaze and frowned. "Shit."

I looked down the path at the lit cavern ahead of us. The glow should have elated us because it would no doubt be the exit we wanted. However, in the center of the sun rays—illuminated like a single stage actor under a spotlight—was a great heaping pile of what was presumably feces. There was no denying what our noses were telling us, and even if we could delude ourselves, the swarm of insects circulating the blob was further evidence of it.

"Oh, no," I moaned and ran forward to confirm what I feared. I went as far as I could before the sea of manure began.

The ceiling of the cavern was open to the blue sky above, allowing us a simple escape—except for what lay beneath it.

I looked around the cavern floor that was covered in excrement. Meters upon meters of feces. Some piles were as tall as me, but even the least inundated areas were high enough to sink knee-deep into. I looked down at my bare feet and legs. I nearly vomited at the thought of walking through so much shit.

Terrin was right. This was a toilet. But not just any toilet. This was the outhouse of a giant. By the looks of it, possibly several giants with very fiber-rich diets.

Even as I felt my will to go forward ebb, Terrin's hand landed on my shoulder. "That should bring us out onto the rock plateau. If we're very lucky, Rey will have a shuttle waiting for us nearby."

"Uh-huh," I agreed numbly. Traversing a pile of shit was by far the least dangerous thing I had ever done in my life, but that didn't mean it wouldn't be the grossest. I looked at Rayne to see if he would have a brave face, but from what I could see behind the hand pinching his nose, he was just pissed. I imagined he was currently rethinking every decision that had led him to this point. Including his relationship with me.

"I see a spot we can climb up," Terrin announced and before I could mentally prepare myself, he trudged directly into the muck.

I let out several stuttered sounds that didn't quite qualify as moans or groans, just short laments that left my mouth gaping like a fish. Rayne fisted his hands and cursed before following Terrin in with matching bravado. With every slurping plunge of his foot, his face twisted into a deeper state of ire.

Terrin made it to the far end of the cavern where the rock face made a sort of ladder we could climb to get out. He looked back at me, expecting my arrival. There was a slight question on his face. I was also asking myself a similar question.

Am I the type of woman that would wade through shit to get where I wanted to be? I had been metaphorically wading through shit for the last few years, but this was literal shit.

Part of me knew Terrin could come back and toss me over his shoulder, saving me from this choice. I assumed that was his question, though. Would I walk, or would he carry me?

It was a stupid moment to be analyzing the modern function of chivalry. How the act of aiding a woman could lead to an assumption of inadequacy and therefore perpetuate an impression of dependency. A stereotype that women all across the galaxy were still fighting.

But come on! It's a huge pile of shit! Where the fuck was my white knight?

I gave up my hopes for a coat big enough to cover this puddle and marched into the poop. I told myself it was only mud. I held my resolve until I hit a warm patch, reminding me that the substance squishing between my toes had recently come out of someone's ass. I stopped and gagged.

My vision dimmed, and for a moment, I thought I was about to pass out. If I landed face-first in this stuff, I would be inconsolable.

"Kit! Look out!" Rayne yelled and pointed up.

I looked up to see what new danger I was being presented with. To my horror, the blocked sunlight was being caused by a mammoth descending bottom. A giant was sitting down to use his toilet, and I was right beneath him.

I grabbed a braided rope from the giant's toga-style garment—which he had not adequately pulled clear before sitting down. I used it to swing clear of the incoming deposit. The splash from the arriving fecal matter splattered shit across my back.

I was finally ready to vomit, but a strong serpentine grip on my leg distracted me from my gag reflex. My lower half slipped out from beneath me, but I gripped the braid of the giant's toga tighter, so I didn't drop into the waste.

I looked back at the vine yanking me toward the waterfalls we had left behind. A pulse pistol fired, but Rayne couldn't get the aim he wanted without the light to guide him. Terrin shot as well, but the vine seemed to be resistant to the energy now. It had a grip on me, and it wasn't letting go.

With so much force pulling on me, I couldn't risk letting go of the giant's clothes, not even to grab my weapon. Then I felt a tug from the rope. Light poured through a widening crack above me. The giant was getting up. He would soon pull out of my grip, leaving me to my fate with the underground creature.

Not to mention the shit beneath me.

"Hang on, Mallory!" Terrin yelled as the tendrils of the garment became as taut as the vine. The weakest link was about to break and that was me.

Terrin ran across the ordure and slashed his sword through the vine attached to my leg. I was relieved to be free, but the sudden change in tension slingshot me upward. As I rose so high, I dismissed my initial dread of falling back into the toilet because I feared a landing not cushioned by shit.

I hit the back of the giant and released one hand to grab a new spot on his garment. The braided net-like structure was easy to hold on to, and I looped my legs through it to ensure I would not drop to my death.

For a few moments, I just rode the back of the giant, unsure of what to do next. It wasn't until we came to a stop; I suspected I was not out of danger. Behind my giant was a second giant. He sat cross-legged on the rock plateau, snacking on what looked like a tree. His features were very much humanoid, although a good deal rounder than I expected. He had chubby cheeks and a bulbous nose—even his ears were puffy.

As he rolled his jaw, chewing on his tree, he stared over at me. I stared back at him. He was watching me like one might watch a rat scurrying around in a cage—curious, but by no means afraid. I, on the other hand, was wide-eyed and shaking, because I knew there was no cage to protect me.

"Kit!" Rayne yelled from below as he ran toward me across the rock ledge, having somehow made it out of the hole. Terrin was only slightly behind him, shielding the baby from too much bobbing as he circumvented the rock crevices.

The sitting giant turned his attention to Rayne, and, like me, he froze in fear. The giant stared at him for a long moment before taking another bite of his tree and then staring off at the horizon.

Rayne moved forward again, and I climbed down. By the time I reached the bottom of the giant's garb, he was just moving again. A quick jump and a dance to avoid his feet left us with only the munching giant to worry about. Fortunately, he had no interest in us.

I checked my tracker and determined our new shuttle was close to us. I was grateful for that small win, since I felt, looked, and smelled like shit. "Come on, this way." I waved Rayne and Terrin after me and led the way past the giant. He took some interest in our passing, sniffing the air. His brow rumpled a bit, no doubt displeased with the stinky insects intruding on his mealtime.

I saw the shuttle in the distance and ran toward it. I wanted off this planet as soon as possible. As I climbed into the waiting shuttle, I took the driver's seat. I had no interest in sitting in the back with either of my love interests. Once they were secure, we ascended from the planet. As I looked out the window, I observed the long rock plateau below us widen into an expansive surface. Dozens of giants occupied the large island of rock. While the peaceful vegetarians snacked on foliage, the carnivorous forest surrounding them was salivating and waiting for its next meal.

Bonding

"Will she be okay?" I asked Kessler as he emerged from the extensive plastic tenting that kept my baby girl from infecting everyone on Rey's ship.

Kessler clicked off his electrostatic barrier and frowned at me. "She is... strong. As I suspected, she isn't so much afflicted by the viruses as she is producing them."

"Still."

"The inoculation has helped, but there's a few I need to reformulate for."

"So, for now, she's the bubble baby?"

"I'm afraid that is the safest protocol. You're welcome to see her, but you'll need to be vigilant with your PPE, so you don't carry anything out to us. I've also put a small receiver in her crib." Kessler pulled a coin-sized pink disc from his pocket and handed it to me. "It's fairly simple. Just press and hold to speak. I know it's not the motherly embrace you desire, but a mother's voice has been shown to reduce stress hormones in children and increase oxytocin, which is a social bonding hormone."

I looked down at the device. It was indeed not a hug, but it was as much as I ever had while she was inside of me. A distant voice eager for her arrival and promising her love.

"Much like our coms, it has a rather significant range—" Kessler's words cut off as I hugged him. Surprised by the abrupt gratitude, he carefully patted my back.

"Thank you," I said as I retracted. He shrugged, indifferent to the comfort he had brought me. "You are a good man, Doctor."

His jaw tightened, and he looked away from me. "Well, history will say otherwise, but thank you." He moved away, unable to tolerate any further accolades.

I turned to the blur of a crib several plastic sheets away and clicked on the device. "Hi... sweetie. I guess Daddy and I are going to have to find you a name. Don't hold your breath, though. We don't agree on much."

I glanced around to make sure I was alone. Kessler had gone into the adjacent lab to do computer work. With no witnesses to judge, I attempted my very first lullaby. It was a doleful one my father had sung to me well into my youth, but it never made me sad to hear him sing it. Unlike me, he had a beautiful singing voice, and I relished the lyrics from his lips. I only hoped my daughter would hear her grandpa do the song justice.

Rivalry

There had never been a greater need for a shower than after taking a walk through a giant's sewer. After nearly twenty minutes of scrubbing between my toes to ensure not a fleck of feces remained, I slipped out of the ship's communal shower area and headed back to my room. On my way down the hall, I heard voices coming from inside Terrin's room. I stopped to see who he was conversing with.

It was Rayne. And though the dialogue was calm enough to be considered civil, it was far from a pleasant exchange.

"I saw what you did to her," Rayne said.

"Are we speaking of the incident on the battlerunner?"

"I'm talking about the bite."

There was a long pause before Terrin responded. "That was a mistake. One fueled by... too many emotions to explain."

"Why are you doing this? Why are you going after her now? I thought you had accepted your shortcomings."

"Believe it or not, I have no desire to compete with you. The very idea of it seems beneath me."

"Then why the seduction?"

Terrin scoffed. "I'm hardly doing anything to warrant that title."

"She's in love with you and you know it—we all know it." I cringed at the suggestion that my adoration for Terrin was so obvious. As if I were a smitten teenager with absolutely no propriety or restraint.

"Yes, I am aware of how Mallory feels about me."

"Then why torment her?"

There was a long pause. "I am reluctant to admit that I enjoy Mallory's attention. And I can hardly stop myself from encouraging her."

It was Rayne's turn to scoff. "You're being just as stupid as she is."

"Perhaps. Perhaps, not."

"What is that supposed to mean?" Rayne asked.

"It means I'm a different person than when I first met her and she has changed as well. I'm not going to stand aside this time, Rayne. I tried that once, and I regretted it immensely."

"Stand aside? Is that what you did? Last time I checked, she chose me."

"Mmm, I think you mean she chose your penis. A logical choice, no doubt. In the competition for virility, you are a step ahead of me. I cannot, as of yet, fornicate with her as two people are intended. I also cannot provide her with children—a factor that becomes increasingly more important to me as I age. However, I do love her and she loves me. I won't relinquish the idea of being with her so readily."

"Whatever your feelings are now, that doesn't change the fact that you are putting the moves on my wife."

"I imagine it's that title of ownership that makes my advances so offensive to you."

"Says the man who bit her."

"I don't expect you to understand that aspect of my culture any more than I can understand love being solidified by paper contracts. But if we are speaking strictly of documentation, then you must know signing a false name to that document will automatically void it. Regardless of the blood stamp—you are an imposter and therefore not legally her husband. You never were."

"And yet we've been happily consummating ever since," Rayne said smugly.

There was a brief pause before Terrin's deep laughter resonated in the room.

"What's so funny?"

"I was just thinking regardless of whose bed she is in; she will always love me. And even though she chose to be with you, you were always just a surrogate for me." There was a long pause. I could only imagine the feral look on Rayne's face as he stared at Terrin.

"I'll be sure to remember that the next time I make her scream out my name instead of yours."

"And when will that be?" Terrin asked. Another long pause. "I don't expect you to step aside, Rayne. If you truly love Mallory, then you should fight for her with every last fiber of your being. However, as I said, male competition does not interest me. I consider you an ally and I don't wish to lose that rapport simply because we are interested in the same mate."

"What exactly do you want, then?"

"At some point, Mallory will have to decide what her future will be and who that future will be with. When she does make a decision, I only ask that you accept it."

"Will you?"

"I want Mallory's happiness above all. I can't provide her with any more children and our intimacy is handicapped, but I do love her and I am finally ready to surrender to that love. If that doesn't overrule being with the father of her child, then I will accept it. Unfortunately, since my heart can only bear so much, it would also mean losing her as a friend—and that is the part I most dread. She has come to provide a great deal of entertainment to my life and I will miss her as dearly as..." Terrin trailed off and for a moment, the room was silent. "At any rate, I have said my piece and made my intentions known. I apologize for my belated declaration, but I wasn't quite certain until recently that I wanted to pursue anything beyond our friendship."

"Am I understanding you correctly? If she chooses me—again, you will leave—for good?" I heard Terrin take in a deep breath. "That's what you meant, wasn't it? If you can't have her as a lover, then you won't have her as a friend."

There was a long pause and my heart raced as I waited for the answer I didn't want to hear.

"Yes, I think that would be my only option."

"Good."

I scurried away from the door and rounded the hall before Rayne could catch me eavesdropping. Inside my room, I considered the ultimatum Terrin had unwittingly laid at my feet. Be his handicapped lover or be his nothing.

It was a cruel choice, one that demanded so much sacrifice on either side. As much as I loved Terrin, I knew Rayne was right about us. Two adults could not live happily without intimacy—especially not at the beginning of the relationship. It was one thing to lose one's love life at the end of a relationship when old age or sickness demanded it. But to never be with them at all. Was there a love strong enough to endure that? Perhaps there was, if the alternative was to lose him completely.

I couldn't fathom my life without Terrin. Even in the years before we reunited, I thought about him so frequently it bordered on obsession. Losing him now would be almost as painful as when I thought he was dead. Worse, possibly, since death at least demands a lack of hope. So long as he was alive, I would long for him.

Queen Mother

Naturally, getting to my mother was not as easy as just showing up on her doorstep. The Coalition's threats against me had put her on high alert and forced her to take military measures to protect me—and, more importantly—herself. Given the infinitely rising threat against my life and the political unrest regarding my loyalties, it was just as dangerous for her to come to me as it was for me to go to her. However, after some debate with her liaisons, we agreed on a safe rendezvous point.

When I stepped outside of the shuttle, a harsh, cold wind hit me with gray sediment from the planet's surface. I pulled my goggles down over my eyes, sparing my corneas the abuse of an unnecessary etching procedure.

A dry storm of angry swirling clouds had blotted out the sunlight of two nearby stars. The only source of light around me, other than the lantern on my belt, was intermittent flashes of lightning. Preluded by an ominous rumble of thunder, each flash afforded a view of the static dust veil all around us. If it weren't for my anti-static garb, I would have been glowing like a light bulb filament.

Besides the weather, a treacherous maze of jagged rocks and deep caverns made the surrounding terrain too dangerous to explore. Straying away from our designated landing site was likely to result in a bloody, if not deadly, fall.

Ayil stepped out onto the ramp with me. He immediately cinched up his long trench jacket and positioned his goggles over his eyes. "This trash planet is where your mother wanted to meet?" he yelled over the howling wind and crackling air. "She really doesn't like you, does she?"

I knew he couldn't see my narrowed-eyed glare, but I could see his wise-ass smirk just fine. "I think this has more to do with protecting herself than it does with getting revenge on me," I defended. "But no, we don't get along that well," I added.

"I don't like this," Rayne said behind us. He peered out over the horizon with every gap in the darkness, searching for the danger that was always around us. He hadn't come out far enough to resort to the diminished visibility of his goggles yet. "This looks like a trap. There could be people everywhere and we wouldn't even see them."

"We don't have a choice. This is where my mother's liaisons wanted us to meet."

"And you trust them?"

I perked a brow at Rayne. "Yes, but I have been known to make bad choices in that area." Rayne paused his perimeter search to give me a sour look.

"There." Terrin pointed his finger over my shoulder, disrupting my standoff with Rayne and directing my gaze to the glow of an arriving shuttle's landing burn-off.

I wiped my goggles off and squinted to see out through the haze of dust. The shuttle lowered its rear loading ramp. As soon as it hit the ground, two neat, organized rows of soldiers stomped out of it in unison. They were each in uniform gear, including helmets and very large pulse rifles.

"Let me get this straight," Ayil said, raising a finger at the arriving squad. "We had to leave our weapons on the ship, but those assholes get to bring cock cannons."

"If we want my mother's help, we have to play by her rules." I sounded and felt like a beaten dog, but I knew better than to fight my mother. I had spent years under her thumb and I knew exactly how hard she could press.

"This is ridiculous." Rayne grabbed my arm and pulled me back into the shuttle. "We can't be sure the Coalition didn't intercept your message. This could be them posing as your mother."

"We don't have a choice."

"Yes, we do. We can get the hell out of here. This is too much of a risk, even for us. Can you honestly tell me, without a doubt, that every person in your mother's employ is trustworthy? How do we know her people won't just gun you down like your father's people?"

I ripped my goggles off and sloughed off his grip. "I don't, Rayne! But you know what I do know? I know, until this is over, my child will suffer the consequences of my creation! I'm not going to spend the rest of my life on Captain Reynard's ship running from the Coalition. I'm also not going to let an attempted genocide go unanswered for. There is only one person who can even begin to deal with the threats against the empire and that is my mother! So, no, we aren't leaving."

I re-positioned my goggles. Rayne's frustration dimmed into an angry bitterness and he put his on as well.

I knew what he was thinking. He was thinking the same thing I was. Asking for asylum with my mother was pretty much like walking into the prison I had escaped from and asking for a room for the night. There was a strong possibility I would never leave Brahama again.

I was certain my mother had accepted I was not fit to be a queen in her stead, but that didn't mean she wouldn't keep me contained for my *protection*. The truth was, I rarely predicted my mother's actions. As my mother, she was an open book, readily affectionate, but the moment she put on her crown, so to speak, she became a ruthless leader committed to the empire—and only the empire.

Regardless of my mother's split personality, I had made a promise to Aresties to get her stolen information to her. I hadn't mentioned the drive to anyone. I was certain Rey would have wanted to decode it and find out what secrets she had uncovered. Since Rey was more of a referee on the sidelines, rather than a player in this game, I thought it would be best to keep him out of the loop.

I took my first tentative steps off the shuttle's ramp. Bracing against the corrosive wind, I immersed myself in the curtain of gray. I could see in the distance a cloaked figure emerging from between the lines of soldiers. Tall, slender, and graceful. My mother. I wasn't sure how she managed to look distinguished and elegant while fully shrouded in amorphous black, but I was already dreading my decision to contact her.

There was no doubt in my mind it was the right choice. I simply wasn't ready to accept the responsibility, guilt, and punishment for the trouble my fleeing had ultimately brought to her doorstep. Not that my escape would be of the remotest importance when compared to the real reason behind my creation, but that didn't matter. She would still take every opportunity to remind me it was ultimately a selfish act that left the empire without a successor.

"Hindsight is not a replacement for forethought." She would say to me at some point.

Oh, how I looked forward to that conversation.

Terrin and Rayne took my flanks less than a step behind me, mirroring my mother and her two Royal guards. Ayil followed in tight behind me.

As we neared the group, the two lines of soldiers broke away from their positions and jogged up around us in two wide arcs, ultimately surrounding us in a loose circle.

"Son of a bitch," I heard Rayne mumble as he shifted to keep the guards in his line of sight.

Intentionally or otherwise, Ayil and Terrin also shifted, leaving us in a rather underdeveloped circle within their larger circle. Despite the organization and the dominating numbers, the soldiers kept their weapons raised high and pointed to the sky rather than at us.

I looked at my mother, trying to peer beneath the heavy draping hood she was using to protect herself from the grating wind. "I thought this was meant to be a peaceful meeting, Mother."

She took a step forward, away from her guards. I also stepped forward, trying to meet her halfway, even though we were still several feet apart. She raised her arms and reached them out as if inviting me into them. I felt relieved that she wasn't going to immediately start laying into me with a guilt trip. I walked toward her embrace. Barely inches from her, I realized something wasn't right. My mother may have missed me. She may have even wanted to forget my indiscretions and go straight to our reunion, but that wasn't what she would do.

My feet skittered to a stop before I reached her, and I backpedaled. "You're not my mother!" I screamed at the unfamiliar jawline peeking through from beneath the black hood. I turned to run and rejoin my circle—tiny as it was, but a small blinking ball landed at my feet, and before I knew it, a bubble of yellowish haze blocked my path to them.

Terrin lurched toward me, but the storm's atmospheric conditions energized the static energy wall, causing him to be thrown back. Rayne pulled a well-hidden knife and attempted to attack one guard, but their weapons descended in unison, aiming at all of them. They each looked around at the multiple threats. Ayil looked at me—as if I might have the answer to this predicament. Our plan was disintegrating quickly.

The shield twinkled with every piece of sand that hit it, unsuccessful in breaking through. The bitter cold remained inside my containment, as well as the cloaked figure and her two best guards.

Despite being unarmed, I turned to face the trio, crouching to prepare for a physical battle. I gritted my teeth and gave them my best snarl when they didn't immediately attack. "Come on! Let's get this over with."

The cloaked figure glanced to her right and the flanking guard stepped forward. I shifted my attention to him and smirked slightly. He tipped his head to the side. The heavy helmet made him look more like a bobblehead doll. "Go on. Shoot me."

The guard turned to the cloaked woman as if needing further orders. I didn't bother waiting for the illustrious queen impostor to give him an answer. I jumped on the guard and we toppled to the ground and wrestled over his gun. The other two frantically tried to pull me off. Their combined yanking only assisted my efforts in pulling the rifle from the guard.

I threw back my elbow, knocking the woman away. I kicked my foot into the chin of the second guard, who stumbled back. The guard below me tried to get up, but I pressed my foot into his chest, forcing him down again. I raised the rifle and aimed it at the bobblehead helmet.

I opened my mouth to rattle off my demands. Among which was, *how the hell did you infiltrate my mother's army?* Before I could spout a single derogatory word about their inadequate fighting skills, the cloaked woman screamed and dove across the guard.

Baffled by the oddity of it all, I didn't notice the second guard had recovered from my kick. He pressed the muzzle of his gun hard against the nape of my neck. A gloved hand reached over my shoulder and gruffly removed the rifle from my possession. He handed it back to its original owner, and seconds later; I was in the same predicament I was a minute ago.

"Do you know what the queen does to traders?" I asked them. "My mother is very old school. She still executes enemies of the crown. Each one of you will meet the edge of her blade before your elder days. If you are very lucky, she won't sentence you to the *nines* as well."

The muzzle resting on my neck dropped, and I heard a shuffle as the guard removed his helmet. "Oh, don't be ridiculous, Kit."

A familiar feminine voice scolded me. "We haven't used the nines in seven generations."

I looked back at my mother in full guard uniform. Her hair was pulled back and slightly sweaty from being under the helmet. She looked a little thinner than I had remembered and she was without a layer of makeup, but it was definitely her.

"Mother?" I turned and gawked at her with a slack jaw. "What the hell?" I looked at the cloaked woman, who I now recognized as her dressing maid. The other guard removed his helmet, revealing the gardener, who was also the maid's husband. No wonder I had beaten them so easily. "I almost shot him—I could have shot you."

"It's not loaded, dear." My mother rolled her eyes as if the idea were preposterous.

"Why didn't you say something?"

"I tried, but the damn helmet muffled me. Although I don't imagine you would have heard me over your macabre threats."

"Why did you impersonate your guard? Why are you holding my friends at gunpoint?"

"Don't get mopey. There are too many threats to count these days."

"My friends would never hurt me."

My mother moved to the edge of the encompassing shield and looked out at Terrin, Ayil, and Rayne. Terrin gave her a slight nod, which she surprisingly returned. Ayil looked at her more severely than I expected. He had never been a fan of my family's situation. It was too far from torturous to warrant pity, but he simply couldn't tolerate anything resembling captivity or censure. Rayne, on the other hand, stared back at her with a cool, almost blank expression, like he was sizing her up. She was sizing him up as well.

"Although your safety is my utmost concern, Kit dear, the reason for my deception has far more to do with protecting myself." She turned to face me again, her eyes dimming with a tenuous sorrow. "You aren't the only one who has assassins knocking on her door."

I frowned, wondering if that was a recent development or just something she always had to worry about. It was true my mother was seldom alone—guards, chaperones, her lady's maid. There was always someone to help, should she need it. I had never questioned their roles beyond that of an over-privileged annoyance. Had I hung around, I might have learned the true burdens of leadership. But I hadn't.

"Well?" My mother raised her hands. "You wanted this meeting. What did you want to speak to me about?"

I glanced at the other two, who were standing tall again, waiting for a command. Had it been a different circumstance, I was certain the maid would have offered me a warm beverage.

"I need your help."

"Is that so?"

I blinked at her. She wasn't going to make this easy for me. "You know the Coalition sent their military after me."

Susan's brow perked as if to say, "*So what.*" "Yes. I heard about the attack on the gattaw ship. I assumed you were dead. I had even begun to mourn your loss." Her eyes brimmed with tears, but not a single one fell. They wouldn't dare. "If it weren't for your Aunt Scarlet and cousin Elder, I wouldn't have even known you were alive. I sent General Sanders out to retrieve you once and for all, but even she let you slip through her fingers."

"I didn't mean to worry you." I took her hand. "I'm sorry."

She looked down at the contact and scoffed. "We are so far past apologies, Kit. I can hardly stand to look at you right now." I wilted away from her, dropping her hand. "I'm still deciding between hugging you and slapping you." She took in a breath and stepped away from me, staring out of the containment. The lightning was still the only light other than the lanterns bobbing around on our belts.

This was the meeting I had expected to have with my mother. A mix of emotions that left us both overwhelmed, even as we starved for more. There was nothing easy about having a relationship with my mother. There would likely never be a middle ground for us. All we had was our separate corners. On the rare occasion we met in the middle, it inevitably led to us fighting another round. Then back to our corners, we would retreat—the cruelest of us declared the winner. My mother was the reigning champ.

"What do you really want, Kit?"

"Asylum for one."

"Asylum?" Susan chuckled. It was a mirthful sound that should have inspired infectious laughter. "You want to come home, is that it?"

"Yes."

"The universe is finally too dangerous for you?" I didn't answer. She was enjoying her power trip just fine without me feeding her more. "I've waited years for this moment. I thought it would feel better." She turned around and rolled her jaw. "Go on then."

"Go on, what?"

"I want you to ask me, Kit." She strolled back to me, eyes hungry for my submission. "I want to hear you make your official request to your mother, the queen."

Despite extensive training in sycophancy, I did not excel at knuckling under. However, disrespecting my mother might ruin my chances of going home. And declining the command of my queen could potentially endanger me.

I squared my shoulders, pocketed my pride, and spoke the words she had wanted. "Your Majesty, I formally request asylum." I paused, looking deep into her narrowed eyes. I swallowed hard, forcing the lump in my throat to drop back down. "I want to come home, Mother."

Susan's face contorted as she tried to reject her emotions. The tears were back and impermissibly fell down her cheeks. She shook her head and groaned. Then she stepped forward and pushed into my space, embracing me. Without her high heels, we were breast to breast, with only an inch or two in her favor. She pressed my head against her shoulder, gripping my hair tightly between her gloved fingers. The almost painful embrace felt more like being held captive than being hugged, but I didn't mind. This was progress, as far as I was concerned.

"I should have put you in prison, child," she ground the words through clenched teeth. "I should have beaten you within an inch of your life. The embarrassment and turmoil you have caused me warrants a death sentence."

"I'm sorry." I cried with her, sniffling like the ten-year-old child she always turned me into when she was mad. "I really am."

Her reserve, what little she had left, caved, and she shifted her arms to wrap around me in a proper hug. It felt good.

It felt like home.

Plan B

As intense as my mother's affection was, it only lasted a moment. She cleared her throat, wiped her eyes, and returned to my view as the same irritatingly stoic woman I always knew. She nodded to her gardener, and he retrieved the flashing orb, the source of our containment. The field disintegrated around us and my mother's maid came to her side, shielding her now exposed face from the gritty wind with her cape.

"Time to go," Susan instructed and ushered me forward with the arm she had around my back.

I walked with her until I heard Ayil yell my name. I turned back, despite my mother's effort to keep me moving. I saw Ayil and the others still being held at gunpoint. The guards had closed ranks, tightening their already tense standoff.

"Mother, call off your men." She didn't answer me and I looked at her. Her expression was cool and evading. "They are coming with me."

"That wasn't part of the deal."

I yanked myself out of her grip and pointed back at them. "I am not leaving without them."

"Yes, you are, because I am not leaving without you."

"If you don't allow them transport to Brahama—"

"They will not step one foot on my planet. I have had enough of this, Kit. No more gats, no more assassins, and no more..." Susan glanced at Ayil. "...whatever he is. Just come with me, so I don't have to make this difficult." Her eyes were pleading, but the tone of her voice told me she fully intended to get my cooperation, one way or another.

"I'm sorry, Mother, no deal. It's either all of us or none of us. These men have protected me time and time again. I'm not leaving them behind." My mother rolled her eyes and raised her hand high in the air. "They deserve your—" I jolted forward from a shot to my back. It stung like a pulse pistol, but there was no current making my teeth chatter.

Rayne roared in objection and even tried to break through the line of guards. The men held their own, ramming the butts of their rifles into his face until it quelled his immediate threat. I also dropped to the ground, feeling the world swirling around me.

I looked up at my mother. "Did you just shoot me with a tranquilizer?" I slurred.

She pursed her lips. "You didn't think I came without backup?"

I glanced around at the landscape, thoroughly impressed by any sniper that could see through a quarter mile of darkness and dust. Then again, there were always night vision goggles with heat signature trackers.

Susan Mallory was always prepared.

Fortunately, I was prepared for her doggedness.

I cuffed the communicator device strapped to my left shoulder. It bleeped to attention and Reynard's voice came across loud and clear. "Hellooo," he sang. "How's it going down there?"

"Time for plan B." My lips blubbered the words, but there was enough intention in them to cause my mother's concern. Plus, the glare I directed back at her alluded that I had an endgame as well.

Susan's head tipped as she examined me more carefully. "What have you—"

Before she could finish her sentence, a torpedo whipped through the atmosphere on a mission. It collided with her shuttle, brightening the land with a momentous explosion. It was a bit overdramatic, and a waste of a perfectly good shuttle, but I was proud to see everyone, including my mother, jump at the display.

While my mother gaped at the damage, I turned my foggy eyes to my friends. Rayne pulled an odd-shaped ring from behind his back, where he'd tucked it into his waistband for safekeeping. He reached it out to Terrin and Ayil, who gripped it with him. There was room for my hand too, but I was too far away. Rayne looked at me to see if I was going to attempt to reach them, but I knew I was in no condition to sprint.

I nodded, giving my consent for him to proceed with the plan. He clenched his teeth and slammed his free hand down on a protuberance in the center of the ring. The surrounding air warbled as if a sound wave had dispelled the surrounding dust. An orange sphere formed around them, humming loudly as it built up energy. The rolling energy became erratic, crackling against the particles in the air.

This was really going to hurt. Luckily, I was almost to the point of passing out, anyway.

"Kit!" my mother yelled at me and I looked up. She was so mad. She was even panting. Had I been any more of a disappointment to her, she might have been wringing my neck with her bare hands instead of aiming her firearm at me. My sinister smile faded as I stared at the muzzle. She had said it wasn't loaded, but I doubted she remembered.

The charge exploded around my friends, propelling outward—not too dissimilar to the way Rayne's ship took out its enemy's shields. However, instead of leaving ships defenseless, this device left people defenseless.

Authority

My mother's hand flew across my face, slapping me harder than I thought her capable of. I hadn't even apologized for knocking her out and kidnapping her in Reynard's vessel. I was hoping to win points with her since I hadn't killed anyone to do it. Even the shuttle was free of passengers before the explosion. It was all just a very harsh negotiating tactic—albeit an expensive one.

However, when the tranquilizer had finally worn off, and I joined the others in the dining hall, my mother didn't even give me a chance to rationalize the situation. The sharp biting sting of her hand gave me flashbacks to other assaults I had endured in my life. Though none were as cutting as this one.

I yelped and resisted the urge to cry. I glanced past my bracing hand to see the looks of discomfort around me. Though my left cheek was throbbing with a welt, it was the humiliation that colored my right cheek a ruby red.

I couldn't remember a time when she had struck me. I had never really been one of those children that required a good whippin' to get compliance. My only rebellious act was running away—twice. Even that hadn't raised her ire enough to strike me.

My father had never slapped me, but he had always been a gentle man. He wouldn't have so much as pinched me under the table for fear of hurting me or drawing my tears—which he actually had sympathy for.

Terrin seemed unfazed by my punishment. I suspected he had a much different measure of discipline than the others. He was also more familiar with my mother and her tactics. Short of her punching me, Terrin was not likely to interject in a family dispute.

Ayil, however, was furious. His face twisted from shock to rage. "You bitch!" He jumped up, ready to lunge at my mother across the table.

I wasn't sure what he intended to do, or how he planned to defend me, but Terrin grabbed him around the chest before he could come to my rescue. Ayil struggled uselessly against the gattaw and demanded to be let go.

"This is not your fight," Terrin grumbled in his ear.

"The fuck it isn't," Ayil seethed. I was certain he would not have been on board for any discipline my mother doled out, but her physical dominance was apparently too much for him to tolerate.

My mother glanced at the strange young man struggling in Terrin's arms, but kept most of her virulence aimed at me.

Terrin gave me a scolding look, as if I were to blame for his reaction. I knew I wasn't responsible for his deep-seated hatred of authority figures. Nonetheless, I took my hand from my face and stood up straight, denying any pain from the incident.

Ayil finally gave up his resistance to Terrin's strength and sat back down. He did not relinquish the salty glare he had aimed at my mother. Terrin straightened his back and sat down next to him—as if to babysit him.

I looked at Rayne to see if he would have any ill will toward my mother. He was sitting beside Mr. Davis, watching my mother with the intensity of a predator. He pressed his hands to the table as if he were mere seconds from pushing himself up to stand.

I noted Mr. Davis was smirking at my mother. Had she been closer to him, he may have patted her on the back for a job well done.

Reynard's eyes shifted to the floor when I looked at him. He was usually oblivious to social awkwardness, but this was obvious enough for even him to sense.

Dr. Kessler was beside Rey, glancing between the two of us with more concern in his eyes than anyone. "Was that necessary, Your Majesty?" he asked. He looked at everyone else at the table—searching for the answer.

"It's alright, Dr. Kessler." I stepped back, giving myself a little more room to look at my mother. I wanted to rub my cheek badly, but I kept my hand down, refusing to reveal how much pain she had caused me. It wasn't as if she would let her sympathy restrict her authority, anyway. "My mother has been holding that one in for quite some time."

Susan took in a deep breath and held it before she released it again. With it went the tension in her muscles. "You shouldn't have brought me here." My mother turned to include everyone at the table.

"I needed to talk to you."

"We were talking."

"No, you were kidnapping me."

"And what are you doing now? When my tail ships arrive, they will blow this ship out of the sky."

Reynard snorted loudly and his stomach jiggled as he tried in vain to keep his sputtering laughter under control. Mr. Davis also smirked beside him, and try as he might, Rayne seemed to struggle with his indifference. My mother eyed them all carefully.

"Mother, this is Captain Reynard Baloch. He was one of the Coalition's more renowned weapons designers. He—"

"You." Susan moved closer to Rey, inspecting him. "You're the one responsible for creating the biomechanoids. They are your abomination."

Rey shifted his gaze to the floor, unable to deny his shame at creating them.

"Rey no longer works for them, Mother. He's an independent..." I glanced at Rey to see what I should describe him as.

"Egalitarian," he suggested.

"He's an anarchist and a murderer." Susan glanced at Rayne. She had already figured out the connection between them. He didn't shy away from the accusation. "The entire universe trembles at the mere mention of Captain Baloch." Rey smiled proudly. "But not me." His smile diminished. "I find your tactics to be that of a coward." Rey frowned at her.

"Mother." I shifted to touch her arm. "Don't."

"I've heard all the stories. Witnessed the bodies you leave in your wake." Susan once again glanced at Rayne. "I'm unimpressed, Captain."

"Is that so, Majesty?" Rey asked. His lips pinched with displeasure.

"That is so. You see, it's easy to kill the men standing in your path. Diplomacy, on the other hand, is a long and daunting process that requires true skill. Perhaps if you had more patience—or less ego—you could understand that."

"You have no idea what you're talking about, lady," Davis sniped.

Susan turned to him and looked him over. His role certainly eluded her, but Mr. Davis certainly didn't evoke the image of a coward. "You may call me Majesty or you may shut your mouth."

"I may call you something else if you don't get your head out of your ass."

"That's enough, Mr. Davis." Rey waved him off his high horse. "The queen believes she is above our underhanded tactics, and that's fine. She can continue to delude herself as much as she wants. Because, after all, she is royalty." Rey added a flourished bow to drive home his sarcasm.

"Delude myself?" Susan couldn't help but take the bait.

"Oh, yes, Majesty. You see, you might be against my guerrilla tactics, but your army isn't."

"My army doesn't conspire with traitors."

"As Mr. Davis said, you have no idea what you are talking about."

"Mother, Rey isn't a traitor."

"I would know if my army is using black market weaponry."

"Clearly not." Rey grimaced. "Speaking of your army. Do you have General Sanders' home coordinates? I very much want to send her a message."

"You can't be serious." My mother took a step back, shaken by any suggestion that her army was not following her guidelines for conduct.

"No, I find her rather stimulating, actually. I'd like to correspond with her further."

"Not now, Rey." I shook my head at him and moved to my mother. "Mother, we need—"

"I will put every one of you to the nines if I am not released at this moment!" Susan yelled, trying to regain control of the situation.

"Just try it!" Rey finally added his volume to the situation. "The only reason you are still a queen is because I have allowed it!"

"You self-important, malefactor! When my ship gets here—"

"I will destroy it! Just like I could destroy every—"

"Both of you, stop it!" I waved my hands between them, drawing their attention to me. "I didn't bring you together to exchange threats and measure your military cocks. I brought you together so you could fight this war together."

Susan pulled her hardened gaze from Rey and gave me a puzzled look. "What war is to be fought?"

"The war against the Coalition."

Susan lowered her head and pinched the bridge of her nose before turning her frustrated, albeit patient, demeanor back to me. "Sweetheart, I can't fight a war with the Coalition. While I don't agree with the charges against you, this battle will need to be fought diplomatically." She threw a glance at Rey.

"What about attempted murder? Is that a charge worthy of war?"

Susan shifted her gaze from mine and wrung her hands together. "I wish it were that simple. The life of one cannot be weighed against the thousands that would be killed in a war."

"What about tens of thousands? Hundreds of thousands?"

"Millions," Rey added.

"What are you talking about?"

"I'm talking about the Coalition attempting to murder members of our empire. Starting with the assassination of the queen herself."

"What?"

"Mother, allow me to introduce Dr. Alvin Kessler." I motioned to Kessler, who stood and reached out his hand for an official greeting. My mother looked him over carefully before consenting to the handshake. "Dr. Kessler is the man responsible for my... creation." My mother gave me a sour look. "He's also responsible for the virus I was meant to infect you with following my sixteenth birthday." Susan frowned at me.

Kessler moved forward and gingerly placed his hand on my mother's shoulder. "Why don't you have a seat, Majesty? We have a lot to tell you."

Proof

I had never seen my mother so quiet before. She was taking Dr. Kessler's explanation of my origins a good deal better than I had. To the untrained observer, she was downright indifferent to the information, but I could see her fingers kneading the fabric of her uniform under the table. She was in shock, but she bravely put on the face ingrained in her since birth. In my youth, I had hated her terse, reserved behavior. As an adult, I hated it even more, but I at least respected it.

Kessler had stopped short of telling her about my daughter. That was my secret to tell, and I still wasn't sure I wanted to tell her. She wouldn't be happy about my relationship with an assassin, much less that he was the father of her granddaughter.

The room remained silent for nearly a minute, though it was not without unspoken dialogue. I looked at Rayne, wondering if this was the time to reveal our child. He shook his head slightly. Rey looked around at all of us as if searching for a cue to speak so he could fill the void of conversation. Kessler looked at me sympathetically—in that fatherly way I didn't like.

"So, is it too early or too late for a drink?" Mr. Davis said when his tolerance for the drama had reached its limit. He stood from the table and headed over to the bar cart to fix himself a drink.

"This virus," Susan finally spoke. "It was destroyed with the medical base?"

"Whatever samples or research were held there would have been destroyed," Kessler said. "But I doubt it was the only location. The Coalition is very thorough. We suspect Agate may still have other research locations we don't know about. Rey and I could only locate this medical station because of Mallory." My mother looked at me, but I didn't elaborate about my surrender to Agate. I was certain she would not have approved of my self-sacrifice when it was at the risk of so many lives. Especially since I had no idea it would come to benefit anyone other than Terrin.

"But if my daughter has the antibodies and you have already created a vaccine for this virus, then our priority is not war. We should be inoculating the empire to prevent this disease from being spread, should Agate choose to release it."

Kessler shifted uncomfortably in his seat. "The problem, Majesty, is the Coalition has had years to devise and create other viruses. Though Mallory's objectives have failed, there is nothing to stop them from releasing something new. Something she has never been exposed to. Something that could kill tens of thousands before we could formulate a cure or vaccine for it."

"Do you understand the risk now?" I asked her. "Do you see why I need your help? Agate has been plotting against the empire the entire time."

"I see nothing. I hear the words these men are telling me, but I cannot go to war simply because they say these things are true."

I frowned and leaned away from her. "You don't believe them?"

"What they are suggesting is preposterous?"

"Why?" Rey asked.

"Because I would know if my daughter was not my own," Susan snapped.

"She is your daughter," Rey insisted. "I took the liberty of comparing your DNA after we got you on board. You're her mother."

"You what?" I did a double-take on Rey. He merely shrugged at me, reminding me that personal boundaries were not his strong suit. "Look, Mother—"

"If what you're saying is true, then the Coalition has been plotting against the empire since..."

"Since they first reached out to make peace with you," Rey said. "Every step leading to Kit's creation has been a step closer to them taking control of the empire. Think about it, Susan." My mother threw him a glare for the familiarity. "The Coalition doesn't care about your religious prophecy. They were using it as an excuse to create a baby that would frequently be in both your possession and her father's. They designed a weapon you would not only never suspect, but one you would love and protect and keep close to you at all times." Rey leaned forward. "I know you are not prepared to go to battle based on the tales of two Coalition defectors, but you must understand we are on the cusp of war already. Agate knows his medical base is compromised. With his plan exposed, he will be figuring out his next move. He will not let decades of planning go to waste."

Susan leaned forward and pressed the tips of her fingers into her forehead. "It's not that simple." She looked at me and frowned as she gave me the speech. "Even with this knowledge, there are protocols to follow. Despite the empire's vast military, the Coalition still poses a significant threat against us. Their technology—"

"I designed most of their technology," Rey said. "Even their new designs are not far from my prototypes. We can assist with your defense."

"For a price," Mr. Davis added from the bar.

Susan frowned and shook her head. "I can't go to my delegates and demand we go to war based on the say-so of two men I have no reason to trust."

"You're the queen," Rayne said, as if she might have forgotten that fact.

"My duty to the empire is not to act without provocation or proof. I must weigh all my actions against those of the greater good. Going to war with the Coalition would be a death sentence for thousands of loyal men and women. That sacrifice must be for a worthy cause."

"I think I have the proof you need." Reaching into my pocket, I pulled out the data drive Aresties had given me. I held it up for my mother to see. "Assuming the information on here will help you."

"Where did you get that?" Rey asked.

I glanced at him. "From Aresties." I watched my mother's eyes light with interest. "Before she died on the medical base." Susan reached for the drive, but I yanked it back. She cast me a look, warning me I was testing her nerves. "Who was she, Mother?"

Susan took in a deep breath and raised her chin defiantly. "Aresties was a spy."

"What?" Ayil volleyed his eyes around the table, seeing if he was the only one surprised by this statement.

"She was one of many loyalists who assisted the empire by keeping an eye on the affairs outside of our reach. I assigned her to watch over you."

"The whole time?" I asked, a little disappointed that my longest companion was yet another rent-a-friend.

"Yes." Susan snatched the drive from my hand while I was stunned into distraction. She leaned forward to speak quietly just to me. "You didn't think I would let my daughter roam the universe without help, did you?"

My eyes flickered over hers, trying to wade through the emotions of inadequacy that her "help" usually provided. However, since I was beginning to understand the strength of the connection between a mother and daughter, I found room for relief in her overbearing nature. Though Mother could have taken me home anytime, Aresties' only task was to watch over me. Just in case. Since I could think of several times she had saved my life, I could hardly resent her presence. The only thing I regretted was not knowing the woman she truly was. Or perhaps she was the Aresties I knew, just with a secret worth keeping.

"Give me that." Susan snapped her fingers, demanding the tablet Davis was occupying himself with. He rolled his eyes but brought it over for her to use. She the drive plugged into it and began scanning the files it contained. After a few seconds, a grimace appeared on her face. She looked appalled by the information she was seeing, but then it turned to a smile—a ruthless one. The information Aresties had attained must have been valuable to her.

Susan ripped the drive from the device and stood up. She turned to Rey, who also rose from his seat. "Set a course for Brahama, Captain. I'll need a secure channel to contact my fleet and arrange a meeting with my delegates."

"Does this mean you will help us?" Rey asked.

Susan nodded. "You'll have your war, but it will be under my direction. Is that understood?"

Rey glanced at me and I gave him a pleading look—hoping he would not let his ego stand in the way of saving the empire. He nodded. "Very well, Majesty. Perhaps I should contact General Sanders to discuss further integration of my technologies," he added eagerly.

"Focus, please, Captain." Susan waved him toward the door with her and he rushed to take the lead to the bridge

Asylum

Memories flooded me from the moment I stepped off the shuttle and onto Brahama's familiar ground. The sweet smell of flowers drifted over to the landing pad from the nearby gardens. The sound of water features burbled in the background even as my mother's guards arrived, feet pounding in unison against the cement.

My mother brushed past me, shouting orders left and right, demanding information from every face that jogged up beside her. I lengthened my stride to stay on her heels. I could feel a certain tension return to my spine as I stood a little straighter and taller than I normally would. Years of mandated poise were rising to the surface, muscle memory as familiar to me as riding a bike.

Two guards settled in just ahead of my mother and just behind me, forming four corners of protection. Unconsciously or otherwise, my steps mimicked theirs. Soon I was marching step for step through the courtyards like part of the military accompaniment.

I noted a few members of my mother's staff glancing at me as they moved clear of my mother's path. I knew I was the epitome of the black sheep to them. Even if I hadn't been wearing a perfunctory space-approved linen uniform with a god-awful striped pattern, they still would have looked at me the same way. I was heir to the most powerful position in the universe. What idiot walks away from that? Moreover, who runs away from it?

I wanted to glance back to see if the others were following me, but I didn't dare lose a step or she would leave me behind. As it was, my mother had somehow gotten several feet ahead of me. She rounded the corner, turning out of the extensive courtyard into the estate. I followed behind her through a set of paned glass doors that were being held open for us.

After another quick turn down a dark hallway, I realized our destination.

The war room.

The room where my mother would meet with the head delegates. The men and women directly beneath her and for whom the galaxy could not run without. In this room, she would, and often had, decided the fate and future of the empire.

She had never allowed me in the war room. I was much too young to be privy to the conversations that happened beyond the double red doors at the end of this hallway. Until now, it would seem.

As we approached, two guards opened the mammoth soundproof doors. My mother crossed over the threshold into the room that was even darker than the hall leading to it. Her black uniform disappeared within, leaving only her bobbing blonde hair visible.

Just as I reached the entrance, two spear axes crossed in front of my face, nearly shaving off my nose. I halted and looked at the two frozen guards. I knew better than to petition them for anything. They were almost as inhuman as the biomechanoids.

"Mother," I called out to her before she could disappear completely.

Susan turned and looked back as if she hadn't even been aware I was following her. Perhaps she hadn't. She returned to the entrance and stared at me over the crossed weaponry.

"Let me in," I said when it was clear she had no idea what I wanted.

Her eyes narrowed slightly, and she shook her head. She took another slow and purposeful step forward. "This room is reserved for members of the royal family and those committed to serving the empire." Her eyes sparkled with contempt. "I'm afraid you no longer qualify as either."

I clenched my jaw, restricting the curse words I wanted to throw back at her.

"Take Kit to her room," she said to the guards at my back. "She needs to get cleaned up." She glanced down at my attire before walking away.

"Mother," I rasped at her back. Before I could object, the two guards at my back gripped me tightly behind the elbows and urged me to move away. "Let go of me," I seethed and tried to pull away. They refused to release me and started pulling me away from the door. "Let me go!" I fought against them, but they only added my wrists to their grips—guiding me away from the war room like an elderly woman unable to stand on her own.

I was in a thorough fit by the time we reached the outer doors. Terrin, Rayne, and Ayil were standing outside conversing in the courtyard when I arrived. As if being slapped in the face wasn't enough of a... well... slap in the face—my friends now got to see me being sent to my room like a misbehaving child.

"What's going on?" Terrin approached, waving Ayil and Rayne back before they inadvertently committed treason.

"They've been ordered to escort me to my room," I snarled, still trying to get the use of my arms back.

Terrin looked over my position, his eyes landing on each of the hands containing me. "I can escort the princess to her accommodations."

"We have our orders," one guard said.

"Get your hands off her!" Ayil yelled over. Rayne pushed him back, urging him to shut up and let Terrin handle it.

Terrin took a step closer to me. "I'm certain the queen did not mean to suggest you manhandle her in this way. Perhaps if you release her, she can voluntarily head to her room." Terrin glanced at me as if letting me know that this was what would indeed need to happen. The men didn't release me. "Or I could assume that my duties to protect the princess extend to the confines of this estate." Terrin didn't glare at the men. He just perked his brow, inquiring about their preference.

"We have our orders," the same guard said, refusing to yield.

Terrin's chest bolstered and his eyes lit with fire. His mouth opened to speak, but another voice filled the air.

"Release her." General Sanders' dulcet tone was unexpected from a high-ranking military leader. Nor was her glowing complexion, bright eyes, and resting smile what should inspire fear in one's enemy. However, over the years, she had continuously risen in the ranks—demanding respect from all of her compatriots. "That's an order, gentlemen," she added.

The guards instantly released me, and I gravitated away from them toward Sanders. I stopped before her and observed her short, wispy blonde hair, a new style since our last meeting. "General," I murmured as I smiled at her.

Her smile grew into a natural, toothy grin. "Hello, Kit," she answered. She raised her arms slightly, inviting me into a hug and I rushed forward—eager to get an embrace from the woman I thought of as my fun aunt. Though we were unrelated and had little to nothing in common, we had formed a bond that filled a vacancy for each of us. In the days when I desperately sought more attention from my mother, and she struggled to completely sever her maternal instincts—we began to socialize. It wasn't much more than small talk, but it was meaningful. Like all long absences—I didn't fully realize how much I missed her until she was standing right in front of me again.

Sanders gave me a tight squeeze before drawing me back to look at me. She looked over my hair with a perked brow. "Haven't you used up the rainbow yet?"

I laughed and self-consciously covered the part in my hair where my roots were showing. Since I hadn't had time between my life and death scenarios to see a beautician, the deep plum color had faded into a dull brownish purple. "Not yet," I answered. "You cut your hair." I reached and touched her formerly long tendrils.

"I had a run-in with a flamethrower." Sanders turned and flipped a layer of her hair up to reveal a rather messy scar that covered the base of her skull and neck. Despite the ugliness of it, she had no qualms about revealing it to me and everyone in the courtyard. Her lack of feminine exhibitionism was one of my favorite things about her. Her concern for presentation did not stretch beyond a hot shower and a wrinkle-free uniform. "I rather liked being bald, so I kept it shorter after that. I leave just enough to keep my head warm."

Sanders' eyes shifted subtly to the right. I glanced over to see what she was looking at and noticed my small entourage was waiting in the wings to be introduced. "Oh, yes, of course. This is my friend Ayil." I pointed to Ayil, and he accepted Sanders' handshake. I noted he was taking in her features—as most men do upon meeting her. Even without her long hair—she was a vision. "He's been my shipmate since almost the beginning."

"Pleasure," Sanders nodded politely and pulled her hand away even as Ayil leaned in to kiss it.

"This is..." I paused, not sure whether to introduce Rayne as the name I knew him by or by his actual name.

"I'm Rayne." Deciding for me, he extended his hand and shook Sanders' outstretched hand. "I'm her husband," he added.

Sanders froze mid-shake. "Husband?" She looked back at me and I shook my head.

"Sort of. It's a long story involving paperwork and—some other stuff." I turned my attention to Terrin, trying to divert the conversation. "And, of course, you remember, Terrin."

Sanders looked at Terrin as she pulled away from Rayne. Her rarely missing smile dropped into a flat line. "Terrin," she said with civil acknowledgment. I noticed she did not raise her hand to greet him.

"General." Terrin nodded at her. His hand also stayed sedately at his side.

She took in a breath and turned back to me. "I would love to stay and catch up, but the queen needs me in the war room."

"Sure." I stepped aside, giving her leave to go.

Her eyes looked me over admiringly. "It's good to see you again, Kit." Her mouth hung open as if she were deliberating her next words. "I missed you." She finally surrendered to the words.

"I missed you too," I admitted.

"Oh, I almost forgot." Sanders waved to a couple of her right-hand men waiting at the far end of the courtyard, near the landing pad. They disappeared into the corridor. "I think I have something that belongs to one of you," she said coyly before settling her gaze on Ayil.

I looked between them, watching Ayil's eyes narrow almost into a ferocious glare before he relinquished to the hope Sanders' smile was putting into him.

"Daddy!" Edric's voice carried across the courtyard, putting a sharp pain in my heart and taking the air out of my lungs.

Ayil's face melted even before he turned his head to look at his son. He clenched his teeth together tight and sprinted to greet the boy being chaperoned by Sanders' guards. Edric broke away, running to meet his father in the middle. He wrapped his arms around Ayil's neck as he lifted him into the air. The scene brought tears to my eyes, and I eventually had to look away to get my emotions under control.

I noted the smiles Terrin and Rayne were wearing as they too moved to distance themselves from the reunion—effectively giving Ayil some privacy. We were all happy for Ayil, especially since he was the one most hurt by Aresties' death. Now, at least, his heart had the fuel to heal.

I followed behind Rayne and Terrin, joining the impromptu stroll around the concrete garden paths. They eventually fell into a rhythm and their footsteps mirrored each other.

"What was that about with Sanders?" Rayne asked. I looked up, but realized he was directing the question at Terrin. Since I was also curious about the interaction, I moved a little closer to hear the answer.

Terrin glanced back, noting my proximity before answering. "Much like the queen, Sanders was disappointed by my efforts to keep Mallory secure."

"Really?" Rayne said, unconvinced. "After all these years, she's still holding a grudge for bad babysitting."

"We had an altercation."

"An altercation?" Rayne asked, even more curious.

"Yes, she tried to kill me."

"What?" I asked.

Terrin stopped and turned back to me.

Rayne stopped and frowned deeply at Terrin. "Why would she try to kill you?"

Terrin turned his attention to Rayne. "She reviewed the security footage of the docks on the day Mallory escaped. She erroneously suggested that Mallory's escape may have been inspired by me."

"You?" Rayne scoffed. "Why? Because she was pissed off at you?"

Terrin's jaw rolled in disgust. "The general accused me of inappropriate behavior."

Rayne glanced at me. "You mean..." Rayne probed delicately, but still couldn't say the words.

"She thought I had abused Mallory during our trip from Brahama and that she was running away from me, not her family." My mouth gaped as I remembered the kiss I had given Terrin to distract him before I ran off. It was a harmless kiss—hardly more than a peck.

Rayne sputtered out a laugh. But then he glanced at me as if my suicidal draw to Terrin might have resulted from some affliction. "That's preposterous, right?"

"Yes!" I crossed my arms and glanced at Terrin. "I gave him a goodbye kiss."

"It was a distraction so she could get away," Terrin corrected.

"It was also a goodbye," I defended, since I could have distracted him in other ways.

Rayne's face seemed to light with understanding. "And naturally, Sanders assumed the kiss was forced or coerced."

"Yes."

I let out an awful groan and pressed my hands to my suddenly queasy stomach. "She doesn't still think that, does she?"

"No, but there is still some tension between us."

"Enough to cut with a buzz saw," Rayne said.

I wanted to drop to the ground, but I found a brick flower bed to sit on before my knees gave out. I looked at Terrin and shook my head. "I'm so sorry, Terrin. I never considered anyone would interpret it that way."

Terrin stared back at me. He directed his ire at me in place of Sanders, or the younger version of me. I held his eyes, silently pleading for him to forgive me. To pardon me for everything I had put him through.

"What's done is done," Terrin eventually said and walked away. He probably didn't want me to know about the accusation, and I was certain he didn't want Rayne to know. I felt awful and the moment I saw Sanders, I would explain that to her, but as Terrin said, what's done is done. We couldn't change the past. I couldn't undo the decisions I had made then. I just had to live with the outcome.

VOICE

As if the culture shock of my mother's home wasn't enough, my bedroom was the exact mirror image of my room at my father's mansion on Vagari. It was an attempt to make my transition between the two worlds easier. However, it sometimes left me feeling displaced, as if the world around me was transforming, but I was staying the same.

Staring at the room now made me angry, though I couldn't fully understand why. Something about the illusion of normalcy within the chaos infuriated me. I stepped up to the small round table in the center of the room. Its sole purpose was to hold a vase of flowers and though it did it beautifully, I still hated it.

I picked up the blue vase and launched it into the wall. I shoved the table over too. I looked at the items sitting on my small vanity next to the bathroom door. A neat row of various hairbrushes lay there, like a setting of flatware at a dinner party. I swiped them all off, letting them clatter to the floor, potentially breaking the pearl plating.

I opened my chest of drawers and pulled out one item after another, searching for a single garment I had picked out. Nothing. Not one shirt. Not one sock.

Nothing in this room or the other one was my decision. This was the part of my life that inspired me to take control. Had I been an ordinary girl with ordinary skills, I could have just developed an eating disorder, but I didn't just want control of my life. I wanted the stars.

I looked at myself in the mirror over the vanity. I looked terrible. And not just the usual lack of makeup and baggy uniform. There were inexplicable bags under my eyes and my hair desperately needed a restorative treatment.

Relinquishing to yet another of my mother's demands, I gathered up my supplies and headed in to take a shower. It was possibly the longest shower I had had since I left home the second time. Clean, shaven, and properly moisturized head to toe, I emerged from the bathroom in a bathrobe.

I froze in the doorway, staring out at the room. The clothing I had ripped from the dresser was back in place, no doubt neatly folded. The maids had replaced the broken vase with a replica. They had swept and mopped the floor. Everything I had done to express the most minimal objection to my situation had been erased in a matter of an hour.

I had forgotten why temper tantrums never worked in my mother's home. The staff's officiousness bordered on creepy. I hated that even in my room—my private space—I couldn't use my voice. It only reminded me that whether my mother cloistered my DNA or Rey quarantined my virus, it had very little to do with me. Everyone kept forgetting I wasn't just a prophecy or a plague. I was a person.

Casualties

"Mother!" I shouted as I jogged across the courtyard to her. Her sentinels shifted, as if they wouldn't allow me near her. That would have been a fine ending to a nearly fourteen-hour wait. The sun of the hot day was long gone, and I assumed the war room had only dispersed out of desperation for food and sleep. However, even that would not be a long break.

I spent much of my childhood standing outside the war room, waiting for my mother to emerge from heated diplomatic discussions. Though she always looked the part of the queen, I could see that some sessions took more of the fire from her eyes than others.

The dim evening moonlight prevented me from accurately reading her mood, but as she marched past, I saw her mouth pressed into a thin line. "Not now, Kit."

Rather than get in front of her and risk being gored by her guards, I walked with her on the outside of the colonnade. "I need to know what's going on."

"This is none of your concern anymore."

I scoffed. "Mother, I'm the one who gave you the proof of this potential genocide. I think I am owed an update."

My mother's feet slowed to a stop, and she turned her tired gaze to me. "The credit for this information shall be wholly attributed to Aresties, or have you forgotten her sacrifice?"

"I didn't mean that she..." I trailed off, feeling ashamed of any suggestion of forgetting Aresties' contribution. I, of all people, knew exactly how much she had sacrificed for her duty, as well as our friendship.

"The crown thanks you for your delivery of the information." She moved again, and I followed her, trying to shake off the white-hot rage that was bubbling through my core.

"I can help you!"

"You mean Captain Reynard can help me? No, thank you. I consider that man to be as much an enemy to the crown as Chancellor Agate."

"It's foolish not to utilize him, Mother."

"No, Kit." She stopped again and turned to me. "It's foolish for you to put your trust in a man with no allegiances." Her gaze flickered over me, no doubt disapproving of something I was wearing. "Your draw to increasingly more dangerous men seems to have left you ignorant of the risks around you. I had hoped you would grow out of that." She walked on, but this time I didn't follow her. Her fangs had cut deep enough to garner my surrender.

"What do you want to know?" General Sanders stepped out of the colonnade after my mother had gone.

I breathed a sigh of relief as I looked back at her. "Thank god, a rational woman."

She chuckled and shook her head at me. "You really pissed her off when you left after the wedding."

"Of course." I meandered over to one fountain and sat down on the edge. "Because, at that time, I was leaving her custody. She couldn't blame it on my father."

"I'm sure it goes deeper than that." Sanders sat down next to me, leaving a little space between us. "The information Aresties obtained has been... eye-opening."

"I take it you know about me."

"Yes, there is a very detailed file on you."

"Several, I'm sure. What is she going to do?"

"We've been discussing options. The first of which is demanding an explanation from Agate."

"You've got to be kidding. The man is orchestrating genocide. Just stick a gun to his head."

"It's not that simple."

"Why not? The empire far out-mans the Coalition."

"We found something else in the files that has us... concerned."

"What, more viral bombs?" I asked.

"No. They're called ultra-bios."

"Oh, right, those."

"You've seen them?"

"Just a few, but they were pretty decked out."

"Agate has apparently been working on them for a while. The tech is an offshoot of the biomechanoids fabrication, so they still use human tissue for the base, but they've added a good deal more weaponry. There are several factories on Vagari, producing them as we speak. It's in everyone's best interest to shut the factories down, but they are being protected by a significant defense system."

"So just bomb it from space," I said, supplying my less-than-expert tactical knowledge.

"We are weighing the pros and cons of that. It would mean entering into an all-out war on Coalition territory. The civilian casualties would be steep, and it would almost certainly mean your father and Elizandra would be lost."

I frowned, not even realizing my sister was with my father. I also hadn't considered that, as the enemy's leader, he could be a target. Even if he were only Agate's puppet, they would likely attack the capital hard to ensure the elimination of the most important political figures first. "I forgot..."

"Our greatest advantage is that Agate doesn't know what we know. We still have time to use all the information to our advantage and make a sound battle plan that will minimize casualties. I'll let you know when I know something more." Sanders squeezed my shoulder and stood.

"General, do you know if the ultra-bios are using the same programming system as the regular bios?"

Sanders' brow dipped as she looked back at me. "I'm not sure. I could find out. Why do you ask?"

"Because—"

"Kit," Rayne called over to me as he approached the fountain. "I need to speak with you."

"I'm kind of in the middle of a conversation already." I motioned to Sanders.

"It's important." He was speaking earnestly and his eyes were burning holes into me, demanding my attention.

Sanders glanced between the two of us and smirked. "Well, far be it from me to stand in the way of a *happy* couple." She said happily, as if she doubted it applied to us. How right she was. "I'll keep you informed, Kit."

After she had gone, I looked at Rayne and shrugged. "What?"

"Come with me."

I followed him out of the courtyard and into the mansion. We traversed the confusing paths of staircases and arrived at the door to my room. "What are we doing?" I followed him inside and watched him search the room. "Rayne?"

"I want to talk about us," he said rather indifferently as he moved to my vanity.

"You seriously want to rehash this again?"

"No, I don't want to talk." He wasn't even looking at me as he spoke. He picked up one of my lipsticks and wrote *"he is listening"* on the mirror. I stared at the words, trying to fathom who, but it wasn't a far leap to know who could spy on me even inside of my mother's house. "I want to do this." Rayne came back fast and grabbed me. He kissed me hard. I pulled away and nearly head-butted him, but he held his finger to his mouth, begging me for my silence before pointing back to the mirror.

He yanked my shirt open, releasing all the snaps in a single swift movement. I gasped, feeling the exposure of my body as both a violation and unwanted arousal. "Rayne," I objected, since I had no intention of putting on a live show for the captain.

Rayne pointed to the inner lining of my snaps. I examined the tiny black disc someone had added to the back of one of my snaps. That son of a bitch had bugged me. I opened my mouth to cuss at the little device, but Rayne kissed me, stopping my words and potentially my thoughts.

I struggled slightly against his disrobing but allowed him to take my shirt and pants off. After which, he removed his shirt and pants.

"Now, let's get that Gat washed off you."

I glared at Rayne for the insult as he dragged me into my bathroom. He shut the door behind us and turned on the shower for added noise. After which, he stood with his hands propped on the trim of his boxers, staring at me.

I leaned against the sink, arms crossed over my bra, trying to not focus on the fact that I was two sheer garments away from being naked with Rayne. "He has no right to bug me."

"Kit, don't even start with that sanctimonious shit. I thought you understood who Rey was. He thought you understood how he operates."

"I thought I could trust him."

"He thought the same of you, but he's not the first man to make that mistake."

"Oh, geez! You have no room to talk about honesty!"

"Quiet," Rayne hissed and pulled me closer to the shower.

"What is going on?" I yanked my arm away. "Why is he listening to me?"

"You screwed up, Kit."

"I screwed up what?"

"That thumb drive."

"What about it?"

"You gave it to your mother."

"Yeah, Aresties told me to give it to her."

"Yes, and you just handed the empire a huge chunk of information without even consulting us about it."

"Why would I…" I chuckled at the sheer drama of the conversation. "I wasn't aware I was required to get approval from Rey for anything I did."

"Kit, Rey is not your friend. He's the man that hires me to get rid of any players that don't play the war game fair."

"Fine, but I'm not a player in his game."

"You became one the minute you handed that drive to your mother."

"So, what, I should have given it to him instead?"

"You should have told him about it. He would have looked it over and decided what the empire should know."

"Why does he get to decide?"

"Because he's Captain-fucking-Baloch, Kit! Because he saved your life and Ayil's life. And because he is currently expending a great deal of resources to keep our daughter alive."

I frowned. "What are you saying? Would he hurt her?"

Rayne shook his head. "No, that's off the table… for now. But Rey expects a minimum of discretion when it comes to his abilities."

"His weaponry? I barely understand what I have seen."

"I didn't think this needed to be reiterated, but no one, and I mean no one, can find out about the backdoor in his biomechanoid program."

"But that could—"

Rayne put his finger firmly on my lips. "I understand the desire to reach for the option you can see, but Rey works on a far more complex level than you and I do. He makes plays years in advance and he doesn't act on emotion. He acts in the best interest of the players."

I pushed his finger away. "This isn't a game. This is war. I can't just let tens of thousands die when I have knowledge that could help end this before it even begins."

Rayne placed a hand on my shoulder before I could consider leaving. "Kit, I need you to listen to me very carefully. I am trying to protect you. You think because he's allowed you to come here, that you're free of him, but you are very wrong. Once you are on his radar, you are never off. You are a player now, and he will use you as he sees fit. And if you do anything to interfere with his game—do anything to imbalance the measures he has taken to equalize the playing field, then he will kill you where you stand… and whoever you have told."

I stared at Rayne, wondering just how close I had come to dying moments ago in the courtyard. The logical side of me wanted to believe my mother's security system would have protected me from any orbital attacks, but I knew that probably wasn't true. Technology rarely deterred Rey, especially when it was less advanced than his own.

"Rayne," I whispered. "You're frightening me."

"That's my intention, Kit. The rapport I have with him will give me some favors, but they are running out. Do you understand?" Rayne asked firmly.

"Yes." I nodded, feeling numb from head to toe. My mother had been right that I was wrong to trust Reynard. She had been right about a lot of things I didn't want to admit to until now. "Should I try to get the drive back?" I asked, even though I had no idea how I would do such a thing since I wasn't even welcome in the war room.

"No, he already has the information. Mr. Davis's pad downloaded a copy of it the moment she plugged it into his device."

"Wow, he's good."

"Yeah, he's the best." Rayne sounded as if he admired the man. The thought of their friendship being amicable after what he had done to me left a sour taste in my mouth, but I saw no reason to dissuade him from his delusions about the man. "I know this sounds strange to you, because you have fought all of your life to be free from the strings that control you, but there are benefits to being one of Rey's players." Rayne reached in and shut the water off, but stopped. "Well, I suppose that was enough time to make you come." His gaze froze on me. "Unless you think it will take longer."

I could see the hunger in his eyes, helped along by the partial nudity between us, but I had no interest in having sex with him. Aside from the obvious trust issues between us, Rayne had just put Captain-fucking-Baloch right in the middle of the tattered remnants of our relationship. My primary concern for our future—bringing a baby onto the ship of a childish, sociopathic warmonger—had just received an answer.

Hell, no.

I would not raise my child anywhere near Baloch. Which meant a relationship with Rayne was not possible.

"No," I answered Rayne. "That's enough for me."

Balcony

My mother's grand mansion, similar to my father's estate, had more rooms than anyone could occupy in a single night. However, the design of her mansion was more haphazard. The structure wasn't flawed so much as purposefully confusing. I had once thought it was strange for my mother to have three separate bedrooms each in a different section of the home, but I was starting to understand the burdens of the crown a little more each day.

Mother had been more than gracious, allowing Terrin, Rayne, Ayil, and Edric a room to stay in while we were *visiting*—as she put it. She had done nothing to hide her displeasure with me and, apart from the prior evening's encounter, I had not seen or heard from her. General Sanders had not reached out to me either, leading me to believe there was probably nothing new to report.

My thoughts about Rey and his disapproval had plagued me since Rayne had told me about it. As angry as I was about his betrayal, I was wondering if I should have put more of my trust in him. Perhaps he could have been the one to help me destroy the Coalition instead of my mother. Or maybe he was already doing that, just in more calculated steps.

Part of me wanted to rush back to his ship and remove my daughter from his custody, but without Dr. Kessler's approval, I knew Rey wouldn't let her off the ship. I wondered if taking her away would be an issue, anyway. How far would Rey go to contain the vault of viruses she and I possessed?

"You look so different when you're here," Terrin said as he came up behind me on the balcony.

I jumped a little, surprised by his presence. I had been standing on a stone balcony overlooking the pool. Ayil and Rayne were playing with Edric, tossing him back and forth in the water as if he were merely a ball. He would scrunch up, as tight as can be, and one of them would launch him up in the air. Edric would splash down into the water, only to do it all over again from the other side. The boy was giggling so loudly and gleefully that neither Ayil nor Rayne could keep a straight face. It was the first time in a while I'd seen either of them in such a cheerful state. Fatherhood looked good on Ayil and I was certain it would look just as good on Rayne.

I turned to look at Terrin and his eyes drifted over me, taking in my hair, makeup, and outfit. My dress was both overdone and boring. The long, heavy beige fabric hugged tightly to my body. There were two wide sashes attached to the shoulders draping down the front and back on either side. There was even a sparkle of gold tinsel threaded in with the stitching to give it a hint of elegance.

"Not that I don't enjoy seeing you in a dress." Terrin moved to stand beside me and look out over the balcony at the same view as me. "But you do look a little like your mother."

I chuckled. "I'm sure that was her intention when she picked it out. But we do have a similar skin tone and body shape. What looks good on her will also look good on me." I didn't mention that the reason for my fashion choice was to avoid Rey's surveillance.

"And the hair?" he asked.

I shrugged, but couldn't bring myself to look at him. It was the first time in over a decade I had a natural hair color. God knows what my original color was, but the auburn waves I had received that morning looked pretty well on me. "It's just hair."

I also didn't mention I was sucking up, hoping to gain favor with my mother. I resented her resentment, but I also wanted her to forgive me. So, on I went, pushing my boulder up the hill that was my mother's love.

A hissing sound emanated from the back of Terrin's throat. He turned to face me, resting his hip against the balcony railing. "It's just clothes. It's just hair. It's just you being swallowed up by all of this. I'm not going to let you do this to yourself."

"Do what?" I continued to stare out at the courtyard like a statue.

"Absorb back into this life."

"It's fine, Terrin. It makes her happy. And mother being happy is always a good thing."

"I know you think I don't see you, Mallory. But I do. I know what this place does to you. I know what she does to you."

"I've always been two people, Terrin. You know that. Kit Mallory or Mallory Kit. I'm just playing the part of the Princess today."

"And which of you is in love with me? Because I'd like to speak to her." I snapped out of my daze and looked at him. He stared back at me with his beautiful reddish-brown eyes, searching for the girl he knew, the woman he loved, and the friend he was devoted to. I let my eyes trace over the distinct pattern of his skin. The smooth scales turned to scutes when they reached his forehead, followed by two thick ridges that apexed into stubby black horns. He wasn't the type of man most human women sought for a mate, but there was still a part of me that found him beautiful, exotic, and alluring. In a different life, Terrin and I might've run away together and lived happily ever after, but that was a much different life. One without the confines of biological imperatives and two condescending nations. That was the fairytale. This was real life.

"What are you thinking about, Mallory?"

"About how beautiful you are," I said, still mesmerized by his features.

I was curious to see his reaction to my blunt honesty, but instead of being flustered by the statement, he simply smiled at me and shook his head. "You always were such a strange girl. Kissing frogs to find a prince." He shifted a little closer, so he was looking down at me. "You know we never talked about what happened on the battlerunner."

"You mean the complete and utter humiliation of having my husband interrupt—" Terrin raised his finger to my lips, pressing away any further sarcastic words.

"I was more curious about what you thought of our intimacies. I was wondering how you wanted to proceed." He pulled his finger away so I could speak, but I didn't have any words. I pinched my eyes shut, remembering the heated kisses we shared, the feel of his body pressing against me, his hand on my breast. I took a breath and shook my head, trying to dislodge the arousing thoughts. Embarrassment bloomed in my face and I looked down. Terrin leaned in and whispered in my ear. "Did you enjoy yourself?"

"Yes."

"Enough to do it again."

I looked up, shocked that he would try to solicit me at my mother's house. If she caught us, she would kill us both. "Are you asking if I enjoyed it enough to do it again? Or are you asking if it was enough for me?"

Terrin's shoulders raised with a deep inhale. "Was it?"

"Was it enough for you? Would I be enough for you?" He stared at me, not finding the words he wanted or not having the words for what he wanted. "That's really the question that we're asking, isn't it?" Perhaps it was the princess inside of me coming through, but as I stared at my frog prince, I found the strength to speak the words I couldn't while in the confines of a ship. "Terrin, I think it's time for us to give up this biological rebellion."

"Yes, we keep saying that, and then we keep ending up back in each other's arms."

"There's a remedy for that," I said.

Terrin's brow flicked down. "What are you saying?"

"I'm saying that I appreciate everything you've done for me, but... I need you to leave Brahama." The words left my lips by the agency of someone else's command. I nearly gagged as they reached my ears.

"What?" Terrin's face could not have been more shocked, but I resisted taking back the words.

"Auntie Kit," Edric yelled up to me from the pool. "Come swim with us."

I looked at him and smiled, grateful he was giving me an out for this conversation. "Be down in a minute." I waved to him.

I looked back at Terrin, who was staring hard at me, still waiting for an answer. "You don't mean that, Mallory." His words barely made it past his clenched jaw.

"I do." I moved to leave, but he shifted into my path. His body was shaking, and I feared if I wasn't careful, I would earn myself a renewed bite on the back of my neck, or perhaps this time he would go straight for the jugular.

"You're running away from me again."

"Don't make a scene, Terrin. You know how that will end here."

His chest heaved with every breath. "I know you love me."

"Yes. You will always have a part of my heart, but for your sake, as well as mine, I am no longer offering my body." I moved to step around him, but he grabbed the side of my neck and pulled my head close to his. From an onlooker's perspective, we were merely hugging, but the hot breath on my ear was no longer the whispers of a lover.

"No, Mallory, I don't think so. Not anymore. I think every last beat of your heart belongs to me now." His voice was so strained, I could barely understand his words. "I know what you are doing. I know you're trying to save us both, but I won't let you. Not this time. I will not let you run away from this."

I pulled away enough to look at him. Nearly nose to nose, I matched his fury. "Do I look like I'm running?"

"We can be together."

"No, we can't. All we can do is leave each other wanting more and I refuse to indulge my childish fantasies any longer... or yours."

"This is by far the cruelest, most selfish thing you have ever done to me."

"It's, in fact, the most unselfish thing I have ever done since I stand to gain nothing from it. Think about what you gain by not being with me—not just a proper mate, but a chance at being a father. That's something I can never give you. Now that I am a mother, I understand the value of being a parent and I refuse to take that away from you. If for no other reason than to protect your lineage, I will not participate in this toxic relationship any longer." I tried to move again, but his hand shifted into my hair and gripped me tightly. I glanced at the guard posted just inside. He was taking notice of our tense situation.

"If I didn't know for certain that it hurts you to speak these words as much as it hurts me to hear them, I would—"

"Highness?" the guard called out to me, unsure of how to react to this situation.

I fought back the urge to beg for Terrin's forgiveness or appease his desire to have his love acknowledged. My heart may have been breaking, but for once in my life, I wasn't letting my emotions make this decision. I had a brain for a reason. It was time to use it. "Terrin was just about to rendezvous with Captain Reynard," I told the guard. "Perhaps you could remind him where the launchpad is."

His eyes widened, but I schooled my features, looking ever more the part of the princess. I needed him to know I was no longer *requesting* his departure.

He seemed to recognize the unyielding expression on my face. Much like my outfit, it was better suited to my mother.

He backed away, letting his grip slide out of my hair. His mouth gaped slightly, but his words disappeared. The tenderness in his eyes vanished, then he stormed off, nicking the shoulder of the guard as he passed him.

"Are you alright highness," the guard asked.

I nodded, and the guard ran off to *direct* Terrin to his exit.

I rubbed away Terrin's touch. I had never seen him so angry. Even in the dogfights, he hadn't been angry so much as energized. It took me, his only love, to bring him to the brink of such fury. I wasn't sure what his threat would have been, but I was glad to be spared his angry slurs. As much as I had hurt him, he was right that I had hurt myself just as much. I panted, unable to control my hyperventilating sobs. On any other day, I would have collapsed to the ground and wallowed in my anguish, but I didn't dare ruin my dress.

Lifeguard

"Auntie Kit, watch me, watch me!" Edric shrieked when I came down to join the fun at the pool. Edric was now doing cannonballs off the diving board while Ayil and Rayne watched. I was happy to do anything that took my mind off my romantic problems.

Since my altercation upstairs with Terrin, I had stifled my tears and powdered my eyes into a false glow. The smile I wore was just as false, but it felt more natural the longer I watched my adoptive nephew play.

Edric splashed into the pool for the hundredth time, and I applauded his performance. I smiled at Ayil, who was content to float in the shallow end and be a vigilant lifeguard. It was nice to see them taking part in normal father-and-son activities.

I stood beside Rayne, who sat on the edge of the pool. He didn't immediately look up at me and seemed to be pointedly avoiding eye contact. "Everything okay?" he asked. When I didn't answer, he looked up and nodded toward the balcony where I had just been speaking with Terrin. "Things seemed to be getting tense up there."

I nodded. "Yeah." I cleared my throat. "I asked him to leave Brahama."

Rayne said nothing at first, though I assumed he was silently rejoicing in my decision to end things with Terrin. "Is that what you really want?" he asked.

"No." I let the answer hang between us, reminding both of us that I was not being cruel by choice. "But it is what's best for my future. For my daughter's future."

"Our daughter," Rayne corrected.

"Our daughter," I remedied.

"Hey, Kit, why don't you join us?" Ayil said, swimming over to the edge.

"Isn't it cold?" I scrunched up my nose, remembering the cold swims of my youth.

"Chilly, but comfortable," he said, kicking his feet behind him to splash Edric, who squealed his objection. "Why are you so dressed up?"

I shrugged. "My wardrobe selection took a dive after my ship blew up, remember? The clothes I brought with me conveniently disappeared somewhere between my hamper and the laundry room."

"She stole your clothes?" Ayil asked, disgust making his eyes narrow into slits.

"She probably burned them, actually," I joked, though it was probably the truth. Even if I had trusted Rey to send me down more clothes, my mother would have probably *lost* them too. She was not a fan of my utilitarian style.

"And your hair?" He perked his brow. "You look... normal." More disgust.

"Yeah, she not-so-subtly suggested that if I didn't change it, she would shave it off." I chuckled, once again thinking it was a double-edged sword since a bald princess was just as bad as one with weird hair.

"You know, I used to have someone who would tell me what to wear and how to cut my hair," Ayil said.

I looked at the legitimate revulsion marring his beautiful face. "It's not the same, Ayil."

"Why? Because you're rich?"

"No, because she's my mother."

"I had to mind my *daddy* too," Ayil said dryly.

I scoffed and shook my head. "Ayil, come on, she's just—"

"Come on, Auntie Kit!" Edric yelled behind me just as he shoved himself into my back. I lobbed forward over the edge of the pool. I narrowly missed Ayil, as I instinctively brought my hands out for the unintentional dive. The water hit me like a familiar frigid embrace and, as annoyed as I was with my adoptive nephew's prank, I rather enjoyed the long-missed pleasure of swimming.

I reached the bottom and gracefully parted the water with my arms to begin my ascent back to the top. My rise stopped abruptly as something tugged on my shoulder. The draping fabric of my dress had snagged on something. Following the sash like a rope, I blindly searched for the source of the problem. I found where the fabric disappeared beneath the return grate and yanked on it.

It wouldn't release.

Seeing no alternative, I reached around to unzip my dress, but I couldn't reach it. The pull tab was too low to reach from above and too high to reach it from below. I panicked and grabbed the sash again. I needed to get free.

Something sharp hit my hands, and I retracted in pain. My gasp forced water into my lungs and they burned, rejecting the fluid. Someone's arms wrapped around me and pulled me upward, propelled by their kicking legs.

I popped out of the water and took a grateful breath.

"Over here!" Ayil yelled, and I reached for him. He pulled me out of the water like a fish and left me to cough and sputter the water out of my lungs.

"I'm sorry," Edric was crying and frantically apologizing, but I didn't have the wherewithal to console him or explain this was just a freak accident no one could have predicted.

"Kit, are you alright!" Rayne pushed me onto my back and I burped in his face before croaking out a response that sounded nothing like a "yes." I gave him a thumbs-up instead.

"Wait, wait, wait, it's not what it looks like!" Ayil yelled at someone.

Before I could see who he was talking to, I felt them. The hands of two guards arrived from out of nowhere. They grabbed me and dragged me back. I watched another slew of men surround Rayne as the guards took me away. They yelled at him to drop his knife. The blade perched in his hand immediately dropped to the ground, and I realized what had happened.

Rayne had jumped into the water to cut me free with one of his ever-present knives. He must have still had it in his hand when he was checking on me. The guards thought he was attacking me instead of saving me.

"Highness, where are you hurt?" I was in a poolside chair now, surrounded by my *saviors*. "Where are you cut?"

"It's fine. He just—" I looked down to examine the cut on my hand that had occurred because I had impeded Rayne's efforts to cut my sash. "—oh, shit." The one minor cut that should not have caused such a stir now looked like a murder scene all over my beige dress. The guards must have thought he was stabbing me to death.

Divorce

"Mother, he wasn't trying to kill me!" I yelled in exasperation when I finally had an audience with the Queen. Surprisingly, she had allowed the three of us into her parlor—though I was certain she would prohibit us from sitting on the furniture with wet clothes.

"You are covered in blood." Mother sat at her small writing desk in front of the window. She had hardly turned to greet me and was continuing to write even as I tried to plead Rayne's innocence.

"My dress was caught in the filtration system in the pool. I was drowning. He accidentally cut me when he was cutting me free."

"Why were you in the pool fully clothed?"

I gaped at her. "That's what you want to know?

"I threw her in," Rayne falsely confessed.

My mother turned around to look at him. He was now in handcuffs with a robe over his shoulders, but still sopping wet. Her mouth twisted in contemplation. "And why did you do that?"

"Because I enjoy getting your daughter wet," Rayne said with seemingly no embarrassment. I meanwhile felt my face heat to a dark burgundy.

Susan maintained her sharp observance, not wavering at his bravado, nor balking at his obscured vulgarity. "I find there are few men who surprise me. You are not one of them, Mr.

Turner." Rayne recoiled at hearing his real name—or at least his real pseudonym.

"Geez, Mother, Edric pushed me in. It was a prank. Do you want to interrogate him, too?" I looked around. "Where is he? Is someone with him?" Ayil nodded, and I relaxed.

"Please don't think that because I agreed to have you all here. The invitation extends further than my patience. I could force you to leave at any time."

"Does that include me?" I asked. She looked at me, not technically answering and yet saying plenty.

"Where Kit goes, I go," Rayne said.

"Me too." Ayil bolstered his chest and moved to stand next to Rayne as if this were the moment to take a stand.

Susan looked between Rayne and Ayil, no doubt thinking little of their declarations. It was rather difficult to take either of them seriously in their swim trunks. She took a breath and stood. With slow, concise steps, she approached Rayne and stood in his face. They were about eye to eye, and had I wanted to place bets on who would win this argument, I still would have picked my mother. She always had the last word. "I can see you have feelings for my daughter. That's good... given your history." My mother glanced at me, putting the lion's share of a whore's guilt in my lap. "Kit is a beautiful, bright girl. There is plenty to like. However, the relationship you had with her prior to coming here is over."

Rayne's mouth twitched slightly as he struggled to maintain his stone-cold facade to match my mother's. "Your Majesty, with all due respect, that's none of your business."

"My daughter's suitors are very much my business." She looked back at me now, though she was still technically speaking to Rayne. "I let her last deviant desires go unchecked for too long and I regret that." My head swarmed with curses and my fists tightened as the word deviant sidled up against my ardent affections for Terrin. "You see, unlike her, I could see her future. I knew how much pain her misplaced affections would cause her. I did little to stop it and I think now that it was a mistake. One I won't repeat." She turned her gaze back to Rayne.

"And how do you intend to stop me from having a relationship with her?"

Susan smiled. "Come now, Mr. Turner, don't play the fool. I despise making threats that have to be spelled out."

"I think you're going to have to spell it out because last I checked, Captain Reynard is still circling the planet. Even the hint of foul play and this little accord is over."

"Oh, don't worry, I haven't forgotten about your captain. He is a rather interesting character. One that might require a good deal of thought to deal with, should the occasion for violence arise."

"Mother, you don't want to make threats against—" She raised her finger at me, silencing my attempt to warn her.

"Ultimately, the lesson I am trying to edify is that I am not just some garden variety leader. I am a Queen. A dictator by birthright, by law, and by the decision of thousands of nations across hundreds of planets. I advise the leaders of half the known races in this galaxy, stipulating laws, settling disputes, and maintaining a continuous flow of goods throughout the systems, so every member of my constituency has food and a job to pay for that food. And in return for those services and mediation, I have access to age-appropriate men and women for military service. I wield the threat of nearly one billion soldiers, so if you think you or your clever captain are going to make me whither, you have sadly misjudged me. As for spelling out the threat against you, just take into consideration the many ways I might remove you from my daughter's company, either in totality or in parts at a time."

Rayne didn't react to her, but he didn't snap back at her, either. As usual, my mother had won again.

"So." Susan turned back to me. "From here on out. There will be no more gattaw, no more assassins, and no more..." She struggled to find a label for Ayil. "... pool boys."

Pleased with her announcement, my mother headed back to her desk.

"You blustering bitch," Ayil said to her back.

I gasped and turned to Ayil. He had been so quiet until then. I hadn't thought about what his reaction would be to my mother's condescension. Unfortunately, he was the one I should have been concerned about. He was frothing with anger, his upper lip curling, and his breath coming in heavy heaves. He despised anything resembling authority over another human being's life, and that was the entirety of my childhood.

My mother slowly turned around. "Excuse me?"

"You heard me," he said.

"Ayil, don't," I warned.

"Don't what?" He looked at me, no doubt shocked I wasn't standing up for myself. He didn't understand that it was safer under my mother's boot heel. "Don't question her? Don't disobey her. Don't step out of line!" Ayil's volume and vehemence surprised me further.

"Careful how you proceed, young man," my mother warned him.

"You don't scare me, you old bitty." Ayil took a step forward.

"Just calm down, Ayil." Rayne moved to touch his shoulder, but Ayil ripped away like the touch had burned him.

"I'm tired of being calm." He took another step toward her. "You are no better than the man that kidnapped me as a child."

My mother scoffed and looked at me. "My daughter is not a kidnap victim."

"Do you know what he used to say to me after he raped me?"

My mother frowned and looked at me with a little more worry in her expression. I suspected it was the same worry my face held. Ayil rarely spoke of his abuses, and certainly not to strangers.

"He told me I could never escape him, because no matter what, he would get me back?"

"I am sorry for your childhood trauma, but it has nothing to do with me."

"It has everything to do with you. When I look into your cold, heartless eyes; when I hear your cocky voice flaunting your power, I see him, I hear him. You can put on a pretty fucking dress and wave a scepter instead of your fist, but you are no better than him."

"That is an outrageous comparison."

"You put her in front of a line of men and said choose. The only difference was, they weren't paying, and she didn't have to spread her legs... at least not right away."

"How dare you!" Ayil had flustered my mother. So much so that she struggled to keep her composure. She was losing, and she didn't like losing. Without warning, she raised her hand and slapped Ayil right across the face.

He was no stranger to a woman's wrath, but something about my mother had him in a frenzy. He didn't even pause before slapping her right back. With a little more strength to back his hit, she lost her footing and landed on the floor.

"Guards!" she screamed.

I ran forward to help my mother. Two men burst in from the patio doors and blocked my path to her. Four more came in through the main door. The two men forced Ayil to the floor, holding guns at his head. Despite his handcuffs, someone detained Rayne.

My mother stood from the floor, casting away any offers for assistance. She touched her reddened cheek and glared at Ayil. "Kill him."

"No!" I screamed and leaped for Ayil, but the two men blocking my path grabbed me and pulled me back.

They cuffed Ayil's wrists and ankles. The guards picked him up and carried him toward the door. It had been a long time since my mother had executed anyone, but I hadn't been exaggerating when I said she still did. Any act of aggression against the queen was considered a threat to the crown and was, therefore, taken very seriously.

"Nooooo!" I shrieked and dropped to the floor, struggling against my captors like a marionette doll. "Mother, no! Please, don't kill him!"

My mother ignored my pleas as she looked after Ayil's exit with venomous eyes.

"Mother, please!" I was blubbering and bawling. I only had seconds to convince her. There would be no ceremony for Ayil's death. Just an old-fashioned metal bullet to the back of the head. "Stop this! I'll do anything! Anything!" I screamed as loudly as I could—hoping my sheer volume could pierce the cold armament around her heart.

"Tell them to wait." My mother motioned for one guard to run ahead and stay the execution. She moved to look at me face-on. "Anything?"

"Yes!" I nodded and mouthed please when my croaking throat only produced a wretched cry.

My mother turned to Rayne. "What about you? Do you want to save your friend?"

"Yes."

"Very well, come over here. Both of you."

The guards released us and removed Rayne's cuffs. We moved to the desk where she had been working. "If you want Ayil's life to be saved, then sign and blood this document."

I looked down at the handwritten script on the paper. Rarely did anyone write out documents anymore, but it was commonplace in Brahama when it was a contract. I read the larger print at the top: Divorce Decree. I looked at my mother and she gave me a thin, contented smile.

"Guards, leave us!" she ordered and the guards swiftly evacuated the room. The doors closed behind them and we were once again alone to speak freely.

"I don't really care what has transpired between the time of your wedding and now, but I have no intention of inviting a known assassin into the family line. Both of you sign and blood this document to make your divorce legal, and Ayil will get to live."

I stared down at the document. It meant nothing. The document was symbolic, much as the marriage had been, to begin with. It changed nothing, and yet my heart seized with a deep ache. I had all but broken up with Rayne anyway. It shouldn't have mattered, but it felt final. Like I wasn't just walking away from him, but losing him entirely.

Rayne stared down at the document a moment, no doubt thinking the same thought as me. Hopefully, anyway. However, it only lasted a moment. He picked up the pen and signed the document with exaggerated loops. He pressed his finger into the disc beside the paper and then moved his bleeding finger to the paper to imprint his bloody pattern onto the contract. When it was done, he stepped back and looked at me. He jerked his head toward the document. I moved to the desk and did the same. I pressed my bloody thumbprint into the paper and made our divorce official.

Before I could even consider picking it up and ripping it to shreds, my mother yanked the contract from beneath me and rolled it up. She said something about accomplishing one thing in her day and stomped out of the room to cancel Ayil's execution. She had won again. Even when she was losing, she was only a sidestep away from winning again.

"This doesn't change anything, Kit," Rayne said.

I looked up at him and shook my head. "You're right, it doesn't." Rayne reached for me, but I pulled away. He frowned at me, baffled by my reaction.

"But I thought..." He blinked. "You said by the pool that you told Terrin to leave."

"Yes, I told Terrin I no longer wanted to pursue a relationship with him. I'm sorry if you assumed that meant I would be returning to you."

"But our..." He lowered his voice to a whisper. "...daughter?"

"We'll figure it out, but I'm done trying to figure you out."

"Kit."

"We don't work. Rayne and I almost worked, but Mr. Turner and I lead very different lives." Rayne scoffed, but I was in no mood to deal with more fallout from my rejections. "I'm going to check on Ayil." He stormed out of the room through the patio doors while I went to see Ayil.

The Message

As I sat in the courtyard on the edge of a fountain, I thought about why I had returned to Brahama. I thought coming home meant I could fix everything that had gone wrong since I left. I assumed my mother—the most powerful woman in the galaxy—could make everything better, but she was turning out to be even more oppressive than I remembered. I had no idea how far she could take her cruelty to get what she wanted.

She saw how attached I was to Ayil and instead of taking pity on me, she used it against me. I was glad now I hadn't told her about her granddaughter. God only knows how she would use her to manipulate me.

Had she at least acted quickly to attack the Coalition, I could have tolerated her abuses. But she was not turning out to be the hero I had wanted her to be. The politics of warfare were hindering my revenge.

A whistling sound above drew my eyes, and I searched for someone trying to get my attention. Something whipped past my head, lifting my hair. There was a splash in the fountain behind me.

Looking back at the mossy green pond, I saw a blinking red light in the water. I gasped and dropped to the ground behind the fountain's stone wall.

For some time, I lay there, waiting for my end, but it didn't arrive. I peeked back over the wall, trying to discern what was lurking beneath the water.

I reached out and tugged the disk that contained the light. I freed the disk from its rod and pulled it from the water.

"Ouch!" I yelped as its heat became more obvious outside of the water. I dropped the mechanical disk, and it clanked on the fountain edge.

I looked around to see if anyone was observing me. There were guards all around the mansion, but the courtyards were relatively safe, so they didn't maintain a heavy presence in them. After all, the only way in was from above, but satellites and a slew of radar systems monitored the atmosphere. Not to mention my mother's planetary armada. Nevertheless, I scanned the sky for enemy vessels.

Perhaps the device was from Rey.

Without regard for one of life's most crucial rules, I pressed the blinking red button on the device. It clicked and hummed. I was about to run, but a flicker of light and a screeching sound indicated this was a telecom device and not a bomb.

I followed the path of the miniature projector and watched the images flash against the backdrop of a small waterfall. After a short signal search and an audio check, it revealed a blank wall.

"Rey?" I asked. "Is that you?" A man stepped into view, just as grainy as the last time I had seen him. "Chancellor."

"It's good to see you again, Mallory." His voice conveyed the same contemptible condescension I had grown accustomed to, but his face looked tired. The same way my mother looked coming out of the war room.

I looked around again, searching for someone to alert.

"I wouldn't," he said. "I can disable this device from here, and I think you might want to hear what I have to say."

"How did you know I was here?"

"Where else would you be? You have nowhere left to run. I knew eventually you would run home to mommy. I'm just surprised it took you this long."

"What do you want, Agate?"

He laughed, staring back at me coldly. "The same thing I have always wanted. You, Mallory. I just want you."

"Not my baby?"

"Oh, so the child survived, after all." I kicked myself for revealing this truth. Perhaps no one ever needed to know she survived. "Don't worry, Mallory, I know a mother would never surrender her own child."

"I'm tired of this game. I want you to leave me alone."

"I'm tired of this game, as well. I've lost an entire research base because of you and your lot. Not to mention an entire infantry."

"Boo-hoo," I mocked.

Agate's face lost all expression, and then he smiled. "I'd like to show you something." He shifted in the image and then I was being transported with him. We moved across his office to a window. The blazing sun made the image white until the lens adjusted. Then I saw my sister.

Elizandra was in the backyard of my father's home, skipping through the gardens like I imagined I did once upon a time. Looking at her evoked hope in me. Hope that I might someday see my daughter running through those cobbled paths.

"She's growing like a weed." Agate's face returned, and I said nothing. "Healthy. Happy. I bet you would like her to stay that way." Still, I said nothing. "Sadly, she doesn't have the resistance that you do. I'm afraid if we infected her, she wouldn't even make the journey home."

My eyes welled with tears, but I still said nothing. There was nothing to say. The people I loved were perpetually being used as pawns against me. They had captured my king and my queen was too gutless to fight for me.

"I need you back, Mallory. The research is at a standstill until we can figure out what Kessler did to make you so fucking resilient." He paused, almost begging me to say something derisive. "It's very simple. You come back to me and I will release your sister. No tricks. No sabotage. Just a girl for a girl."

"Okay," I whispered.

Agate looked taken aback. "I mean it, Mallory, no tricks. If I smell a rat, I'll just kill her outright."

"I said, okay." Agate still looked unconvinced. "I'll make the arrangements. Just keep everyone else out of it. No hurting my friends."

Agate snorted. "I've never given a second's-worth of thought about your friends. As long as they stay out of my way, I'll stay out of theirs."

"Fine. I'll just need a few days to—"

"You have forty-eight hours to leave Brahama. I'll expect you on the fastest transport you can find."

"Fine."

Agate looked like he wanted to lay down another threat, but he just signed off and the tiny device hissed as an internal self-destruct sequence deteriorated it from the inside out.

Bargaining Chips

Susan yelped when she came into her room and found me lounging on the bench at the foot of her bed like a patient lover. However, the look on my face was not that of any type of love. Alerted by her cry, her sentinels arrived seconds later to save her. They must not have recognized me with my new updo. The bright orange tips sticking out of my high ponytail made it look as if my auburn locks were on fire. They matched my mood perfectly.

Her guardians leaped forward, ready to extract the intruder from my mother's room. I didn't panic, even though they were several times bigger than me. I simply raised the two pulse pistols I had stowed behind the pillows my arms were resting on and fired at them.

The two men seized and grunted before falling to either side of my mother. She looked down at the two unconscious men and then at me. She was livid and barely able to get her words out. "Where did you... How did you... Why?" She finally settled on the last.

I kept my guns in hand and leaned forward to rest my elbows on my knees. I had given up on the dresses my mother had provided for me and was instead wearing the uniform of one of her very own guards. Although made with the same puncture-resistant fabric as the biomechanoid's, the cranberry uniform with black trim wasn't nearly as confining. I found I could move rather freely in it.

"Get out or I'll call for more guards," my mother warned, but I could see she was feeling a little insecure with the position I was putting her in.

"I really wouldn't advise doing anything that would put me on the offensive, Mother."

Susan snorted dismissively, and her fear evaporated. "Are you really going to shoot your own mother, Kit?"

"That depends. Were you really going to kill my best friend yesterday?"

She chuckled with relief. "Is that what this is about? You want an apology?" She moved away from me and sat down at her vanity to remove her makeup and get ready for bed. "Your friend was out of line, you know that."

"He was out of line, and I've spoken with Ayil. I can't exactly say he will treat you with the utmost respect, but he won't touch you again."

"Well, thank God for common sense."

"Speaking of common sense, he made some interesting points, don't you think?"

Susan groaned and pressed her fingertips into her brow. "Please, Kit, I beg of you. Can we not rehash your childhood? Not tonight."

"Mother, I had to disguise myself as a guard and shoot two of your sentinels just to get a private audience with you. If you think I did that out of some outlandish hope for an apology, you're being naïve."

"Then what do you want?"

I stood and holstered my pulse pistols on my hips. I leaned against one column of her poster bed and spoke to her reflection. "I want an update on what you plan to do about Agate. How are you going to stop him from infecting half the galaxy?"

"I can't speak to you about that."

"Why? Because I'm not your daughter anymore?"

"No, because I can't trust you." She turned to look at me face to face. "You have been collaborating with an enemy."

I shifted uncomfortably, no longer able to claim confidently that Rey was not an enemy. Had it not been for her stubbornness, I might have taken my bug directly into the war room and inadvertently allowed Rey to listen in on their entire meeting. "If you knew what these viruses could do, you would understand why I feel compelled to be involved with the decisions being made in that room."

Susan turned around and continued with her routine. The silence stretched out for a moment. "What about Elizandra?" I moved to sit on a hamper next to her vanity so I could see her face as she scrubbed away her mask of beauty. "Have you considered rescuing her and Dad?"

"There will be no rescuing your father. As far as the people are concerned, he *is* the Coalition."

I stood and circled the room, frustrated that even at this moment she could be so cold to the man who raised me. Who loved me in a way she never could have. "So, if Agate disposes of him, you won't retaliate? I thought if I came here, you would fix this." I touched the painting of my mother that hung over her faux fireplace.

"I'm sorry, Mallory, a mother can only fix so much."

"Sometimes I think I hate you." I let the words hang for a moment and didn't look back to see her reaction. "But I always respected you."

Susan laughed, and it surprised me. I looked back and saw genuine mirth on her freshly exposed pale face. "You had a funny way of showing it."

"I respected you as a woman—as a queen. I never wanted to follow in your footsteps, because being a queen meant I had to be unyielding and yet surrender to everything." I shook my head. "I couldn't surrender. Not until now." My thoughts slipped back to my memory of Terrin confessing to Rayne that he was finally ready to surrender to his love for me. I hadn't thought about what that truly meant until now. It was as much about giving into passion as it was about giving up on finding a better, more suitable partner.

"Are you suggesting that you are ready to be a queen?" my mother asked tentatively.

I blinked, realizing I had perhaps misled her with my statement. "No, but I am ready to make a stand. I'm done running. I'm done hiding. I'm going to save my sister. With your true heir safe and sound, maybe you can finally be the queen I thought you were."

I headed for the door, stepping over the downed men as I did.

"What are you talking about?"

I paused at the door. "He's given me an ultimatum."

"Who?"

"Agate."

Susan knocked over her stool as she stood and moved to me. "When?"

"Yesterday, in the courtyard. I got a communication—"

"Why didn't you tell me?"

"I tried." I motioned to the downed guards.

"If I had known what it was about—"

"This has to stay between us, Mother. If the others know I am intending to sacrifice myself, they'll try to stop me."

"Forget the others. *I'm* going to stop you."

"No, you won't," I said somberly. "Rationally, I am the bigger bargaining chip. Holding onto me is the only way to keep leverage on Agate. But while he has Elizandra, he has *your* biggest bargaining chip."

Susan stared at me. "I have two daughters, Kit."

I nodded. "Yes, but one of them needs you more."

"I won't allow it." She moved behind her changing screen. I moved over to her bed and sat down as I watched her shadow dance behind the screen. I massaged the plush fabric of her bedspread, considering what the right level of objection was in a situation like this. She couldn't outright say yes because that would mean admitting her preference. She had to convince herself it was a logical argument.

"He won't kill me, Mother. That's the difference. He gets what he wants, and you technically get what you want. Both of your daughters will be safe.

"Alive does not mean safe." She came around the screen in a mauve gown that could have passed as evening wear. "However..." She looked at me, evaluating me. "If we made it public, that would be a different story. The Coalition has made a stink about you running off since day one. The people consider you a traitor. Handing you back as a prisoner would require news footage and trials. It would be necessary for them to keep you in the public eye. They couldn't just bury you—in a lab, I mean."

I nodded. "That's true."

My mother looked proud of her brilliance for a moment, but then her face fell as she realized what she was saying. For a moment, she just looked at me. I kept my face stoic, not allowing her to see the fear I felt. "I'll call a press conference tomorrow morning," she said, finally caving to the logic we had established. Her eyes fell on my more casual ensemble. "Wear something nice."

The Press

I took my position among the aids, just to the right of my mother, and stared out at the crowd in the press room. Everyone in the room clicked their cameras, taking the first photos of me since my wedding day debacle. Two cameras hovered near me, taking footage of me and my mother. I could feel the warmth of digital laser scans as well. They would take 3D images of me down to the very last pore. Good thing I had put on makeup.

This was the part of public life I hated. In my early childhood, laws protecting children from published photos spared me the torment of cameras. But when I turned fourteen, the examination began. The entire galaxy debated if I looked more like my mother or father. They critiqued my clothing, my hair, and my body.

Unlike Elizandra, I did not desire to be the center of attention—at least not for an empire.

In the presence of cameras, I found my chest would seize, and I couldn't breathe. Forget speaking or presenting an image of stalwart grace. If I didn't keel over into the crowd, it was a good day for me.

Even now, with assassins at my back and Agate in my future, it wasn't the fear of death making my breath more labored; it was these blasted cameras. I regretted not having at least one familiar face in the audience, but I couldn't risk Ayil making a scene. I hadn't told him my plan. He was going to be furious with me. He hated it when I gave up.

Was I giving up or was I standing up? It was becoming harder to tell now that my options were so few.

My mother began the speech that was to announce my return to the royal fold. That was the excuse for the press conference. Everyone was eager to hear how the queen was going to clean up my mess. Little did they know, she had no intention of doing so. I was going to clean it up myself.

"As you all know, my daughter has betrayed the trust of not only her mother and father, but also the empire and the Coalition."

I glanced at my mother, a little surprised she wasn't holding punches. She didn't need to add fuel to a bonfire.

"But I have convinced her to do what is right."

I had to bite my cheek not to smile. Even at this moment, she had to make herself look good. It wasn't my decision. She had to convince me to do it. This was the part of my mother I loathed. More than the absentee mother or the cruel queen. I hated the politician in her the most.

"My daughter will be surrendering herself to the Coalition."

Gasps filled the room and camera flashes blinded me. The reporters erupted into questions about when and how I would deliver myself. My mother began explaining that an armada of ships would peacefully deliver me home. It was a clever plan; I thought. By making my surrender public and on the nose of a battle cruiser, Agate was not likely to renege on his end of the deal. My sister would be home soon, and my mother could concentrate on how to protect the kingdom from whatever the chancellor had up his sleeve.

I blinked away a few of the little white stars in my eyes, but the moment I thought I could see again, someone put a laser in my path. I raised my hand to block a particular nuisance beam and glared at the cameraman, aiming it at me.

My handicapped vision landed on a man in the back row. While everyone else was wearing business casual clothes, he was in full business attire. I narrowed my eyes and leaned a little to the right to see past his scanning device. Mr. Davis met my gaze and beamed at me.

I looked for Rayne, but he wasn't with him.

Mr. Davis held his index finger to his lips, demanding my secrecy. As he pulled his hand away, he kept his finger raised, now pointing an imaginary gun at me. My brow dipped, perplexed by his ill-timed comedic drama.

The air around his hand warped and disfigured until an object appeared in his grasp.

A gun.

At that moment, I remembered Rayne had told me not to make major plays without consulting Captain Baloch. He didn't want the viruses I was carrying to fall into the Coalition's hands. And he was making sure that didn't happen.

"No!" I yelled, but it was too late. The *poof* of the weapon's discharge hit me hard in the chest.

The sting reverberated around me, an exquisite pain that forced a scream from me as I toppled to the ground behind my mother.

More screams followed mine and people scrambled to escape. The guards tried to contain everyone, searching for the person with the weapon. Meanwhile, several of the elite troops swooped in and yanked my mother away from me.

"Kit!" she yelled. "Wait! Is she okay? Kit!" Mother's heart-wrenching demands overpowered every other sound until they dragged her out of the room.

For a moment, I was alone. I could feel my heart thumping, but my lungs were not filling. My scream had depleted the last of my air and nothing I did would allow another breath to be drawn.

I looked down at my chest, horrified by the blood. I could have sworn Mr. Davis had used a pulse pistol, but it must have been a projectile weapon. The bastard had shot me.

When the remaining screams died down, I heard clicks again. I turned my head and found several brave reporters who hadn't fled the room yet. They were taking pictures of me. I was dying, and they were photographing me. Parasitic scum! I tried to raise my hand to flip them off, but my motor functions were failing.

Mr. Davis pushed between two of the reporters and looked down on me with satisfaction. Not only was he pleased with his new status as an assassin, but he was just sick enough to stick around and watch me slip away.

I wasn't ready to die. Tears sprung to my eyes and I let out a gargled cry as my head fell back. The paralysis had reached my face and my lips went numb. My eyes drifted out of focus and I could no longer feel my body.

Someone near me, I couldn't tell who said, "Her heart has stopped. She's gone." They pulled my eyelids down, putting me into the darkness of my death. Soon after the sounds disappeared, I drifted away from the only reality I knew.

GRAVE

Sometime later, sounds penetrated the darkness. I could hear the soft whistle of my inhalations and muffled voices. I couldn't feel anything except the cold. For a moment, I thought I had arrived in hell. Even as the thought came to me, I felt my heart jump into overdrive.

I was alive.

I couldn't move, couldn't talk, and couldn't see anything, but I was alive.

Another thought occurred to me. Was I in my coffin? Did they bury me alive?

Footsteps approached, followed by the sound of metal being hit. The impact sent vibrations through me. "You son of a bitch!" It was Terrin. "Why didn't you tell us it was a ruse?"

"We needed everyone's reactions to be sincere." Mr. Davis was speaking. "We needed the empire to believe she was dead, so the Coalition would believe it, too."

"You want my sincere reaction?" Terrin asked. Something clanked as it hit the ground. Mr. Davis, presumably, started making grunting sounds. "I have been in mourning for eleven hours. You could have mentioned this sooner."

"Terrin," Rayne said calmly. "We need to get her out of here before she wakes and someone mistakes her for a zombie. You can kick Davis's ass later."

Davis made some kind of whining sound, like his partner's disloyalty appalled him. A moment later, he was coughing and breathing again. "I don't know what the big deal is. She's alive. I've given you good news."

"I doubt a cockroach-like you could even understand the pain endured by even a single second of imagining the one you love is dead."

"Whatever, Rayne, is right. We need to get this done. We're losing time. Her stasis only lasts so long." After a clatter, I felt my body move away from the strict darkness around me. Someone pried open one of my eyes. I could just make out Mr. Davis before a light flashed in and out of my vision. "Come on, before the hypothermia sets in too deep to save her toes." Mr. Davis closed my eyes and put his hands under my back. I felt hands on my legs as well.

"Out of my way," Terrin said, and I felt his arms scoop up my body. For a moment, his heat embraced me—like the desert come to life. My body begged to be wrapped up in him, but he placed me on a different surface. It was softer, like a bed, but not warm. "Mallory?" Terrin patted my cheeks.

"She won't be awake for another few hours," Mr. Davis said.

"Davis, help me with the other one." A door creaked open and the sound of footsteps diminished.

Terrin touched my cheek. "Is this what you felt like, Mallory?" he whispered. "That day in the pit, when you saw me die and reborn again. I thought the ache in my heart would subside once I saw you, but it's sharper than ever." He paused, his breathing becoming ragged. "I know you're trying to dig me out of your heart. You're smart to do so, but there isn't a knife sharp enough. I will find a way back in. Because it is quite clear to me now. I cannot live without you." His arms wrapped around me and he mumbled something in his language. The warmth he provided lulled my mind into sleep and I disappeared back into my temporary grave.

Corpse

I inhaled sharply and grappled against the surrounding water. I was drowning, but only in my dreams. The bed sheets tangling around me were not water, and the bed beneath me was not a coffin.

Only the darkness was real.

I heard a shush, and a hand touched my forehead. It gently combed back through my sweaty hair. I remembered Terrin's warmth and sweet words and instantly relaxed. "You're okay now." I looked toward the voice in the darkness and recognized the features that matched the voice—Mr. Davis.

My relaxation instantly diminished. I leaped at him, full steam, without regard to what my condition was. I pushed him to the ground with my weight, but my flailing was useless. I could barely raise my arms, let alone hit with them.

He rolled me back over, pressing me into the cold metal floor with his weight. He leaned into my ear and whispered. "Is that any way to treat the man who saved your life?"

"You shot me."

"Mmm, technically, but had I not shot you, you would already be in the hands of the Coalition. Dissected on a table and contributing to the death of nearly half the galaxy. You're lucky your corpse is just as valuable, or Rey would have just had me execute you."

"What did you do to me?"

He shifted and turned on the light. I winced and blinked against the bright light. He tugged open a couple of snaps on my shirt to reveal my sternum. He traced his finger over the circle of tiny red dots just over my breastbone. "Bio-dampening nanobot injection. They get into your central nervous system and reduce your body function to just shy of death. Without a very extensive examination, no one would know you were still technically alive." He rested his hand between my breasts. Since I couldn't slap him for the offense, I just glared at him.

"Get off her, Davis," Rayne said from the door.

He rolled his eyes. "Just playing." He chuckled and rolled off me.

"You've got plenty of toys of your own." Rayne helped me off the floor and hugged me to him.

"I'm not a fucking toy!" I pushed away from Rayne and stumbled back on my wobbling legs. Davis grabbed me before I could drop to the floor again.

"I like her better like this." Davis grabbed my wrist and shook my hand out in front of me. "Rayne, you've been a bad, bad boy," he said in a mock female tone. "I'm gonna have to spank you." Annoyance flickered across Rayne's face, but a smirk still tugged at his lips. Too many years of hanging out with Mr. Davis had made him susceptible to his tormenting humor.

"I will kill you, you jackass." Despite my effort to pull away, I was too weak to do anything to stop the involuntary puppet show.

"Or maybe you can spank me." Davis moved my hand back to my open shirt and forced me to grope my breast.

"Alright, that's enough." Rayne lost his amusement and came to my rescue. Later than I would have preferred, but it would have to do. Davis handed me off to him and he helped me loop my arm around his neck for support. "Do you have much feeling back?"

"Everything feels numb."

"Good." Rayne grabbed my arm, much as Davis had, and whipped my hand across his face. "That's from Kit." Davis hissed, no doubt feeling a bit more sting with Rayne behind the strength of my blow. "And this" Rayne punched him in the chin, making Davis's head twist the other way. "...is from me."

"Hey!" Mr. Davis blinked and rubbed his chin, glaring at Rayne.

"Are we good?" Rayne asked.

Davis pinched up his face. "Yeah, we're good," he grumbled.

"Let's go." Rayne assisted my limping body out into the hall. I immediately recognized Captain Reynard's ship. "Why are we back here?"

"Because you're dead," Davis answered. "And we intend to keep you that way."

Leverage

I stood at the bridge console looking out over Brahama. My maternal home planet was beautiful from space. Though I had only been ashore for a few days, I was glad to get back aboard a ship. I didn't feel nearly as trapped here. Even though I technically was.

"What did you expect me to do?" I asked Rey without looking at him.

"I expected you to take your role in this more seriously."

"She's my sister." I turned back to face the room of unsympathetic faces. With Rey sitting in the observation chair and Davis and Rayne behind him, they were the epitome of the Captain Reynard Baloch triad—his mind, his face, and his shadow.

"She's still just one person," Rey said.

"I'm the only leverage the empire has."

Reynard made an odd sound that might have been intended to be a laugh or a scoff. He pressed his hands together and pinched his tongue between his teeth—literally biting his tongue. "If you are anyone's leverage, you are mine." He slipped out of his chair and stood next to me in front of the viewscreen. He pressed on my back to turn me so we were both looking out on the planet. "We've had a series of miscommunications and I blame myself for that. You see, I thought we were coming here to give your mother a forewarning about a potential viral attack. You, however, thought we were coming here to start a war with the Coalition. Little did I know you had a massive piece of information that could help the war effort."

"I'm trying to save my people."

Rey groaned and knocked his fist against his forehead. "You don't save people by giving them more guns."

"It was just information."

"It was—" Rey suddenly moved away from me. "Someone please explain it to her."

I rolled my eyes and looked back at Rayne. He was about to speak, but Davis looked up from his pad and pointed to the viewscreen, which was now acting as a monitor to mirror his screen. He stepped up behind me, flipping up more and more documents, enlarging diagrams, and highlighting important text.

My eyes flitted across the genetic data I was certain applied to me. Then another set of images came up for the biomechanoids and what was perhaps the beginning stages of the ultra-bios. "What am I supposed to be seeing here?" I asked, nearly bored to tears by the maps, satellite photos, encoded messages, and photos of diplomats.

"Aside from a slew of crucial personnel information and tactically relevant targets, the information on that data drive contained the exact specifications for making biomechanoids."

"So?" I turned my dumbfounded question to all of them.

"The empire has people," Rayne summed up. "The Coalition has tech. If your mother had both, she would have too much power."

I scoffed and shook my head. "Okay, I get that balance is important, but the empire would never make a biomechanoid army." There was a long pause as everyone stared at me like I was stupid or naïve.

"They've been experimenting unsuccessfully for over a decade," Rey said.

"What? No, I don't believe that."

"It's not for you to believe or disbelieve. It is fact."

"The people—"

"—would forgive her if they knew the Coalition was plotting genocide," Rey interrupted. "What wouldn't you forgive if the lives of so many were at stake?"

"But…" I shook my head in disbelief. "You mean I just gave the empire the permission and the ability to fight a war with the dead?"

"No," Davis said snidely, and tapped his pad. "I tagged the data and deleted it off the drive before she could get access to it. All your mother got was proof of your experimentation, the coordinates for the bio-factory, and enough tactical info to put a few important delegates in danger."

"So just enough to keep the empire safe, but not enough to facilitate a war. No wonder she hasn't made a move yet." I slumped down in a chair in front of the bridge console. "Now what? I'm dead and I stay that way."

"Yes." Rey moved back to me, while Davis poked at his pad, making the information disappear. "I'm afraid that was the only option left, besides actually killing you."

"My mother thinks I'm dead."

"Yes."

"What about Ayil and Edric?"

"We'll send for them. I can't have Ayil running around on his own, possessing information about my ship and the like."

"So, I'm back to being your captive."

"You never weren't my captive, Kit," Rey said.

I looked up to see what manner of sadism might lurk in his eyes, but he had meant the statement as a fact. He really felt that while I may have been moving freely from planet to planet, I was never outside of his grasp, and therefore was always under his control. This notion should have truly appalled me, but his authority on technology gave him the capacity to do this with anyone. So even as his designated captive, I was not so very special. "All the power in the world and not an ounce of good to do with it."

"What?" Rey's brow creased with his confusion.

"My mother was right. You are a coward."

The room seemed to go cold as I watched Rey's face darken. Rayne moved forward, but didn't interrupt his boss's burgeoning anger. "I am no coward," Rey said with barely contained contempt.

"You are Rey. You have the power to do anything you want. To save people—"

"I stop wars! I save millions!" he bellowed, nearly ready to throttle me.

"And you never risk anything to do it. Rayne and Davis put themselves on the line for you to mettle in politics, but all you do is hoard your treasures of knowledge like an old miser." Rey was turning red, but he didn't interrupt me. "You may have me as a captive, but you don't have me as a slave. You want my devotion, my allegiance? Do something that will inspire it?" I shifted the seat away from him and slipped away from him while I still could.

"I won't gamble my one advantage just to save a little girl."

"You did once." I turned back to see his baffled expression. "I suppose it's not the same. My sister has no value to you. But, with me dead, she is the next in line for the throne." I grimaced. "I guess that means one of my cousins will get the job. How is that going to factor into your game?"

Rey considered this, his jaw rolling around and his eyes flickering as if he were calculating my family lineage to see who the best choice for the queen would be. I already knew the turmoil of our royal line would not be enough to garner his sympathy for my sister, but I was desperate.

"Have you ever considered just destroying them all?" I asked.

Rey looked up and frowned at me—appalled by the suggestion. "I don't do genocide."

I winced at his misinterpretation and before I could respond, Rayne coughed and stepped forward. "I think she was referring to the biomechanoids."

"Oh." Rey's displeasure ceased and embarrassment flashed across his face.

"You could—couldn't you?" I crossed my arms and tipped my head, baiting his ego to admit the power he held.

"It's not that simple."

"Isn't it? The backdoor program must give you access to a shutdown sequence or a self-destruct."

"That would only shut down the active ones," Davis jumped in. "And besides that, blowing up a bio doesn't make it go away. They just get a new corpse and another one."

"At the factory? On Vagari?" I asked. "Is there any other location that makes them?"

Davis narrowed his eyes and shook his head. "No—not full construction, only repairs."

"I presume that's a strategy of some kind. Keep the factory on the home planet, so any attack on it becomes an act of war against the Coalition."

"Yes," Davis answered reluctantly.

"Destroying the factory knocks out their military. With the factory gone, they'll be, at the very least, hobbled. I'm certain the Coalition would send every available ship to help fight. You could knock out the entire fleet and rid the universe of the damned things." I looked at Rey, hoping some aspect of my impromptu amateur war planning made sense to him. He was glaring at me—not angry, but more scolding. He knew I was trying to push his buttons. I was certain he of all people wanted to eliminate the technology he and Dr. Kessler had created.

"That's a nice thought, Kit," Rayne said rather gingerly. "But as we have discussed before, the captain doesn't make short-sighted decisions. He always looks at the long term. Eventually, the Coalition would rebuild the factory and—"

"They couldn't. Not without ore, copper, and nickel." I turned to him, almost excited now because the full scope of my plan was just coming into focus, even as my words were pouring out. "They will be financially ruined. They won't have the capital to get it running again without starving their people."

"Son of a bitch," Davis grumbled. He looked at me with a sour face and said two words that I imagined he would have rather chewed up and spat out. "She's right."

Rayne looked at him, perplexed. "What?"

"The Coalition buys nearly a quarter of its food supply from empirical planets," Davis explained. "Not to mention just about everything else. That's how this all started."

"How what started?" Rayne asked.

"The Coalition," I answered, adding fuel to the fire by dredging up my long-forgotten history lessons. Something I never thought I would need. "They were originally a branch of rebels who feared the empire was becoming too strong. At that time, the empire had pretty heavy demands on all planetary resources—especially those new to the alliance. The rebels also didn't like that the empire mandated an undeclared army. At any given moment, 60% of the people had to be ready for war, but none of the infantry actively worked as soldiers. They lead normal lives until called upon."

"It was a draft system?" Rayne asked.

"Yes, same as it is today. Everyone, apart from the very young or old, can be enlisted at any given time. That didn't sit well with some of the wealthier members of the alliance who thought they should be able to buy their way out of the military."

"The Coalition wanted a volunteer army, ready at all times, with no surprises," Rayne said.

"Exactly, so they unionized and defected. There were eighteen uninhabited planets in the system not under the claim of the crown."

"For good reason," Davis said. "They were practically inhospitable." I could tell he was on the same track as me and he didn't like it.

"They were," I agreed. "It took the Coalition well over a century to gain the footing to even call themselves a planetary alliance. By then, the empire had gone through a series of honorable queens that dedicated their efforts to goodwill and balance." I glanced at Rey, reminding him that the empire was the one that originally advocated for balance in the universe. He was taking in everything Davis and I were saying, though I wasn't sure if it was making a difference. Much as I had advocated for war with my mother, I imagined this conversation was going to fall on equally deaf ears. "Since the Coalition's population was growing exponentially, and the planets had limits on how much food could be produced, they petitioned the empire to help feed their people."

"In exchange for technology," Rayne surmised.

"Exactly. The Coalition was making great technical advancements, but they were still at the mercy of..." I trailed off as Terrin entered the room. He glanced at everyone, noticing the meeting he hadn't been told about. His gaze caught on me, but slipped away as he moved around us to take a seat at the bridge console and listen in. I cleared my throat and returned my attention to the conversation.

"They were at the mercy of the land they had chosen to live on. They couldn't grow plants, but they could cultivate minds. For a brief time in history, the Coalition was renowned to have the greatest minds in the universe." I glanced at Rey again, a little effort to suck up to him, but his mind was long gone now. He was back in his imaginary game of chess. I was glad for it, but I was hoping his checkmate didn't involve me losing my sister. "Since the Coalition had gone through such a long period of struggle to get their alliance functioning, they remember the details of their history a little differently. Despite noble efforts on my mother's part, most of the Coalition's population still believes the empire pushed the rebels out and exiled them to these lesser planets. I presume that's why the Coalition is fighting so hard to dismantle the empire. They still blame it for their current state of reliance. They think the empire is enslaving them."

"The Coalition wanted to turn the tables," Rayne said. "They wanted the empire begging them for medicine, just as they once begged for food." I nodded. "But your mother isn't going to starve the people."

"That's the problem. That's why Mother won't make a move against them, even with the evidence I've given her or the captivity of her heir. Just as the Coalition is reliant on her food, she is reliant on their tech. Going to war would starve them and put the empire into disarray. Neither of them wants to risk upsetting the balance, even though they clearly have barrels pointed at each other's heads. What they really need is someone for mutual hatred. A rebel among rebels." Once again, I looked at Rey, hoping he would volunteer to be that person. This time, he was looking directly at me. I smiled at him, knowing he was thinking the same thing.

"You do realize what you are suggesting?" he asked in a somewhat fatherly tone.

I nodded, knowing exactly what I was suggesting.

"What are you suggesting? Rayne asked.

Rey and I spoke our words, not quite in sync. "We're going to stage a coup."

The Pact

Rey was, by all accounts, gleeful. I had never seen such enthusiasm in his movements. So much so that I expected he might jump up and clack his heels together at any moment. I followed him through the ship as he barked orders about getting this ready or that. Rayne and Davis did as instructed and ran off, leaving only Terrin and me chasing after him.

"I don't understand. How did we reach the conclusion of a coup?" Terrin asked.

Rey laughed. "It's the only thing left to do. If the empire won't attack, then we have to attack from within. Thereby a coup."

"And what makes you think the people will just do as they are told?"

Rey snorted and turned his amusement to me. However, I wasn't entirely sure how he was going to do it, either. "You two really don't understand what I do, do you?" he asked, almost sadly. "Don't worry, I have plenty of avenues to get under the skin of the Coalition." Rey tromped away. He was still barking orders over his com, but none of them were for me, so I didn't follow him.

I looked back at Terrin, suddenly aware we were alone. He was looking at me with the same uncertainty I felt. This was our first encounter since I had effectively told him to get out of my sight. A mistake, to be sure, but one I refused to fix. From now on, I made my decisions as a mother first. I had to stop thinking only for myself.

But then I remembered the determination in his voice as he spoke over my mostly dead body. He was likely not aware I had heard him, so there was no point in acknowledging the statement. No point in letting him dismantle my resoluteness with more romantic confessions.

I opened my mouth to say something—anything to make the tension between us ease. However, at this point, even "how are you?" felt like a passive aggressive question.

Before I could utter a single word, Terrin turned on his heel and walked the other way. I watched him leave, stifling any sound that might have come from the stabbing pain in my chest. When he was gone, I leaned against the wall and breathed slowly, demanding my eyes not to cry. It was arrogant of me to assume I was the only one who could wield the sword of heartbreak. He had every right to turn that blade back on me.

Did I really expect him to cower before me and beg me back into his life? The words he spoke at my bedside were the words of a grieving man. Now that I was alive again, he could go back to hating me.

That was just fine—for the best, even. The feeling that my soul was being ripped out of my body would eventually go away.

"Kit!" Rey called down the hall as he jogged back toward me. "Mr. Turner tells me you and General Sanders are close."

"Yes."

"How close?"

I shrugged, not wanting to make any assumptions about her feelings toward me. Rey narrowed his eyes, waiting for my answer. "She's like a second mother to me."

"Good, good, good." Rey's eyes gleamed with childish delight. "Let's make a phone call." He pressed his hand to my back and, with surprising force, ushered me down the hall and back to the bridge. He shoved me at the communications station and instructed me to call her. I shielded my hand, not wanting to give him access to call the General any time he wished.

The system beeped, indicating that we were awaiting the General's approval of my communication on the other side. The beeping stopped and just as the image connected, Rey jumped into me, sending me flying out of the camera view. I landed less than gracefully and threw him a glare. He was far too entranced by Sanders to even notice.

"Kit! Is that—Oh." Her voice drained of all hope as she stared at Rey's image.

I moved to a chair and sat down quietly. I was well out of camera shot, but seeing her face blown up on the viewscreen made me want to call out to her. Especially since I could see the disappointment in her eyes. I thought they looked a little red and swollen as well. It made me wonder if my mother had cried for me. Not in public, of course, but maybe in private. It was awful that we couldn't tell her the truth, but since she was the focus right now, it was too big of a risk. The less she knew, the better.

"General." Rey smacked his hand against his chest. "The magnitude of your beauty startles me every time I see you."

I nearly snorted at the Shakespearean delivery of his pronouncement. If this were a time of castles, his affections might have been better received; however, Sanders was the knight in this story, and Rey, merely a peddler.

"Skip the antics, Baloch, I'm in no mood. If you haven't heard, the princess has been assassinated."

"I have heard," Rey said somberly. "A tragedy, to be sure. A loss that hurts me more deeply than I wish to admit."

I glared at the side of Rey's head. More Shakespeare, but this time aimed at me. I didn't believe a word of it.

"Save your performance. I'm not entirely convinced you didn't have something to do with it."

Rey chuckled to himself and then turned a cold, vacant expression to Sanders. "Kit Mallory has been under my scrutiny for nearly every moment of her life. If I wanted her dead, she would have been dead long ago." Rey's head turned to the side, putting me in his peripheral view. "The fact that I didn't should say at least a little about my character."

"I think it says a lot about your character. It says how patient you are."

Rey rolled his eyes. "I wouldn't have killed her in plain sight. You should at least believe that."

"No, I suppose you wouldn't have done that. Why are you calling me? What are you selling this time?"

Rey groaned. "If only you were buying what I have for you." I wasn't able to resist a slight snort at hearing that. Rey's jaw clenched, and I sensed that had he not been on camera, I might have gotten a stern look for my insolence. "But I do have an opportunity for you."

"What sort of opportunity?"

"I want you to convince the queen to give Kit's body to the Coalition."

Sanders' face hardened, and she didn't speak for several seconds. "I will do no such thing. She deserves a proper burial with her—"

"Burial!" Rey laughed, and let out a slight snuffle as he contained himself. "She's just as valuable dead as alive. Her DNA can be harvested, tested, and reproduced. Hell, if this ship didn't have incinerating toilets, the Coalition could have just collected the shit we left behind."

I grimaced at that thought. Surely my shit wasn't valuable. Had I known, I could have saved my time at the egg banks. I could have just fiber-loaded my way toward a fecal fortune.

"That's why I'm not going to hand her body over to them."

"Well, no, not her real body. I mean, everyone else will believe it's her. That's part of the act, but you and I will know it's a fake."

"Why? What's your plan?"

Rey folded his hands and twiddled his thumbs. "I plan to infiltrate the capital and release the other princess from her confinement." My heart leaped, and I stiffened in my chair. Rey flared his fingers on his hand, silently demanding I be still or quiet or something. "What's her name again? Ella, Elfred...?"

"Elizandra," Sanders corrected him dryly. "Why do you want to save the princess?"

"Well..." Rey bit his lip. "I wouldn't exactly call it saving her."

"What exactly would you call it?"

"Perhaps confiscate is a better word."

Fire rose from deep in my bones, and curses that had no meaning bubbled up into my mind. I was nearly ready to leap at Rey when he leaned forward on the console. He pressed his hand over mine, pressing it hard enough that I couldn't readily pull it away if I wanted to. His thumb shifted over my skin, drawing my attention away from his two-faced words. The soft caress was barely anything and yet I knew he was signaling me to be calm and not react. I tried to remind myself that everything Rey did was for a greater good. When that didn't work, I reminded myself I could throttle him when the camera turned off.

"You are a parasite, Baloch. Why would I agree to let you kidnap the Princess?"

"Dr. Kessler believes the Coalition is holding her because she has the potential to be a carrier for their newest strain," Rey lied—or perhaps he had lied before. "I want to get a look at her before returning her to her mother."

"We didn't find any evidence of a new strain in the data Kit brought."

Rey smiled broadly and winked at her. "Of course, you didn't, my precious. You didn't think I would let such a beautiful and thorny rose go, did you?"

Sanders stared blankly at him. I recognized the futile frustration that came with communicating with Rey. "What happens if Elizandra is a carrier?"

Rey tipped his head. "Now, now, General, let's not pretend we need to discuss that. You and I both know if you knew then what you know now, I wouldn't have been the one to dispatch an assassin, would I?"

To my surprise, Sanders didn't argue with this. "We could arrange an exchange. As we did before."

"No, from what I'm hearing on the news, the Coalition suspects the empire killed Kit. They are already up in arms. Offer them the body on a temporary basis."

"Temporary?"

"Yes, pretend like you have no idea about her DNA's value. Say you'll deliver the body by armed guard so her father can have a dignified funeral for his daughter." My heart clenched as I realized my father also thought I was dead. This was pure torture, and I hated to put either of my parents through it. I only hoped whatever Rey had planned could happen soon, so I could ease their pain.

"Assuming I can convince the queen to do this, how do you plan on getting into the capital, let alone smuggling the Princess back out again?"

"I can help with that," Terrin said from the door.

"Who's that?" Sanders asked, unable to see Terrin past Rey. He moved forward and Rey shifted to share the picture with him. "Terrin," she said with the same displeasure she had the last time they had met. "My two least trusted associates want me to participate in a plan to deliver a fake body and kidnap a real princess. Why do I suspect you're not telling me everything?"

"You have my word, General. I will bring Elizandra back to her mother," Terrin said.

Rey looked at Terrin, no doubt annoyed he was taking responsibility for the operation.

"And what is that worth from you?" Sanders asked.

Terrin's jaw clenched, but he didn't answer her.

"Well, perhaps we should discuss the details on another call. Thanks so much, General." Rey blew kisses at her and slammed his hand over the cut-off switch. As soon as Rey saw "Call Ended" on the screen, he flipped around and pushed himself chest to chest with Terrin. It was, by no means, a physical intimidation, except that Rey's maniacal eyes were a threat in and of themselves. "What the hell was that?"

"I was helping."

"You aren't helping."

"I can get Elizandra," Terrin said.

"We aren't going there to get the girl back."

"What!" I shrieked, but the argument was now between Terrin and Rey.

"No one is breaking into the capital." Rey's laugh sounded breathy and nervous. "Even I have my limitations."

Terrin's brow dipped and his eyes narrowed. "Then why do you want to get access to Vagari?"

"I don't want access to Vagari." Rey's mouth twisted into a smirk and he shook his head. "I want access to General Sanders."

"Oh, geez," I groaned. "All this is about your damned crush."

Rey snapped his head to look at me. "Crush!" The word came out strained, and he laughed to himself. "You two know, as well as I, that unrequited love doesn't crush you. It consumes you and drains you of all rational thought."

I glanced at Terrin, but he was keeping his gaze intently on Rey. I wasn't sure our love was unrequited so much as just plain tormented, but it was just the difference between one pain or two.

"I was eaten alive by mine once. And now it's my turn to do the biting." Rey chomped his teeth together.

"Are you saying this is some kind of revenge plot?" Terrin asked.

"I'm saying you two should leave the politics to someone more equipped to understand the nuances of civilized warfare."

Terrin stared down at Rey's gloating face. "Very well." He nodded slowly. He turned and headed to the door. I was furious. He was just going to give up on retrieving my sister. If he believed there was a way to get to her, I would risk it. It was the least I could do to help my father. Terrin stopped at the door panel and punched in a code that closed the sliding door and activated the lock sequence.

"What are you doing?" Rey asked, positively perplexed.

Terrin didn't answer. He moved back to the bridge control panel and, after entering another code, opened a new window that gave him access to the ship's security cameras.

Rey saw the images pop up and lunged to stop Terrin. "How did you—"

I barely saw Terrin's hand move to chop Rey's throat. The man went down coughing and choking, before sliding across the floor to get away from him.

"You are done talking, Captain." Terrin continued to maneuver the screens and sub-screens with far more alacrity than I would have expected. I watched as the doors to the quarantine area, the weapons "shed," and the shuttle bay shut and locked Kessler, Rayne, and Davis into their respective rooms.

"How are you doing that?" Rey croaked from the floor.

"You assume because I have strength of body that I have no strength of mind. You've also apparently forgotten that gattaw have eyes."

"Son of a bitch!" Rey rasped. "You've been memorizing our codes."

"I've been patient with your presumption of superiority up to this point, Captain, but you are right. I will leave the civilized warfare to you and your crew." Terrin turned to face Reynard, who was now wide-eyed with worry. "As for the uncivilized warfare... I think you should leave that to me."

Terrin reached down and lifted Rey by the collar. Out of nowhere, Rey pulled a hypo-spray device. Terrin grabbed Rey's wrist and twisted it. I gasped when I heard it crack. Rey let out a wretched cry that made me take a step back. I knew I should break up the fight, but I wasn't entirely certain Terrin would let me. Though he didn't seem angry—he looked determined.

Terrin slammed Rey against the wall and his shield activated. Rey smiled, slightly smug, knowing he could not pummel his face. But instead of using him as a punching bag, he raised his thumb and showed it to him. The baffled look on Rey's face was no doubt the same as on mine. "Yes, you have many toys. You conquer the universe with your assassin and your worm because you consider your mind much too valuable to risk. I respect your intellect, Captain, but I do not respect your methods. Mallory was right. You are a coward."

I stiffened, not realizing Terrin had heard that portion of our conversation.

"You use others for your dirty work because you know, as well as I, that once you are stripped of your gadgets... you are just a man." Terrin pressed his thumb into Rey's rib cage, making him wince. "And a weak one at that."

Terrin must have pushed harder because Rey cried out. I moved forward tentatively. Though Reynard hadn't secured enough of my loyalty for me to risk myself, I couldn't help gravitate toward the sound of a wounded animal.

"Stop this! I will end you, you stupid fucking Gat!"

Snap.

I gasped and covered my mouth as Rey's eyes went wide and he doubled over with a groan. Terrin pushed him back up and shifted his thumb to a higher rib.

"Terrin," I whispered, but I wasn't sure if he could hear me over Rey's agonizing bellows.

"What do you want!" Rey screamed.

Terrin eased the pressure, allowing the man to breathe even though that now seemed to hurt him. "I have given my blood to both the Coalition and to the crown, but my loyalty always has and always will be to Mallory," Terrin declared with more conviction than romanticism. "As I've said, I have been patient with your assertions, but no more. From now on, Mallory is no longer your property, your project, or your leverage."

"She is too valuable! I must—ahhh!"

"Her value is as a living being, not a science project." Terrin's voice showed signs of emotion. Rey's moans of pain were further evidence that his anger was getting the better of him. "If you want our cooperation in your little coup, then we want yours. We are going to save Elizandra, and that is final."

Rey hissed, but nodded. Terrin reduced his pressure. For a moment, the captain just panted, but then his weary eyes captured Terrin's and he smiled. "You realize you have made a very risky move—making an enemy of me."

Terrin shook his head. "I have not made an enemy of you. I have proved myself to be a worthy ally. If you disagree, then I shall strike you down here and complete my negotiations with Davis and Rayne. I'm sure they know enough of your ship to coordinate a plan to help us."

Rey chuckled as if Terrin were crazy. Terrin drew his copper sword quickly and smoothly. The tip slipped between his ribs and Rey gasped just as I leaped forward. I grabbed Terrin's arm and squeezed it as I watched the first drops of blood seep into the captain's shirt. For a moment, there was a stalemate between the three of us. Even an inch of movement would irreparably damage Rey's heart.

"Look at her," Terrin whispered. "Look at her!" he yelled, making me jump. Rey looked at me, baffled by his command. "Show me you have an ounce of compassion and I will let you live. Show me you are more than the machines you invented."

Rey's eyes flashed to Terrin, startled by the accusation and then angered. He looked at me again and then around the room as if there might be another option he hadn't considered to get him out of the grip of death.

"I will make a pact with you," Rey said to me. "I will assist in the retrieval of your sister and I will release you as my captive, but you must stay dead."

"What?"

"When this is over. When I have saved your sister and begun my coup, Kit Mallory, and Mallory Kit will cease to exist."

"How will I" I shook my head, realizing the details weren't important now. "Yes, fine. I will take on a new identity." I looked at Terrin, but he didn't remove his blade.

Rey stared at him. "I give you my word, Terrin." Rey dragged his finger over the blade in his chest to gather the blood. He less than gracefully flicked it on the floor. It wasn't as dramatic as the usual gattaw tradition of a blood oath, but it was more than one could usually expect from a human. "You are both now my allies, not my enemies." Rey raised his hand to signify a more human oath. "Death upon me if I am untrue."

Terrin drew back suddenly, releasing Rey and pulling away from my grip. He moved to the computer and undid the locked door, and opened the rest of the ship. I tugged on Rey's arm. "Come on, let's get you fixed up."

"Later." Rey waved me away and shifted with increasing pain away from the wall. "How do you expect to get into the most guarded home on Vagari?"

Terrin leaned against the computer panel, holding his sword across his lap. He glanced at me, giving me more attention than he had so far. It was almost jarring enough to force my eyes down. When his gaze returned to Rey, he looked very pleased with himself. "The same way I planned to get out of it."

Fear

"I will blow that planet to hell before I allow those wretched people to desecrate my daughter's body with their experiments!" My mother slammed her hands on her desk. The conversation had been going on for nearly an hour. General Sanders was desperately trying to convince my mother that offering my body to the Coalition for a funeral was a step toward diplomacy. However, Mother was certain they would take advantage of the situation. She didn't want to risk doing anything to help them with the efforts to destroy her legacy.

General Sanders glanced in my direction. Apart from Rayne, who was also donning a soldier disguise and face shield to change his identity, Sanders was the only person in the room who knew I was alive. It was a necessary admission to make sure our plan worked properly.

Standing in the same room with my mother following my death was surreal. Even with blood being pumped through my veins by the heavy beat of my heart, I still felt like a ghost. I felt like an intruder in my own life, seeing something I shouldn't have.

Never mind that her eyes were red and swollen, or that she had done nothing to repair her smeared mascara. I was more surprised she was in a pair of black slacks and an ill-fitted, untucked blouse. This was the equivalent of a normal person's baggy sweatpants and t-shirt smeared with food. My mother was a wreck, and I was to blame... or Reynard was... or we all were. I wasn't even sure there were enough people to share the behemoth of blame that my death had created. Suddenly, nothing seemed right to me. Every step forward felt like a hole was being dug. I was no longer moving forward or backward, just deeper into a pit I would soon have to call my grave—regardless of my living status.

"We both know war is not an option, Majesty," Sanders explained. "It would be devastating to both alliances and invite a treacherous amount of black marketing into our planets. The unrest in the far colonies has already brought about a surge of smuggling. If we don't show the people our trade will not be interrupted, they will panic."

"This will give us an opportunity to do some reconnaissance," Sanders added. Rey had made it clear that she should mention nothing about saving Elizandra to Susan. I wasn't sure if Rey distrusted my mother, or if there was some aspect of the plan that required her to be in the dark. Perhaps it was simply an effort at plausible deniability.

"And what do you think Kit would say about this?" my mother posed the last question I ever thought she would speak. Never once had she cared what I thought in life. Why bother caring after my death? "How would she feel about her mother selling her off like a goddamn piece of furniture? For a peek at the capital!" Susan roared and I could see Sanders was losing her steam. If the plan hadn't appealed to her at the beginning of the hour, nothing was likely to change her mind at the end. And if my mother didn't agree to the plan, there was no plan.

"I think..." My voice came out strange through the vocal scrambler jammed into my collar. The rough manly tone it produced didn't match my figure, but there was only so much padding I could add beneath my uniform. And only so much height I could add to my boots. I cleared my throat, trying to find the blend between myself and my disguise.

My mother's face snapped to me, her expression already a death sentence for speaking out of turn.

"I think she—"

"Soldier, hold your tongue," General Sanders commanded.

"No, let him speak." Susan threw her hands up as if she had suddenly thrown caution to the wind and changed the pecking order around her. "Go ahead, boy."

"I think Princess Kit would want you to give her father and sister an opportunity to say goodbye to her. She's traveled back and forth between these two planets for much of her young life. What difference does one more trip make?"

"We'll never get her back. She will be cut into pieces, put through a blender, and pipetted into test tubes. At best, we will get a coffin full of rocks."

I frowned at that thought. It wasn't far off, but they wouldn't waste me in a blender. They would take me bit by bit, over the course of years. A specimen preserved in a freezer for occasional harvesting. It was a disgusting thought.

"I'm sorry, Your Majesty, I don't mean any disrespect, but" I glanced at the General. She wasn't happy about me besmirching the image of her normally loyal officers, but since I was the only one who could convince my mother to do this, I had to try. I looked at my mother's angry face, debating if I wanted to have my death re-enacted with her as my murderer. She tipped her head to one side, analyzing me with the curiosity of a wolf watching its dancing prey. "I don't think she would have a problem with that."

"Excuse me?" My mother recoiled, standing high and lifting her chin. She was seconds from striking.

"My apologies, Majesty. I don't know what has gotten into my lieutenant," Sanders directed the statement to me, squeezing the words between her clenched teeth. "I'll remove him immediately."

"No, no, no." Susan waved her away. "I am intrigued. Do tell, young man, what expert knowledge of my daughter do you possess? I would be thrilled to hear about how your limited interaction with her compares to my birthing her and raising her."

"I don't mean to make comparisons. I just wanted to point out that she was raised in this house and in her father's house. She is loyal to both the empire and the Coalition."

"You arrogant little twit, my daughter had no loyalty to either alliance. That's why she left!"

"No!" I yelled back at her, unable to contain my correction.

My mother scoffed and let her mouth drape open. "General, take your soldier away and discipline him before I do."

"Yes, Your Majesty." General Sanders stood, wrapped a firm grip around my shoulders, and started pushing me out of the room. "Shut up," she whispered to me.

I needed to shut up, but I couldn't. All this time, she had thought I was against the people—against the duty. "She didn't leave out of disloyalty! She left out of fear!"

"Stop it!" Sanders cautioned me again.

"Wait!" my mother called after us, her gaze more curious than angry now. "What do you mean, fear?"

Sanders released me, but gave me a scouring look. I tugged down my uniform and moved back to face my mother. I stood at attention, not sure my mother was ready to hear the truth—even after my death.

Susan stepped out from behind her desk. She came up close to me, eyeing the fear on my digitally manufactured face. Her eyes flickered back and forth, a question rising in her eyes, but falling away before it reached her lips. She clenched her jaw and took in a deep breath before speaking. "My daughter was stubborn, belligerent, and uncompromising. She never knew when to give up." She scoffed. "Even when it was for her own good. She was a clever and resourceful woman."

I felt a tennis ball's worth of emotion build up in my throat as my mother spoke. Tears welled up in my eyes and I was thankful my disguise would hide the unapproved emotions from my mother's view.

"She was not afraid of anything," my mother said proudly.

"Except you," I whispered the words, but from my male voice, they sounded more sinister than servile. Susan frowned and once again looked me over for signs of who I was. She was no doubt thinking she should recognize this man with intimate knowledge of her daughter. "She knew she could never live up to your standards. That she could never be the magnitude of leader that you are. So instead of staying and watching your disappointment grow with each and every day, she decided to fail you all at once and sever your hope of her success."

I felt the build-up of my tears release, and one errant drop hit my uniform. My mother's eyes instantly fell to the spot beneath my collar that was suddenly wet for no reason. My heart thumped heavily. She was not a stupid woman.

Her eyes returned to her usual icy demeanor, and she stepped away from me. I waited for her to demand my true identity or invoke my containment.

"Your soldier is right. My daughter would want her father to see her one last time. A cruel, *cruel* goodbye." My mother ground out the second cruel as if the word itself disgusted her. "But perhaps one that will save him the trouble of looking to the stars every night, in hopes of seeing her again. Do whatever you need to do, General," Susan said dismissively and returned to her seat behind her desk.

"Thank you, Majesty." General Sanders led the rest of her men out the door and I filed along behind them.

"Lieutenant," Susan called out to me just as I reached the door. I looked back, wary of her intent. "You are wrong about one thing." She looked up from her work and pinned me with her sternest motherly gaze. "She would have made an excellent queen." She held me there a moment more before returning to her work. I had no room to deny the correction since she believed it so wholeheartedly, but neither one of us could ever know for sure, since dead women can't rule empires.

Snow White

I stared down at my lifeless body through the raindrop-textured glass coffin as I walked alongside it. The imagery of Snow White had long since melted away. Now my pseudo remains were just getting creepy.

Super creepy.

Super duper creepy.

I shook away my childhood nightmares and irrational fear of zombie clones and took a few fast steps to keep ahead of the casket. I sidled up next to one of the other no-name soldiers who was marching my body toward the cathedral for my funeral.

It was strange being back home as an outsider. Even stranger to be arriving as a dead woman. The people were cheering the military-led funeral parade like I was a rock star on tour. I hadn't expected people to weep openly or throw themselves on my casket, but I definitely hadn't expected cheers. This wasn't a football game. This was my life—or rather, my death.

"Is anyone else a little disappointed no one minds that I'm dead?" I murmured.

I heard a static snap from the communicator in my ear. "They just want... your brains," Ayil's sadistic voice came over the line.

"Knock it off, Ayil. I told you that in confidence."

"No, you told me about the clone make-out dream in confidence. I made no such promises for the zombie one."

I scoffed and rolled my eyes. "It was the same dream. And trust me, if you had seen what I saw on that med base, you wouldn't find zombies so humorous anymore, either."

The parade came to an unexpected halt. I peered between the soldiers ahead of me and saw a line of Coalition biomechanoids blocking our path. "Oh shit, they've blocked us."

"We see them," Rayne's voice chimed in my ear. "Just hold your position. We were expecting this."

I watched the men ahead of me part, letting a man through with a device that looked like a miniature megaphone with a calculator attached. I moved aside and watched them approach the coffin. I cringed as they unlatched the lid.

"Shit, shit, shit," I hissed under my breath. "It's a DNA check." I discreetly started looking for somewhere to disappear to, even though I knew no one would recognize me.

"It's fine," Rey assured me.

"How is it fine?"

"Tissue DNA degrades very fast. They'll use hair for a positive I.D."

"Again, how is that fine?"

"I grew some of your hair just for this purpose."

"You grew my" I watched in fascination as the man took a gob of hair from the body and sucked it up with his mini megaphone. After a few clicks and a tweet, the device cheerfully pinged. With my identity apparently confirmed, he walked away. "How the hell did you grow my hair? And while we are on the subject, where the hell did you find a body to use as my corpse?"

"I always have a few extra in my freezer," Rey said.

"I'm going to pretend I didn't hear that."

"Why?" Rey asked nonplussed.

"Never mind," I said, dropping the point. I didn't even want to ask why the body conveniently looked just like me, though I supposed a little bone sculpting was all that was required for that feat. No one had seen me in years, anyway.

The line continued moving, and I noticed a group of people on the sidelines with signs that read, *"Treason is a sin of the heart"* and *"Heroes die as martyrs, traitors die as infidels."* My people's anger toward me didn't surprise me. The Coalition had made sure I was a pariah in their eyes. How else could they justify what they would do to get me back?

All deviant behavior must have a scapegoat.

A thumping sound to my right alerted me to a group of people at the back of the crowd with red flags. They waved them in the air several times, displaying the skull and crossbones before simultaneously tapping the wood handles on the cement. The wielders of the flags had been blindfolded and their mouths taped shut. "Are they protesting me, too?" I asked.

"No," Rey responded. "They are one of several factions on Vagari that believe the government is abusing the dead to fight their wars."

"I didn't know there were any factions."

Rey chuckled. "There are always factions, my dear. You'll be glad for my knowledge of them when this day is done." I ignored the questions forming in my mind and reminded myself that Rey was a brilliant man, who was almost always three to ten steps ahead of everyone else.

As we climbed the wide semi-circle steps of the cathedral, I caught sight of my father waiting at the doors. My feet came to a halt as I stared at him. He looked even older than the last time I saw him. He had lost weight and the hunch in his back was now permanent. I could see a slight bruising around his eyes and an old cut on his lip. I could only imagine what he had suffered for trying to help me—trying to warn me.

"Keep moving, Kit," Rayne cautioned me, but I wasn't listening anymore.

When Richard's eyes caught sight of the display coffin coming up the steps behind me, his mouth quivered. As guilty as I felt watching my mother endure my death, seeing my father was ten times worse. When the casket reached him, his attempts to maintain austere grief shattered. Seeing my face through the tear-soaked glass, his legs wobbled and collapsed beneath him. His aids tried to raise him up again, but he bent forward and let out a direful lamentation that shook me to my very core.

"Stay with us, Kit. You're drawing attention," Rayne grumbled, but I was outside of myself now.

Tears pricked my eyes and my jaw quivered. My legs were about to give out as well, putting me in the same abject position as my father.

"Be strong, Mallory," Terrin's soothing voice came over the com. "I know this is difficult, but his pain is limited by our success. Focus on your mission. Just keep walking and this will all be over soon."

It was barely enough to bolster me, but I bit the inside of my cheek hard and passed my bereft father with my head held high as an indifferent soldier.

I followed the coffin down the center aisle of the church. The pallbearers placed it before the altar and I took my place behind it, along with the other soldiers. We monitored the onlookers to make sure nobody took advantage of my corpse. Though most people here were ignorant of my value, I wasn't entirely sure some of them wouldn't be interested in taking some potshots just to ease their anger.

Thankfully, those attending the funeral actually seemed to be legitimately mourning me. A processional of people stepped up to place flowers and various trinkets on the coffin. I recognized a few of them as my father's staff, including my former teachers and entourage of *friends*. I even saw a few distant relations that my cloistered lifestyle barely afforded a name to a face, let alone any meaningful attachment. Still, it was nice to know not everyone on Vagari hated me.

Once everyone had made their tributes, I looked around the church in search of my sister. I had not seen her with my father and was hoping she might be on her own with her chaperones.

"She's not here," General Sanders whispered through my earbud. I looked around and saw her standing near a column at the start of the crossing. She was the only one on the team I could recognize, since everyone else wore a disguise to hide their identities. "They wouldn't risk having her in the same location as your father."

"Of course not. That would make this too simple," Ayil responded.

"Everyone, just relax. We can't make a move until after the funeral," Sanders reminded us. "Once your father has been escorted away, we can figure out our next move. Assuming Terrin can live up to his claims." Sanders made no effort to hide her disapproval of leaving the next step of our plan in Terrin's hands. Though we all had a vague understanding of what we were going to do next, Terrin, partially at Rey's command, had not revealed the details of our break-in point.

"I'll get us in there, General," Terrin said. "You just worry about getting us off the planet."

I looked around the room, searching for Terrin or anyone I might recognize. Everyone looked the same to me. However, Ayil threw me a couple of double digits that made him stand out from the goons next to him. His imaginary blond buzzed hair and pale skin looked nothing like him, but that was the point. He was standing catty-corner to the general, in clear view of me. His childish movement drew a glare from Sanders, but I smirked just a little. Only Ayil could make me smile at my own funeral.

For another hour, I stood tall, ignoring the mewling sobs of my father and the frightful sight of my own pale face. The preacher granted me all the concessions a dying person might want. My path to heaven was guaranteed by virtue of several long-dead men and a book that had warped my ancestors into medical marvels. His description of my heroic journey ending too soon only reminded me I wasn't actually the hero they thought I was. I was a medical wonder designed to be an abominable weapon.

Richard was the first to leave the church. As expected, several biomechanoids escorted him, making it impossible to get a message to him or to warn him about our upcoming *visit*. As I watched him go, I realized his life had never truly been his own. His obligatory duties were a sentence as much as an honor.

Seeing him flanked by guns at every turn was too much. It made my skin crawl. He was a prominent leader. As an arbitrator, he balanced the chaos of opposing powers. He deserved better than this.

The Coalition planets may have combined their efforts to manipulate my father's genetic line into something worthy of a brokering with the empire, but they were incapable of running this world without a defining voice of reason. Someone had to whisper while others were shouting. And that someone had always been Richard Kit.

Once the funeral attendees had filed out, the only remaining people in the church were perpetual worshipers, the church staff, and a few biomechanoids stationed to monitor us. Sanders' men disassembled, moving less mechanically—no doubt to stretch out the cramps they had from standing still for so long.

Meanwhile, I searched for the door to the sacristy. That would be our most obvious exit point. Assuming Rey was comfortable redirecting the bios for a while, we could get outside with little more than a broken lock and a perturbed priest.

I was about to say as much when the heavy wooden doors to the church squawked open and another group of soldiers entered. I glanced at Sanders to see if she was expecting this. She moved forward to meet up with the group—no clear sign if she was happy about these impromptu churchgoers or not.

General Sanders shouted out an order and everyone in uniforms, including myself, jolted back into a strict stance. The soldiers filed around the coffin and I did my best to follow suit, playing a good little soldier. We formed a loose cluster in front of the coffin—protecting it. The remaining people in the church sensed something was about to happen they didn't want to be a part of. They slipped out of their pews, escaping via the outside aisles.

I recognized the leader of the new group as Admiral Powell. Although technically retired from the military, the Coalition appointed him head of security for my home district, rather than letting his skills go to waste on golf and sunsets. He and his team were effectively a private security unit dedicated to the capital. Well, and above the authority of the police, they maintained the peace through more militant methods.

They were also the ones responsible for delivering me to my weekend appointments. To say I was unhappy to see the admiral was an understatement.

Powell came marching through the nave with nearly a dozen of his prancing puppets behind him. He stopped at the head of the aisle where Sanders was waiting for him.

"Admiral." Sanders saluted.

"General." Powell saluted back. "A shame we have to meet under these circumstances, but better here than on the battlefield."

"Agreed." Sanders nodded. "Do you have it?"

I glanced toward the only figure I recognized, asking the most obvious question with a dipped brow. *Does he have what?* Ayil's shoulders twitched only slightly, indicating he didn't know. This was not part of his briefing, either.

"Of course." Powell gave Sanders a small smirk and pulled an electronic tablet from his front pocket. He poked the handheld screen a few times before turning it to Sanders. "The number we agreed on."

The hairs on the back of my neck went up. Something wasn't right. They were clearly talking about money. This meeting wasn't by chance. Powell and Sanders were expecting to see each other. They were planning to make a monetary exchange. "What's happening?" I whispered, no longer able to stay silent.

"Just stay calm. I believe the general is trying to profit off your corpse." Rey sounded calm, almost wistful over the com. "Perhaps her pension isn't living up to her expectations."

"I thought we were only giving them the body for the funeral," Ayil whispered.

"That was the plan." Again, Rey didn't sound at all disturbed by this sleazy deal.

"And my merchandise?" The Admiral asked, slipping his tablet back in his pocket.

Sanders turned to look behind her, but her eyes were not searching for the coffin. She was searching the faces of her men. When her eyes landed on me, she paused before raising her finger to point directly at me—the real me. "That one," she said without ceremony, then backed out of the admiral's path.

"She isn't selling the corpse." Terrin's voice came in low and serious. "This is a double-sided double-cross."

"Oh, no," Rey muttered, as if his ice cream had landed on a dirty floor.

"Mallory, run!" Rayne yelled, but his order came too late.

I tried to get behind Sanders' men for protection, but they grabbed me and yanked me back toward Powell. The other soldiers in the room scrambled about, pushing and shoving until three soldiers, presumably my friends, were being held in place, just like me. Our own team had ambushed us.

One man pushed the adhesive button under my chin. My male mask disappeared, revealing my feminine face behind it. I stared at Powell with my own eyes and he looked at me with such delight it bordered on carnivorous. "Good to see you again, Mallory."

"What is going on?" I looked at Sanders, hoping against hope this was part of a long con. Something they hadn't told me about to keep my reactions honest and believable. I wanted it to be a trick. I needed it to be a trick.

Sanders gave me an indifferent shrug. "Sorry, Kit, I hate to do this to you. I really am fond of you, but my loyalties lie elsewhere. They always have."

"What?" I had a million more questions, but the only one I could voice was my monosyllabic inquiry.

Powell's men came forward and retrieved me from Sanders' men. They were no less gentle and my struggles only made them tighten their grasp on me. "I trusted you," I seethed at my betrayer. "I loved you!" I screamed at her, but the damage she was doing didn't faze Sanders. She had been like a second mother to me. For her to do this now—in my most vulnerable moment. But, of course, that was why she had been so kind to me. She needed to keep me close.

"I'd advise you to take care of her men now," she said to Powell. "They tend to be problematic."

"No!" I screamed and struggled futilely as they dragged me down the aisle.

Ayil, the shorter buzz-cut blond, fought ferociously against his containment. Rayne had since lost his mask and was also straining to free himself from his captivity. However, the large black man had liberated himself and was barreling toward my captors. "Get away from her!"

Pulse weapons aimed at him, but that didn't stop his charge. It wasn't until I felt cold metal being pressed to my temple that he finally skidded to a stop. I turned just enough to see Sanders was the one holding the gun on me—adding further cracks to the saintly veneer she had constructed over the years.

"Why?" I whispered. "Why are you doing this?"

"It's a long story." She winked at me, but it wasn't a secretive *I'll-tell-you-later* wink—it was a *nice-knowing-you, -I'll-see-you-in-hell* wink.

"Oh, come on, Sanders, it isn't that long," Rey said over the coms. It was frustrating to me that he was so calm. Disrespect for his meal preparations caused him to flip out, but betray him and threaten to take his most valued DNA repository and he's just peachy. "Would you like me to tell it?"

"I'm not sure it really matters now," Sanders said dismissively.

"Oh, history always matters," Rey said, once again sounding wistful. "You see, Kit, I met General Sanders a long time ago when she was working for the Coalition."

Despite the gun still pressed to my temple, I turned to look at her. "You worked for them?"

Sanders chuckled as she shifted her gun to meet my temple again. "I never stopped working for them."

"But you're a general," I said, as if that should have meant something. The thought of anyone rising to the ranks of an empiric military officer without being discovered was incredible to me.

"Oh, but that's the tipping point," Rey said. "She had risen through the ranks by getting just enough information to make her look better than her counterparts. It's easy to subvert attacks when you know precisely when and where they will happen."

"That means the Coalition knows *everything* the crown knows?" I asked, even as this reality hit me like a punch to the gut.

Sanders nodded.

"You see, Kit," Rey said. "This is why it is so important you put your trust in the right people."

"I thought I had," I whispered, but my somber expression had no chance of melting the ice around Sanders' heart. "So now what? You just slink away and hide with your riches."

"Don't be ridiculous, Kit. I've attained a position directly beside your mother in the war room. I have recruited loyal followers." She motioned to her men whom she must have hand-picked for this mission. "You don't slink away from that. I have a duty to my people."

"You bitch!" Powell's men held me tightly, preventing me from lunging at her to slap her or claw her eyes out. My bucking did nothing more than earn me a punch in the stomach. Sadly, that was enough to silence all of my rage.

"Do you remember what I said to you when we met that second time?" Rey said over the com in a soothing tone. "When I met you as General Sanders?"

"You agreed to stay out of my business if I stayed out of yours."

"No," Rey snapped, showing his first inkling of anger. "What exactly did I say to you?"

Sanders rolled her eyes. "You said as long as I didn't interfere with your work, you wouldn't have to blow my brains out."

"I hate to break it to you, my beautiful rose, but you are definitely interfering in my work."

"You always did have a flare for the dramatic, Rey."

"That's true, but this isn't one of those times."

I heard the faintest click over the com, followed by a high-pitched whir coming from Sanders' direction. Her eyes widened, and she opened her mouth to object to whatever attack she sensed coming.

Then she... popped.

I flinched from the onslaught of skull and brain pieces that ejected into the air like shrapnel. Against my better judgment, I looked back at Sanders. Her body stood there, momentarily upright, blood spluttering from her like a fountain. As her body flopped to the floor, I let out an anguished cry leaning over the containing arms of my captors.

The sudden shock of their leader being killed launched Sanders' men into a frenzy. Brandishing their weapons, they demanded that everyone, "Get down!" They didn't understand the attack had come from inside her head. They thought someone had double-crossed the double-crossers.

Powell's men responded in kind, shouting back and demanding they lower their weapons. After several seconds, everything went silent and the only communication between the two groups was intense eye contact and darting glances.

The tense testosterone stand-off ended when one itchy trigger-fingered soldier fired his weapon. Then everyone started shooting as they dove for cover. Powell's men ducked behind pews and statues of blessed saviors. Sanders' men leaped behind the coffin and altar.

Amid the melee, my captors tossed me aside, leaving me to fend for myself. I scrambled behind a black marble donation box to save myself from the deadly hailstorm of planetary projectile weapons. I wiped the blood from the side of my face, along with whatever else had been deposited there from Sanders' head. My mind was still reeling from her betrayal, so it was hard to pinpoint how I felt about her death.

"Rey!" I wailed, pressing my com deeper into my ear and plugging the other to avoid tinnitus. "Why did you do that?"

"She knew the rules," Rey responded, unagitated.

"How the hell did you do that?" Ayil's voice chimed in over the line. I was relieved he was still alive. I tried to peek out from my spot to see where the others were, but I quickly regretted it as a nearby pew splintered from a much too close impact.

"A sonic atomizer, built into the earpiece. My own invention," Rey said proudly.

"Please tell me that doesn't come standard in your earpieces!" I yelled.

There was a slight pause. "Yes, why?"

"Ahhhh," I growled and yelped as a stray bullet chipped away at my marble fortress. "What the hell do we do now?"

"Wait five more minutes and they will kill each other off," Ayil pointed out.

"This gunfire is going to draw the police and every soldier in town to us," Rayne added. "We need to get out of here."

"I can still get us to the estate undetected," Terrin said. "But we need to get outside."

"Kit, where are you?" Rayne asked.

"Behind the donation box on the south side."

"Good, stay there. Everybody else, get behind a column, not the pews. Rey, can you lock onto my com?"

"Of course," he answered, as if the question were stupid.

"Good, fire a laser discharge at it now."

"Will do," he answered calmly.

"What!" I yelled and looked around the corner of my box. Rayne stepped into the center aisle and tossed his earcom like a stone over water. The tiny little pebble slid down the aisle, stopping at the steps leading up to the altar. Seconds later, something crashed through the ceiling, adding to the church's desecration. A harpoon-like shaft dug into the cement floor. There was a slight pause in the gunfire as everyone investigated the device. On its back was a long cylinder. It bloomed open like a flower, revealing dozens of tiny laser stamen within. They began to glow and spin.

"Get down, Kit!" Ayil yelled over the com, no doubt seeing I was stupidly staring at the dangerous device instead of hiding from it.

I slipped back behind the box and watched the laser light show burn tracks all over the walls and pews around me. Screams of agony filled the air, but they soon turned to moans and then eventually stopped altogether. Smoke filled the room, along with the smell of burning flesh, which made me cough and gag. Even after the light show had stopped, I stayed behind the donation bin and listened to Rayne's roll call to confirm everyone's safety.

"Kit!" he yelled, more frantically the third time. His footsteps raced down the aisle and he stopped before me, searching me for injury. "Damn it, answer me when I call," he whispered and pulled me upright by my wrist. He dragged me up the aisle toward the altar, which forced us to sidestep multiple downed men who each looked like they had spent twenty minutes lying on a hot barbecue. Irrationally, I started yanking away from him. I didn't want to be anywhere near these men. I wanted to get out of this church and never step foot in one again. I had seen so much death and yet this was the worst of it, because amongst the smell of bonfire and acrid plastic was the smell of... food.

I gagged on my thoughts of barbecued meat and searched for somewhere to puke.

"Just breathe through your mouth," Rayne said, pulling me closer even though I only wanted to be away from everyone at the moment. I finally wrenched myself from his grip and ran into an empty pew to vomit.

"Is she okay?" I heard Terrin ask Rayne when he reached the altar. He hadn't asked me since I was on the verge of a breakdown. I had lived to see my own funeral, lost a lifelong friend in more ways than one, and witnessed the aftermath of a laser-powered butchering device. My capacity for sanity was shrinking.

"She's fine, just shell-shocked," Rayne sloughed off Terrin's concerns.

"No, shit!" Ayil approached from the west side, back to his beautiful, bronzed face. "Does that man eat, sleep, and wet dream about carnage?"

"I can hear you?" Rey grumbled into the com.

"It was my call," Rayne said. "Rey's toys aren't pretty, but they are effective."

"He's right," Terrin said diplomatically. "This isn't a dinner party. We can't get squeamish now." I looked up at Terrin, but instead of the sympathy I so often thought I might see on his face, he was scolding me. I opened my mouth to beg for a little slack, but the last of my stomach contents came out instead.

SEWAGE

"And I thought the smell of fricasseed soldiers was going to be the worst part of my day," Ayil complained as he climbed down the ladder into the belly of the Vagari sewage system. I stepped aside and let him take up some of the space on the small walkway that traversed along the wastewater river below us.

"What exactly is our plan?" Rayne asked as he put the manhole cover back into place and slid down the ladder to join us.

Terrin clicked on the shoulder flashlight built into his uniform. It gave the tunnel an eerie green glow, making me think of so many more horrors than zombies and clones. "When I was first installed as Mallory's guardian, I was given strict orders to defend against all manner of attacks," Terrin explained as he shuffled down the concrete path, stepping over the occasional blob of debris I didn't want or need to identify. "The sanctity of her womb, though important, was not my primary function."

"Sanctity of her womb?" Ayil mocked me with an adenoidal voice. I looked back and saw his fingers fiercely pinching his nose in defense against the smell. "Well, I guess they can't very well put Pussy Protector on a name tag."

"Knock it off." Rayne shoved his shoulder, and he stumbled into me, nearly sending both of us into the stream below.

"You knock it off." Ayil sniped back at him. "I almost fell in. Oh, wait, I have another one." Seeing the lack of amusement on Rayne's face, Ayil leaned forward to whisper into my ear. "The Cooch Control." Ayil snapped his fingers. "Oh! Oh! Snatch Security." Despite the glares Terrin was now tossing back at us, I couldn't help but snicker at Ayil and the ridiculous nature of my childhood.

"What was your primary function?" I asked Terrin before he sought to defend his dedication to his former job.

"My primary function was to prevent your loss. Whether that be assassination or kidnapping, I was to keep you safe above all else. I planned for every scenario."

Ayil scoffed. "Every scenario, but one."

Terrin stopped and looked back at Ayil. "I planned for *every* scenario. I just didn't plan for every emotion." Terrin looked behind Ayil to Rayne before continuing to escort us. "As part of my duty, I prepared several escape routes to exit the city. I reported them to the Coalition as part of our agreement. However, since one of my possible imagined scenarios was for a coup or an inside informant, I determined Mallory and I might need to flee the city alone without being detected. That route was kept secret, and it is known only to me."

"You don't think the government would have thought to check the sewers?" Rayne asked almost sarcastically.

"There is no need for them to check the sewers since they are impassable." Terrin raised his hand to display the upcoming wall that would prevent us from continuing on our footpath. "The entire compound is protected for this very reason. The wall is nearly a foot thick and embedded with rebar. Even with proper equipment, it would take us hours to get through it quietly. Anything that would get us through quickly would draw too much attention to us and probably risk a cave-in."

"So why did you bring us this way, if we can't get through?" Ayil asked.

"I admit, I never intended to break back into the compound. But the course of action is still the same, just reverse the direction. Unfortunately, the gear I stowed to make the trip more tolerable is on the other side of that wall. Which doesn't do us any good here."

"Gear?" I asked.

"Yes." Terrin turned back to me. "A set of goggles and rebreathers."

I stared at him, slowly turning green with realization.

"No fucking way!" Ayil pointed to the flow of drainage that included many bodily discharges, not to mention possible chemical contaminants. The bacterial count alone could make us sick for days. "I am not going in there."

"It's the safest way."

"Safe!" Ayil shrieked.

"There are a few twists and turns to get to the proper tube." Terrin spoke more to Rayne now than to Ayil or me. "I've traveled it at least a dozen times to memorize it."

"You've done this before!" Ayil shrieked. "By choice!"

"I'll go through first to ensure it hasn't been changed, then I'll return with the rebreathers." Rayne nodded in agreement and Terrin jumped into the flowing water without a moment's hesitation. Ayil groaned, but it turned into a wail when Terrin's head dipped below the surface and didn't return.

"Oh, god in heaven!" Ayil pawed at me, hugging my head into his shoulder. "Let there be another way. I can take the mud. I would relish a garbage chute. Just not this. Let there be a path not paved with piss, shit, and—" Without further warning, Ayil turned from me and vomited into the waterway—adding to its foulness. I stroked his back to comfort him. Had I not already just lost my meal, I would have added to his contribution. When Ayil finished retching, he wept quietly.

I knew exactly how he felt. Waste water wasn't as disgusting as a giant's outhouse, but at least I didn't have to swim in that.

Ten minutes later, Terrin returned wearing goggles and a rebreather, though I wasn't sure it mattered at that point since he was already covered head to toe in unimaginable filth. He handed me a bag with a second rebreather and a pair of goggles. Thankfully, they were still in their packaging. But since he only had the two, I was going to be the only one with the privilege of a fresh set. As he handed them to me, he kept the bag pinched between his fingers. I looked at him, seeing why he wouldn't release.

"You could stay here if you prefer. Rayne and I could do this alone." I glanced at Rayne to see what he thought about this. He nodded in agreement.

I realized my earlier display must have left them nervous about my level of functionality. Since I too was wondering how much more close combat I could take, I considered their offer. Then I remembered my sister. She was already being detained by mean men. How would she react to two stinky ones coming to collect her?

"I'm okay," I said to Terrin, taking the bag from him. "Really," I said to Rayne.

In truth, I probably wasn't, but with my sister's welfare at the forefront of my mind, I could hold off my mental breakdown a little longer.

I opened the bag and slipped out the goggles and rebreather. Terrin instructed me on how to adjust them to fit better. I put them in place as tight as they would fit, covering my eyes, nose, and mouth.

Terrin helped me into the tepid water and per his instructions, I grabbed onto his waist. He dipped us down into the water, and with most of the effort in his arms, he pulled us into the darkened world of underground plumbing. We shifted left, then right around in a circle, diverting through the large pipes, pushing against the natural flow of the water until we, at last, emerged. I cleared some goo from my goggles and looked around the shallow water section that was fed by several waterfalls of wastewater.

When I removed my mask, I was relieved to smell soap above the smell of bodily refuse. Someone, somewhere, was emptying their bath or laundry water, and I was grateful for the slight reprieve. Terrin took me over to the walkway and helped me boost myself onto it. He brought over a plastic backpack and set it beside me.

"Everything you'll need is in this pack."

I removed my protective gear to donate it to the next scuba diver and opened the pack. I found a bottle of soap and a liter of water. I smiled at Terrin, but he was busy adjusting his goggles and couldn't see how thrilled I was that he had indeed planned for everything.

I dug through the rest of the items he had packed so many years ago in case of an emergency—a pair of clothes I would not likely fit anymore, a first aid kit, including antibiotics and pain meds, protein bars, matches, candles, rope, a pocket knife, and a black box. I pulled out the hinged box and opened it.

Inside, nested against white felt, was a silver locket. Elaborate etching adorned the locket with the letter M and several decorative embellishments. I couldn't help smiling at the thought of my teenage self receiving such a beautiful gift, especially from Terrin.

"What's this?" I asked, holding up the box to display the locket.

Terrin narrowed his eyes to see what I was looking at. He scrunched up his nose. "It's a tracking device. I have the monitor in my pack. That was before I upgraded to an implanted device."

"Oh." My smile dimmed as reality once again smacked me in the back of the head. Of course, Terrin hadn't purchased jewelry for me. He wasn't my boyfriend, or even my friend at the time. He was just my bodyguard. I closed the box and shoved it to the bottom of the pack.

"Open it."

I looked up and found him staring at me. I couldn't place the emotion on his face. He wasn't insistent I open the locket, but more daring me to.

Curious, I retrieved the box and removed the locket. I carefully popped open the silver pendant and found two photographs inside. One was of my father—a younger man than I even remembered. The other was of my mother. Unlike my father, she looked nearly the same—beautiful and serene.

I looked at Terrin. He was still watching me. Gauging my reaction to the gift. Had it been a decade earlier, I might have thought nothing of the gift or considered it a bribe. But it was much more meaningful than that. Terrin didn't have to make the tracker a locket—certainly not one so beautiful or etched with my initial. He also didn't have to cut and painstakingly place two tiny photos of the most important people in my life. I may have only been a child to him and I may have been the focus of his duty, but he had cared for me. Enough to consider how much this would mean to me if unforeseen reasons suddenly ripped me from my home.

Terrin moved over to me and took the locket from my hand. He lifted the chain over my head and looped it around my neck. He adjusted the bobble resting against my chest to face the M outward. When I looked back up, he grabbed my chin. For a moment, he looked angry, but it subsided. He released me and stepped back. "Stay here," he commanded and slipped his gear back on. Then he disappeared under the water.

I noticed a second bag sitting farther over on the walkway. It was below a large hole in the wall. Terrin had removed the bricks to access his secret hiding place. I pulled it over and peeked inside to see if it was the same as mine. I noted a change of clothing for Terrin and similar cleaning supplies. First aid and food. His bag had the addition of a pulse pistol, the monitor for the tracking device, and a box of preloaded syringes. I pulled the box out and examined the formula on the label.

Tranquilizers.

I grimaced as I realized he had intended them for me. I wasn't sure if I should be flattered or insulted. He really had thought of *every* scenario.

Terrin and Ayil sprung up from the water. Ayil immediately ripped his rebreather off and started coughing. A spasm followed and then he contributed another load from his stomach into the water. Terrin noticed me snooping through his bag and eyed the tranquilizers in my hand. He approached me and took the box from me. "You were rather difficult at the time."

I smirked. "What's changed?"

"A lot." He shoved the box into his pack and tossed it away. He gave me a scolding look. "A lot has changed, Mallory. Get washed up." Terrin took Ayil's gear and headed back underwater.

Ayil transitioned from sickness to a stupor. He was shell-shocked by sheer grossness.

"Come here." I waved him over.

He meandered to me, barely capable of looking me in the eye. I reached down and pulled his shirt off. He didn't fight me, since he was ready to be rid of anything holding the stench on him. I retrieved the soap from my pack and pooled a gob in my hands. I scrubbed it into his hair, digging my fingers deep to remove any debris. Then I moved to his face and shoulders.

"Oh, I love you so much." He exhaled contentedly and spoke through sudsy lips. "If you didn't smell like shit, I would kiss you."

I chuckled. "Likewise, pal," I mumbled and kept scrubbing.

Shelter

After our partial showers in gray water, we all headed down the remaining length of the sewer toward my childhood home. When we reached a fork in the road, Terrin directed us to the right and we headed into an alcove with a ladder leading to the surface.

We arrived in what I would have assumed was a basement. It had solid concrete walls lined with multiple rows of piping and exposed electrical wiring. There were a few passageways heading away from us, but they were too dark to see the end of. "What is this?" I asked, surprised I didn't recognize my home.

"This is your father's bomb shelter."

"I didn't even know this existed?"

"It was on a need-to-know basis."

"Need to know? I was living on top of it."

"Your father did everything in his power to make sure you were oblivious to the dangers around you. The need for a bomb shelter suggests one might be at risk of being bombed."

Ayil came up out of the hole looking a little more than worse for wear. Until he had new clothes and a battery acid bath, he would not be himself. Since he refused to put on his stench-filled shirt again, he was making do with my pink unicorn shirt. Apart from cutting the sleeves to make room for his more ample arms, it fit him rather well.

Rayne, on the other hand, wasn't in the least bothered by this covert project. He was in assassin mode and ready for a fight.

He surveyed the room, searching for traps I hadn't considered. Satisfied the area was secure, he closed the trapdoor and looked at Terrin. "Now what?"

"We find out whose home." Terrin touched his ear. "Rey, are you there?"

There was a short static burst in my ear that made me worry the water had damaged the devices after all, but then a few cuss words came over the line. "Just a second."

"What's happening?" Terrin asked. Rayne leaned into my ear to listen, because he had destroyed his device to save all of us.

"Oh, nothing, just a few cruisers and an armada." Rey's voice cracked over the com. "I guess they noticed that laser missile shooting through the atmosphere."

"Are you okay?" I asked.

"He lives for this stuff," Rayne assured me.

Rey cackled. "They can see me, but their radar can't. They are firing off the cuff and their aim is shit. A few lucky shots." The connection fizzled for a moment. "...be on your own for a little while ... call when it's safe ... send ... help you." The com snapped and went dead.

"He's left the atmosphere," Rayne said. "His coms won't work until he returns. We'll be working blind for a while."

"No communications, no backup, and no ride," Ayil summed up dismally. "Great. Some rescue this is going to be."

I looked at Terrin for an answer. "This shelter is fully equipped and fortified against attack. The only problem is, we used the only unlocked door. If we want to get up into the mansion, we have to access the main controls. I was hoping Rey would handle that remotely, but we'll have to give it a try ourselves."

Terrin headed off down a passageway. As he moved into the darkness, lights flickered on, accommodating him with illumination. We all followed him down to a room at the opposite end. He pushed open a set of double doors and the room awakened for its arriving guests.

Besides the lights, a set of computer screens came to life on the back wall. Below them, a control panel with keyboards, dials, and meters glowed. Terrin waved his hand toward the chair in front of the panel. "Care to give it a try?"

"Me?" I grimaced. Hacking was not my specialty.

"It was designed for you," Terrin added. "All of this was designed for you."

I sat down in the desk chair and instantly an image popped onto the screens above. My father's youthful face loomed before me, overlapping the screens. "Welcome to the Vagari bomb shelter. Please enter or say your 12-digit security phrase." I shrugged at Terrin.

"It would have been created before my time. He would have asked you to remember it."

I pinched my lips together and typed in my name, but it wasn't long enough. "I'm sorry. I don't remember learning a security phrase."

Terrin rolled a chair up beside me and rested his arm on the back of mine. "He wouldn't have asked you to remember a security phrase," he explained. "He asked you to tell the computer something about yourself." I protested, but he hushed me. "You would have been eleven or twelve, not quite the mature adult you were the second you hit your teen years." I snorted at his obvious sarcasm. "Don't tell me what you would say to the computer. Tell me what she would say to it."

I reached up and fiddled with the locket that was terribly out of place on this mission. I considered my parents' names, but that was just me thinking like an adult again.

What would my childhood self want to tell a computer I was meeting for the first time?

"Hello, my name is Mallory Kit," I said, remembering a game I used to play with my father that never made a lick of sense until right at this moment. "What's your name?"

"Hello, Mallory Kit." The computer responded with stuttered syllables. "My name is Computer. Do you want to play a game?"

"Yes."

"What is your favorite color?"

I laughed and put my hand over my mouth, impressed by the way my father's mind works. I smiled, leaned forward, and clearly said, "Pumpernickel."

"Security phrase accepted," the computer responded and started going through a series of loading screens.

"I got confused between periwinkle and pumpernickel," I told Terrin, even though he hadn't actually asked for an explanation. "My father thought it was hilarious, so I kept saying it that way to make him smile."

Terrin nodded, and the slightest smile appeared on his stubborn lips, as if he too couldn't help but be charmed by a miniature Mallory Kit.

The system hummed and an image of my father came onto the screen. He was sitting in a chair by his favorite hearth. I half expected to see him pick up a pipe and start puffing on the smoke. "Hello, sweetheart," he cooed. "Can you tell me, are there any soldiers around to help you?"

Terrin put his hand over the microphone. He shook his head vehemently, making me wonder what would happen if I said yes. He moved his hand, and I leaned in again. "No."

"Okay, let's keep playing our game." I frowned at the childish program. "All the doors are locked, so you can't get out. Not unless there is no one outside that will hurt you. Is there someone outside that can hurt you?"

I looked at Terrin, and he put his shoulders up and mouthed my response.

"I don't know," I answered.

"Okay. If you want to see who is outside, you'll have to push the button to your left that's blinking." I pushed the button and black-and-white video footage of the entire mansion replaced

Richard's face. Each room or section of the grounds had a dedicated screen. The only areas free from spying eyes were the bathrooms and some bedrooms. I could hardly believe the number of guards posted. This was a security detail well and above containing a little girl and her father.

"I guess Sanders told them we were coming," Ayil asked.

"Look at that." Rayne pointed to a lower right video image as it appeared again. "Protesters. I think Rey's coup may have taken seed."

"How did he" I trailed off, not needing or wanting to know how he was fueling his coup.

"Is there anyone dangerous outside?" my father asked.

Terrin shook his head at me. "No," I said.

"Would you like me to unlock the door so you can come back into the mansion?"

"Yes."

The computer hummed for a moment, then it showed me a map, guiding me to the exit. There was even a little cartoon of me following the line. I smiled at my theatrical little avatar with long rainbow hair.

"Where do we go?" Ayil asked.

I pointed to the monitor displaying my little sister's room. She was curled in a ball on her bed, sleeping or crying, I wasn't sure which. "First, we get Elizandra out, then we can work on my father." I pointed to another screen displaying my father sitting in his study. His tears had since stopped, but his vacant stare worried me more. This stunt was putting more than a few gray hairs on his head.

"Kit, your father wasn't part of the plan," Rayne said. I twirled my seat around and found Rayne staring at me with his don't-make-me-be-the-bad-guy look.

"I'm not leaving him behind."

"He's the face of the goddamn Coalition. We can't take him with us. We'll never get off the planet with him. From their perspective, we would be kidnapping a world leader."

"We'll use a mask," I suggested. Rayne shook his head and clicked the button under his chin. The identity shield shimmered partially before disappearing. Unlike the coms, it was not immune to water. "I'm not leaving him," I said firmly.

"And I'm not risking my ass for him."

Terrin held up his hand, stopping me from retaliating with a remark I might regret. "Let's focus on getting Elizandra, then reassess our options. We don't want to risk—"

"I'm not leaving him behind," I said in no uncertain terms.

Terrin stared at me with an exhaustive annoyance I hadn't seen in a while. "Then I'm glad I brought these." He held up the box of tranquilizers before slipping them into his back pocket. Before I could find out if he was joking, he was on the move with Rayne directly after him. Ayil pressed on my back, urging me to move. We followed them up and out of the basement, into the heart of my home capital.

Sidekicks

Sneaking through the mansion was the only way to operate without being inundated with security. Thankfully, they had opted to use human soldiers rather than bios, but around every corner was a new face Rayne or Terrin had to subdue. For the sake of keeping things clean, Terrin used the tranquilizers to keep them out rather than killing them. I noted he deposited the last syringe into his pocket—saving it for his resurrected plan B escape. I resented he was actually considering knocking me out, but this was not the time or place to discuss my rights.

With a trail of sleeping men and women in our wake, we arrived at Elizandra's door. I pushed inside and she jumped off her bed. "I said stay out!" she yelled at me venomously before she realized it was me. "Kit!" She ran into my arms but instantaneously recoiled. "Eww, you stink."

"I know, honey. We need to get you out of here. Mommy wants to see you."

"Mommy!" Her eyes brightened with a joy I no longer possessed at the prospect of seeing my mother. I wondered if she would grow out of it or if she truly had a different relationship with her than me.

"Yes, but listen, nobody wants you to leave, so we have to sneak you out. Can you be very quiet so no one knows you are leaving?"

She nodded. "Why do you stink?" she whispered.

"Don't worry about that right now." I pulled her along and stopped in front of Ayil. "This is Ayil. He's my *bestest* friend in the whole wide universe." Ayil smirked at me and put out his hand to shake. Elizandra shook it tentatively. "He is going to take you someplace safe."

"What?" Ayil asked.

I glanced at Rayne and Terrin to see if they were going to object to my plan. They were gnashing their teeth hard, but neither of them objected as I took over the plan. "Just go back the way we came and lock yourself in the bomb shelter."

"How will you—?"

"Just keep her down there and monitor us. If something goes wrong—"

"Kit!" he scolded me.

I grabbed the back of his neck and pulled his forehead down to press against mine. "—take care of her."

"Of course I will," he whispered, glancing at Elizandra.

"No, Ayil." I shook my head and leaned back to look at him. "If something happens, I want you to take care of *her*... like your own," I whispered, trying not to allude to the specific *her* I was referring to in front of my sister.

Ayil's mouth gaped, and he nodded, unable to scold me for being dramatic when he was so flabbergasted by my request. "Come on, Elizandra. You and I are going to be sidekicks for a little while."

My sister placed her hand in Ayil's outstretched hand. "What about Kit?"

"She's gonna be a hero for a little while."

"I want to be the hero," she complained.

"But you just got upgraded from damsel to sidekick. You have to play that part for a little while first." Ayil's logic confused her, but she nodded, understanding that even in games, there was a natural pecking order.

Ayil started out the door, but Rayne stopped him and handed him a pulse pistol they had taken from one of the more recent downed soldiers. With a breadcrumb trail of sleeping men, I had no concerns Ayil would make it back to the bunker safely. We, however, still had a long way to go, to get to my father's office, and many more guards to deal with. Since there weren't enough tranquilizers to go around, I knew things were about to get bloody.

Ꝺaddy

We made our way through the remaining posted guards, this time leaving behind dying or dead men in our wake. The glossy white floors of the museum-like mansion were turning red, but there was nothing to be done about it. Much like the massacre at the church, it was necessary for our survival.

"That was too easy," Rayne whispered once we reached the door to my father's study. Since there were nearly six men behind us, I didn't agree, but apparently, Terrin did because he was shifting warily to look behind us and even above us.

I ignored their concerns, only focusing on my task. I stepped inside the room slowly, checking the corners for guards. The wide white pillars lining the walls were nearly a mirror image of the cathedral, just on a smaller scale and without the pews. The semi-Grecian theme was beautiful, but it made the room difficult to secure. I crossed the length of the marbled floor on tippy toes, noting the two biomechanoids standing just outside the patio doors behind his desk. Because their programming restricted them to monitoring the exterior, they were unlikely to enter unless something alerted them.

I reached the desk where he was working, but he still hadn't looked up. "Daddy." I reached across the desk and touched his hand.

When he looked up, he frowned, as if in disbelief. "Mallory?" He rose from his seat slowly and examined me. Satisfied I wasn't a mirage, he rushed around the desk and embraced me. I buried my face in his shoulder, weeping with relief.

"I'm so sorry," I mumbled repeatedly, hating myself for causing him the pain I had witnessed at the funeral.

"You shouldn't have come here," he said.

"I had to." I looked up at him. "I had to save you."

"Brave girl." He kissed my forehead and as I stared up at him, tranquility poured over me. I hadn't felt a protective, fatherly embrace for far too long. One that was unconditional and didn't lord the expectations of possession over me.

"*Kit!*" Ayil's voice cracked over the com, distracting me from my pleasant moment. "*Get out... there! That's not...!*"

"What?" I questioned through the static connection. Apparently, even Reynard's equipment was susceptible to some ground interference. I uselessly pressed my finger into my ear to help the transmission quality. "Say that again."

I waited several seconds before Ayil's voice came through loud, clear, and breathless. "*That's not your father!*"

I drew back to look over my father's face more carefully. It was him; I was sure, but there was a slight difference in his body. I had assumed his weight loss was from stress or simply the frailty of aging. However, the arms embracing me were not weak from malnourishment—they had strength hiding behind the tailored suit he wore. He was smiling down at me, though now it looked more like a smirk.

"Where is my father?" I pulled away from him, taking several long strides back to the door where Rayne and Terrin were standing watch.

"I'm right here, Kit." He expanded his arms, offering another hug.

"Where is he!" I yelled.

"*He's gone, Kit.*" Ayil's voice came over the com softly.

"Gone where?"

"*No, Kit. I'm so sorry. He's... gone. They killed him.*"

The silence that followed that statement rang in my ears, and the room spun. Paralyzed by shock, my thoughts went a thousand different directions and nowhere.

He couldn't be dead. My rock... My foundation... My constant... The seedling to my compassion, self-confidence, and the very core of my heart had just been ripped from my grasp.

The reality of never seeing, speaking, or touching him again stamped out my hopes of saving my father. A truth so cold that it sent a shiver back in time to the many times I had thought of him. Now, in retrospect, I was right to be concerned about his welfare. Not that they mattered, because he was probably already gone by then.

I floundered, searching for something or someone else to grab onto. But there was no one and nothing that could replace him or satisfy my need for him.

"He's dead?" I whispered, begging it to be a lie. Let it be a terrible misunderstanding. Let the face staring back at me be real. "My father is dead?"

"Now, how did you figure that one out?" Richard's face asked. "Did that little birdy in your ear tattle on me?" Richard reached up and pressed the button under his chin. With a flicker, the digital mask dissipated, revealing Chancellor Agate.

I took another step back—repulsed I had been hugging him just moments earlier. I shook my head, trying in vain to stop the tears that were clouding my vision and preventing me from focusing on my survival.

"Where did you get that technology?" Rayne asked.

"I bought it off a black-market trader. I never thought I would need it, but lately, it has been quite useful."

"Not smart." Rayne chuckled and raised his pulse pistol.

"Oh, I wouldn't do that," the chancellor said, just as two biomechanoids arrived through the door behind Terrin and Rayne. They held guns to each of their heads, keeping them from defending themselves.

I watched their fury reabsorb as the reality of this trap drained them of hope. Before Agate could take away my last vestige of revenge, I grabbed Terrin's short sword and ripped it from his belt.

Summoning bravery I rarely possessed and acting on the skills I had hardly perfected, I ran at the chancellor. His eyes widened, but there wasn't time for him to get away from me.

I could sense movement behind me, but I dove before a pulse blast could stymie my plans. I slid the remaining few feet on my knees—just as I had done many times in this office when I was a child desperate to be entertained. Never had I considered that I was training for a tactical advantage.

I stabbed the sword upward, prepared to gut Agate from the naval up as I had seen Terrin's father do in his final battle on Miorita.

The blade only narrowly missed its target. It was close enough to rip his pants as another of its likeness propelled my copper blade down.

The tinny clang of a competing sword preceded the vibration of mine striking the floor. My gaze traveled up the intrusive copper blade that had foiled my efforts, and I found Agate's personal bodyguard. The smug-looking gattaw was pleased to have denied me my blood.

Agate stumbled back, huffing out his relief, and checking his crotch more than once for damage.

I ripped my sword from beneath the gattaw's sword and stood. I raised it, ready to fight him. The gattaw guard laughed.

"Mallory, no!" Terrin yelled behind me.

"Will you just grab her!" Agate yelled at his guard.

I abruptly cut off the gattaw by throwing a sword at him. I was far from accurate and it only pissed him off, but that was really all I was going for.

"Don't underestimate her!" Agate snapped as the gattaw lunged forward to grab me.

I yelped and ran to Terrin. I wrapped my hands around him tight and cowered helplessly against him. He instinctively wrapped his arms around me.

Buried in his chest, I looked at Rayne. There was a look of subdued jealousy on his face until he noticed I was groping in Terrin's back pocket. He smiled slightly and struggled against his captor, distracting him from my true motive in grabbing Terrin.

The bodyguard placed a heavy hand on my shoulder and Terrin's hand followed, stacking on his. He said something in his native tongue, which predictably sounded like a threat. The gattaw ripped me back. If I hadn't bounced against his body, I would have been on the floor. He leaned forward to look at my face before saying something, no doubt insulting, back at Terrin. The final insult was spitting on me.

Irritated just on principle, I tried to strike him, but he quickly lassoed my arms, preventing me from kicking. I was immobilized.

"Put her in my shuttle and kill the other two," Agate instructed.

"No!" I struggled to fight the gattaw, but I could do nothing to stop my progress to the patio doors behind my father's desk. I looked at each of their calm faces as the gattaw dragged me out. "No!" I screamed again as daylight hit me. "Rey!" I turned my hopes to the only other man who could help us.

"Oh, yes, I forgot." Agate reached in my ear and yanked out the tiny com device. Agate crushed it between his fingers. "Come on."

Agate led the way to his shuttle, while his bodyguard pushed me behind him. I slipped the syringe I had snagged from Terrin out of my sleeve and positioned it away from my back. I lunged forward and the gattaw instinctively pulled me back toward him. The moment I hit something solid, I depressed the plunger.

I couldn't entirely track the events that followed, but it resulted in me lying on the landing platform with a burning ache in my face. Agate looked back at me and then to his bodyguard, who was wavering back and forth trying to fight the sedative I had injected him with. It probably wasn't an adequate dose for him, but it would have to do.

I jumped up and ran back toward the house, but I was quickly back on the ground, pushed by the impact of an explosion. My ears were ringing, and I was trying to figure out why I was in even more pain. I coughed dust from my lungs and pulled myself up to look at what had happened. The explosion destroyed the office I had just left. Remnants of fire and charred columns were all that remained.

"Rayne! Terrin!" I screamed into the smoke.

I stood, ready to run into the rubble to check for survivors, but my leg demanded I not put weight on it. I looked down and saw a piece of wood sticking out of my thigh. I touched it, testing its depth, but it was too deep to risk removing.

Agate looped his arms under mine and dragged me away. With unseen injuries, I wasn't able to fight him as I wanted to. Another bomb hit the mansion just as we reached the shuttle; Agate threw us both through the hatch before more shrapnel hit us. I was close enough to him to hear his ragged breaths and see the worried look on his face. Whatever was happening was not part of his plan.

"Go, now, you idiot!" Agate yelled to the front of the shuttle, where his pilot had been waiting at the ready.

Another bomb hit, making the ground beneath us tremble. I shifted in Agate's arms to see what was becoming of my father's mansion. Fire and smoke were taking over the view, but I could see broken windows on the upper and lower levels. The hatch closed just as the shuttle lifted.

"What the hell is happening?" Agate yelled, holding his finger over his ear to listen for a response. "What? Who is this?" Agate's frustrated face turned grim and his face sobered. "How nice to hear from you. I was hoping you were dead. ... You should have surrendered her to me while you still had a chance to profit from it," Agate said. He glanced at me, a certain determination on his face. "Yes, you always did have a soft spot for broken things. ... I have no intention of doing anything of the sort. ... Good luck with that, Reynard. You aren't the only one with tricks and toys." Agate frowned and then glared at me. "Go ahead! Try it! You'll kill her too." Agate screamed at the heavens.

I laughed and rolled my body back to lie against the diamond plate metal floor. That was when I realized Rey wasn't intervening to help me. He was going to destroy me before the Coalition could use me to destroy the universe.

Burn

I stared out the shuttle's window at the capital. Everywhere I looked, I saw smoke and fire. Agate was looking at the same carnage. His lips pinched as tight as his asshole.

"What's happening?" I asked, since I didn't understand the randomness of these attacks.

"Riots are breaking out all over the city."

"Rey?" I asked.

"Yes. Seems he's released some damaging information to some naysayers of biotechnology."

"What sort of information?" I asked.

"We're almost there. I'll show you."

Well past the city center, the pilot landed our shuttle on a tall building in the factory district. Agate shuffled out and demanded I follow. With some effort, I limped across the roof until we reached the stair access. I stared down the flight of steps ruefully.

"Come on." Agate reached for me. I pulled away, but he shook his head. "Don't be ridiculous. Your legs cut to the bone. Let me help you."

I surrendered to his help and leaned on him during the slow, agonizing trip to the elevator. Once inside, I rested my head in the corner, trying to cool my forehead and ignore the overwhelming heat taking over my body.

"You didn't have to kill him," I said, mostly to myself.

"He was becoming a liability. His devotions had long since converted to the empire. Had he known about your origins, he would have pitted the entire Coalition against itself."

"Seems like that's happening already." I breathed, trying to control my dizziness. I knew better than to look at my leg, but I was curious if it was as bad as Agate was claiming.

"Please, even if all the factions rebelled, I have enough bios to put them down. The people understand our technology is what feeds us."

"The empire feeds them."

"Tit for tat."

"For fuck's sake, how slow is this elevator?" I turned back and noticed the numbers were in the negative now. I hadn't noticed the air was getting cool because my body was so feverish. The elevator finally dinged and Agate helped me out of the carriage.

We stepped directly into a lab that resembled every other lab where doctors had poked and prodded me, except this one contained dead human specimens floating in jars instead of pig fetuses or random organs. I stared at the death aquariums as we passed, wondering if everyone eventually ended up on the Coalition's parts list.

"I don't feel so good," I reluctantly admitted, even though I was certain my face was probably three shades lighter than it ought to be. Since my temperature had caused me to break into a sweat, I was now shivering in the cold lab. "I need to go to a hospital."

"I don't think there is any need for that," Agate said as he sat me down in a chair. "It occurred to me after I heard about your death—your faked death. I didn't necessarily need you alive. I mean, it was smart to make your surrender public, so I was obligated to put you through a trial and all the like, but really, now that you're dead, I think I'll just keep you that way."

I couldn't help but chuckle since that seemed to be the consensus preference. However, since Agate probably meant it literally, I quickly lost my humor. "DNA degrades quickly after death. You'll want to keep me alive." I sputtered out what sounded like a good excuse for not killing me.

"That's easy. I'll keep your tissue alive." He motioned over to a set of hospital beds on the back wall. I could see the basics of life support equipment and two small isolation tents, but that was about it. "Go on," he urged me as he leaned against the counter he was standing next to. "Take a peek," he said, practically double-dog daring me to witness the truth.

I stared at Agate, not wanting to take part in another one of his show-and-tells. Nothing good had ever come from opening the curtains of his operations. However, I still wanted to know what information had spurred the bio-opposers into a riot.

I pushed with my good leg to roll my chair over to the beds. I glanced back at Agate before peering into the first one. The body of the man inside was for all intents and purposes dead, but he looked to be asleep to the untrained eye. I maneuvered to the other tent and cried out as I ripped myself clear of the horrible image I had just scarred my eyes with. I wept for the woman inside the tent. With no eyes, half a skull, and no brain, she was clearly not sleeping. The life support system that was traditionally used to keep coma patients alive was being used to keep her remaining organs and tissues viable.

"You're evil!" I screamed, not even pulling my face from my hands. "Do you know that?"

"One man's evil is another man's—"

"No!" I screamed at him, lifting my head to stare at him from across the lab. "There has to be a line, Agate! We can't just keep defiling our humanity by turning ourselves into parts."

"You sound like those religious zealots."

"This isn't about religion, Agate! This is about humanity. When people die, they should be treated with dignity. Is this what you would want for yourself? To be lying on this bed in pieces?"

"I would be dead. Who cares?"

I stared at him, trying to comprehend what it was he couldn't understand. I slapped my hand against my chest. "I would care." I pointed at the bed next to me. "I don't know her. But I care! Because I'm not a machine, Agate." I shook my head at his blank features, realizing my words were meaningless to him. "You're not even a sociopath, are you?" I asked.

Agate smiled and chuckled to himself. "Maybe." He shrugged.

"No, you're not. You're just the guy who kept taking the next step. One more. One more." I was feeling numb in my brain as well as my body, and I suspected I wouldn't be conscious much longer. "One more," I murmured.

"Come on." Agate moved to me and started wheeling me back to where I had started. "There's *one more* thing I want to show you before I put you out of your misery."

Agate slid me back down a dark hallway and placed me in front of a large window. He looked at me and smiled. "This one is really going to piss you off." He moved to a box on the wall and flipped on a light inside the viewing room.

I leaned forward as the people inside came into view. They were all just standing in a row as if they had been waiting in the dark for me to arrive. "What is this?" I asked, even though I knew I didn't want the answer.

"This is the next step," Agate said mockingly. He pressed a button on the power box. "Everyone, this is Mallory. Say hello."

"Hello." The row of people said in fairly synchronous voices. They sounded human, but they didn't sound authentic. There wasn't an ounce of emotion coming from any of them. They were speaking robotically.

"What did you do, Agate?" Again, I didn't want the answer, but I needed it.

"Show us your tops," he commanded his puppets.

The entire line reached up and grabbed fistfuls of their hair. Then they lifted off their *tops*. Their skulls separated, revealing brain matter implanted with electronics.

I stared at the soft tissue merged with blinking LEDs and wires. Nothing about it truly surprised me. The fact that they were more human than robots didn't even really matter. They were still bios, just less obvious ones. "Spies?" I asked, coming to the only logical conclusion for wanting less tech.

"Very good," Agate rewarded me like a child or a dog. "They actually work pretty well, except for one minor issue."

"Their tops fall off when they bend over?" The flat, morose sarcasm spilled from me on autopilot. I had completely disconnected from this moment.

Agate chuckled. "Sort of. We can't seem to keep the infection away. Even when fully healed, they still can't fight off the bugs."

"That's because you put antennas in dead brains."

"Oh, they weren't dead." I turned to look at Agate and saw the anticipation on his face. The bastard was feasting on my astonishment like a parasite. "The dead ones weren't working, so we started *recruiting* live specimens."

Though my pain had subsided, I knew not to attack Agate. Beyond not wanting to finish breaking my leg, I didn't want to give him the satisfaction of my outrage. "That's what Rey told the factions, isn't it?"

"Yes. It was the final straw, I'm afraid. They've been looking very hard for solid proof and Rey gave them the list of our conveniently disappearing volunteers."

"I can't decide if monster to murderer is a sideways move for you."

"This is what I'm going to do to you, you know?" I stared at Agate, still fighting my instincts to run or fight or cry. "I'll stick you in that box with them." He watched me for a reaction. "I bet you won't have an issue with infection. You know why?"

"Why?" I asked, just to play along.

"Because you're *special*," he said with irritated enthusiasm. "I have no fucking clue, because Kessler is either a genius or a complete idiot."

"What do you mean you don't know? I was in and out of your possession for years. You've tested me a billion times."

Agate sighed and scrunched his face. "Kessler reprogrammed so much of your existing DNA it's hard to understand what bits do what. Most everything about our bodily functions is caused by several genes, not just a single one. We can't simply reproduce his results on any DNA strand. It has to be yours."

"What about my baby?" I asked, out of curiosity.

"Worthless. Apart from her being the carrier of your previous plagues, she provided me with no help. Whatever created your immunity is thus far still unknown. But in time, years perhaps, decades, I think you will tell all your secrets." He smiled and wheeled me deeper into the building.

We arrived in another cold room with beds, but these were empty. With some effort, Agate lifted me onto the bed, which I didn't fight. I looked around the room as he hooked me up to IVs. "Just like old times," he said as he taped off my line.

I looked down at the line as he attached an IV bag. "What is that?"

"Fluids."

He pulled a syringe from his pocket and injected it into the bag port. "What is that?"

"Pain medicine." Agate perked his brow. "I'm not actually going to kill you." He tapped my head. "I need you in healthy condition if I'm going to turn you into a good little spy. Which means we have to heal this leg up before we can proceed."

I watched as Agate cut open my pants to reveal what looked like a saw blade had taken a bite out of my leg. "Mmm," he mumbled as he sprayed the area with cleanser. I expected it to hurt, but I was a little beyond pain now. I was just a patient observer at this moment.

After a careful inspection, Agate removed the wood fragment, rinsed the wound, staunched the bleeding with freeze spray, and placed a bone filler and tissue mesh, followed by a metal clamp cast around my thigh.

"Would you get a message to her?" I asked.

"What?"

"My daughter. I'd like to tell her something, anything. She shouldn't grow up without a single word from me."

"Have some deep wisdom to share, do you?"

"Not really, I guess. I just wanted to say hi and bye." Agate smirked at me, unimpressed by my plea for sympathy. "Do you have a pen and paper? You can throw it away when I'm dead. I just really need to write it down." My eyes watered, but I turned away so he didn't see me cry.

He sighed and rummaged around in his pockets, searching for both. He found a pen and handed it to me, along with what looked like an old grocery list. I glanced at him and he shrugged. "We discouraged paper in the lab after Kessler."

I nodded and maneuvered myself, trying to find a surface to support the thin paper without exerting too much strain on my leg. I looked around and pointed toward a surgical tray stand. "Could I—shit," I cussed when the pen dropped to the floor.

I shifted over to the side of the bed, trying to reach for it, but was too far away. Agate leaned down to grab it. While he was reaching down, I quickly looped my IV line around his neck and jumped on his back. He threw himself backward, toppling the IV stand. With very little strength left to stay attached to him, I put all my effort into holding onto the two ends of the throttling tubing.

Agate elbowed me and scratched at my hands, but my pain meds and determination were making me untouchable. Something stung my thigh, and I saw a needle sticking out of my leg. It could have been more pain medicine or a sedative or heroine, but it didn't matter. All that mattered was holding onto the tubing.

I tried not to think about the act itself—the murder I was committing. I focused on keeping the garrote taut. When he let out a strangled plea for help, I reminded myself of how many lives were at stake because of his leadership. He was far too embedded in his quest for power to stop. Only death would prevent him from committing greater and greater atrocities against the dead... and the living.

I had no choice.

I had to kill him.

Agate's frothing and choking lessened as the oxygen to his brain waned. He dropped to his knees and fell over, but he wasn't yet dead. That took more time.

My eyes blurred, and I worried I wouldn't be conscious, or possibly alive, long enough to finish what I had started. I pulled both ends of the tubing as tight as my strength allowed and tied them into a knot.

Even if I was spiraling toward death, Chancellor Agate would be right by my side. I would stand before the great gates of the hereafter and bear witness to his misdeeds. Even if I had to march into hell right alongside of him, I would be content knowing I had rid the world of another Dr. Frankenstein.

SAVIOR

"Tell him he has to wait!" Terrin's voice sounded strained and distant.

"I'll deal with it. Just find her!" Rayne yelled back at him even further away.

"Mallory!" Terrin was closer now.

I lifted my head off Agate's back, but the surrounding darkness was not eased when my eyes opened. "Terrin," I croaked, still feeling drugged up by whatever Agate gave me. I lifted my hand and waved it around. The power-saving lights flickered on.

I shifted and pulled Agate over to check him. I immediately wished I hadn't. His bloodshot eyes stared back at me, accusing me of murder. I reminded myself I had done this for my people—both the Coalition and the empire, but it didn't make me feel any better.

"Mallory!" Terrin was closer now, running toward the light in the distance.

"I'm here!" I yelled as loud as I could.

Terrin came into the room and rushed toward me. He saw Agate just as he reached me. He noted the tubing around his neck, the obvious means of his demise. He said nothing and wrapped an arm around me to assist my rise. I limped along beside him, happy to endure any amount of pain so I could get out of this hellish lab.

"How did you find me?" I asked, not terribly sure how long it had been since I had left them.

Terrin raised his hand, displaying a small monitor showing two blinking dots, one green and one red. When I didn't show any sign of understanding, he tapped the locket on my chest. I pressed my hand to it, grateful for once that he was such a controlling man.

"We have to hurry. Rey is eager to blow up this building."

"Good."

We met up with Rayne and they both assisted me up the stairs to the roof, where a transport pod was waiting. Before I even made it through the door, Elizandra was on me, hugging me and making it impossible to walk. "Kit! You're alive! I thought you died again."

"Come on, E," Ayil dragged her back and buckled her up again. Before Ayil situated himself, he hugged me. I was certain he intended it to be a brief thank-God-your-alive hug, but I draped my body against him and cried.

Ayil pulled me in close and kissed the side of my head. "I got you," he whispered and guided me to sit with him.

An alarm went off and Rayne cussed as he brought the engines online and took off.

"Is he insane!" Terrin yelled up to Rayne.

"He had to fire. He's losing ground. The fucking empire just put their ships on him. They think he's the one responsible for all of this." I nearly laughed between sobs because Rey *was* responsible for all this. And yet he wasn't. "Buckle up! This isn't going to be fun."

Terrin forcefully parted me from Ayil to get my safety belt on. Ayil strapped himself in and Terrin narrowly reached his own seat before a bright light filled the pod. Barely a heartbeat later, the shuttle flipped from a blast wave and a loud explosion vibrated the hull.

Elizandra screamed.

Above the squawk of metal and banging of shrapnel hitting the hull, I heard Rayne yell, "Brace for impact!"

The already lurching ride became a jolting one as we impacted several hard objects before coming to a sliding halt. As soon as we had stopped moving, I stripped off my seat belt and moved to Elizandra, who was wailing tearfully. "It's okay, honey, it's over," I assured her.

"Rey? Come in, Rey. Shit!" Rayne threw his pod's handheld communication device against the already broken window.

"Is he really in danger?" I asked.

Rayne looked back at me, his eyes filled with equal parts worry and anger. "Yes."

"The entire city is rioting now," Terrin explained. "The protesters are heavily armed. They broke into the mansion and took it within a matter of minutes. We barely made it out alive. They were killing everyone."

I nodded, knowing that he meant absolutely everyone. The mob was not likely to distinguish between guard and gardener. I pushed away the memory of more than a few familiar faces in my father's employ.

"You wanted a coup; you got a coup." Rayne moved to the back and opened the hatch with a push of a button. The open door revealed the trail of debris and fire we had left in our wake. Not all of it was from us, though. There were people scattered throughout the streets vandalizing and looting. Molotov cocktails were on tap.

I stared at the vacant space behind us. Rey's bomb had leveled more than just the factory. Besides the sounds of alarms and breaking glass, I could hear people screaming and calling for help. The city was no longer rebelling against its leaders. It was descending into anarchy. I was a fool to think that this would be any less devastating than a war.

"We need to move," Rayne said. "We're drawing unwanted attention."

"We need to find a host telecom," I said.

"What? Why?" Rayne asked.

"Because I'm going to put a stop to this."

I climbed over several cement chunks before reaching a flat surface. I ignored the increasing carnage as I walked down the street in search of a public communication station.

"Kit, wait," Ayil hollered after me, but I continued to walk. No one paid any mind to the strange woman limping down the street that smelled vaguely of sewage. I was no one to them. I was never more than an image in their mind, anyway. I represented a societal-level delusion of grandeur leftover from the empire. They wanted a piece of the god they had lost, so they created a child to live as a myth.

"We need to get to a transport," Rayne said as he caught up with me. "I need to get to Rey."

"You can't help Rey right now. He's surrounded by two planetary armies and regardless of how clever he is, he doesn't have enough firepower or gadgets to get himself free. Does he?" I turned to confirm this, but Rayne just pouted. I hadn't seen it before, or had at least ignored it, but Rayne cared for his employer. He was, after all, his savior. He hadn't just put his trust in him. He had placed his life with him.

If Reynard Baloch died on this day, it would be my fault for dragging him into a war he didn't want to fight. It would be my fault for not sticking to the plan.

As usual, everything from the day I was born was my fault.

And it needed to stop.

A man darted at me from the side and snatched the locket right off my neck. He disappeared in an instant, a yelp sounding his departure. I didn't bother to look over to see what Terrin had done to the man, but I suspected my locket was no longer in his possession.

Nearly a quarter mile down the road, we arrived at a communication station. The machine was remedial, with very basic options, but it had interplanetary connectivity and the city grid supported it. Which meant that I could call any planet under Coalition rule.

"What are you going to do?" Rayne asked, but I didn't answer.

I dialed in a basic I.D. and password that essentially told the device who was calling and who to bill. I wouldn't look forward to the debit this phone call caused. After that, I typed in a very special code which brought me to a very special screen where I typed in yet another *very* special code.

There weren't many tricks in my bag, but this was the pièce de résistance. I never thought in a million years I would ever need to use it, but today was that day.

A series of accumulating numbers filled the screen. Hundreds, thousands, millions. Each line of data followed with the words "live connection." The last line listed the largest number and indicated "In queue." All totaled, there were more than a trillion communication devices connected to this one machine in the middle of the capital city.

"What did you just do?" Ayil asked.

"She called everyone," Elizandra answered. "Look!" She pointed above us to an electronic billboard several blocks away that showed my face. The rioting people stopped and stared at the images filling in on their devices and public screens. "It's for emergencies only," Elizandra added.

"This is an emergency," I mumbled.

I turned and looked into the camera that was witnessing my revival from the dead. For a moment, the sheer exposure of this moment overwhelmed me. Who was I to be addressing an entire nation? Who was I to be standing in the middle of chaos and demanding attention?

Then I remembered exactly who I was.

"My name is Mallory Kit, Kit Mallory daughter of Susan Mallory the foreordained queen of the empire and President Richard Kit." I heard my voice echoing through the city streets, as my voice rose above that of the gunfire and detonations.

"There is a war brewing and a coup in progress. It is for a good reason. We have been lied to, manipulated, and forced into a corner by our leaders. The technology that was meant to save us is destroying us.

"I know many of you see me as a savior or a traitor or perhaps just a failure, but I am none of those things. I am a woman who was lied to, just like all of you."

"I was told all through my life that I was special. That I was meant to replenish the human race. Bring it health and intellect, in the form of a child. But that wasn't what I brought." I paused, debating how much to say. How much would the people believe?

"Instead, I brought the capacity to carry a plague. A sickness that was created by the Coalition. I was never meant to bring life. My true purpose was to be a conduit of genocide.

"The future that we all wanted—that we believed in—isn't in here." I tapped my chest. "It's out there, in the stars!" I pointed upward. "There is no point begging for miracles when they are all around us. And there is no point killing each other when all we gain is more bodies to fight our wars!"

I swallowed hard, pushing back my emotions. "I have been betrayed by my countrymen today! Richard Kit... my father... is dead. He was a good man. He was loyal to his people, and he died because of it."

"I know I have never been the savior any of you asked me to be, but I beg you today to be mine. People of Vagari, lay down your arms and mourn with me today. Not just for our president, but in reverence to those who have died and not been allowed to rest."

"I ask all of you—the people of Vagari, the empire's armada, and Captain Reynard Baloch—to be penitent for the atrocities we have allowed to happen through silence and passivity. Stand down so that you might see the turmoil that we are *all* responsible for." I could sense the looks being passed between my friends. I was taking a significant risk by publicly calling out everyone to share the blame for the Coalition's underhanded tactics.

"Queen Mallory…" I stared into the camera, feeling her angry eyes on me from halfway across the galaxy. "I beg you to be a mother today. Not just my mother, but the matriarch of a galaxy starving for compassion. We need to know that you are here for us. That you will protect us—even from ourselves. Stand down."

"Captain Baloch." I considered what I could ask of him to bait him into behaving, but there was no negotiating with a madman. As I stared at the lens before me, I swallowed hard and hoped he had more humanity left in him than Agate. "Rey," I whispered. "There has to be a line. One that we won't cross. One that can't be mechanized or monetized. There has to be a time when we use diplomacy because the alternative is just too painful. There has to be a time for peace. If for no other reason than to wash the blood from our hands."

With all of my pleas used up and not a shred of dignity left to strip from myself, I disconnected the call. I didn't wait to hear what anyone thought of my efforts in mediation. I just limped back down the road, hoping to find somewhere to sit and pass out until someone picked us up.

An explosion behind me sent me tumbling to the ground. I looked at the others and found them scattered, but unharmed. They had left the public communicator before its destruction.

"So much for diplomacy," I mumbled to myself.

Two jetships descended from above, settling into a dust-raising hover on either side of me. They aimed their glossy black noses, and consequently their missiles, right at me. Not only could they not miss, they couldn't hit anything but me.

It was the end of the line, and no one could do anything about it. Ayil had yanked Elizandra onto his shoulder and was running her to safety. Rayne and Terrin were moving toward me, but I put out my hand, waving them off. They both knew it was futile, but they needed permission to not try.

I mouthed "I'm sorry," to them both and lowered my eyes so I didn't have to see the missiles coming.

I waited for an eternity, but nothing happened. I looked up, confused by my lack of halo. One ship veered decidedly to the left and bumped into a building.

Rayne pressed his ear and then motioned for me to come over to them. I didn't hesitate and walked right past the other hovering jet to get to them. "What happened?"

"The bios are down," Rayne said as he urged me and Terrin toward a nearby building.

"Rey shut down the pilots?"

"No." Rayne stopped and looked back at me. "He shut them all down."

"All?" I asked, though I didn't need confirmation of that since the look on Rayne's face said it all.

"Ayil!" Rayne called him over from hiding. Rather than risk any problems, he carried Elizandra over. "Rey sent us a ride."

We all ran—or rather they ran and I hobbled to the elevator. We rode it up to the top floor and took the stairs to the roof. In the mere minutes it took us to get upstairs, our shuttle had already arrived and was landing on autopilot.

"Rayne?" He looked at me. "Am I in trouble?"

He paused. "Yeah." He answered honestly. Despite the wrath of Rey and undoubtedly my mother, I boarded the shuttle and prepared to go face them both. My days of running away were over.

Broken

I stared down at the shower floor, waiting for the water to run clear, but much like my tears, the bleeding wouldn't stop anytime soon. Kessler had given the gash in my leg a more effective bandage and insisted I keep the cast off until he was sure there would be no infection. I trusted his judgment, but was having a hard time justifying walking on a nearly broken bone. The pain killers were doing little to nothing for my leg pain and even less for the ache in my heart.

When the water turned cold, I twisted the valves off and stepped out of the shower. With shaky hands, I wrapped a towel around myself and limped out of the bathroom. Anticipating an empty room, I jumped when I saw Terrin sitting on the edge of my bed. The sudden jolt of movement made me wince.

He stood and shifted a little closer to me. The way he stared at me, I expected him to reprimand me for some misdeed. When I took a step forward, putting pressure on my bad leg, I nearly collapsed from the pain.

Terrin was next to me then, holding me up at first, but then just holding me. There was something rare in his eyes. Something I had only seen in my worst moments... sympathy. My stoic, sometimes cold, friend was giving me his most sincere expression of remorse.

When his lips parted to speak, he said something in Gattish. Though I had picked up a few words here and there, I didn't recognize the phrase. All I knew was that he spoke them in earnest before caressing my cheek.

"What does it mean?" I rasped.

He blinked as if he hadn't realized he had said it out loud. He shook his head slightly. "It doesn't translate well. It means I have known your pain and endured it, so I will endeavor to shepherd you through yours."

It hadn't occurred to me until then that Terrin did indeed share my pain. I had been with him to witness his father's death. And he had been there to witness the grief of my enlightenment.

"I'm so sorry, Mallory." Terrin's hands were on my face, cupping my cheeks and wiping away fresh tears. "Your father was a good man, and it was my honor to know him."

I was beyond speaking now, breathing heavily and nearly ready to succumb to blubbering like a child. I pressed on Terrin's chest and turned to leave his excruciatingly kind embrace before my rising emotions crushed me.

I yelped when I once again put too much weight on my leg. Terrin moved behind me and scooped me up into his arms. He carried me to the bed and set me back on my feet. He pulled a night robe out of the dressing cabinet and assisted my arms into it. Once it was in place, Terrin stayed at my back while I shifted my towel off and finished tying the robe.

I turned to thank him for his kindness, but he was gone. The mattress creaked beside me and I realized he had crawled into my bed. He raised his hand, gesturing me in with him. Since I knew his intentions had nothing to do with us and everything to do with my grief, I scooted into the bed next to him. His body enfolded me in warmth and I felt safe.

Even as my eyes dragged shut, I mumbled, "Speak to me."

Terrin's head shifted, no doubt surprised I was communicating. "What would you like to talk about?"

"No, just speak... in Gattish. I like hearing you speak your language."

"Wouldn't you rather know what I'm saying?"

"I can just pretend I know what you're saying. Then you'll always say the right thing."

"And what is the right thing for me to say, Mallory?"

"You should say that no matter how much I screw things up, you'll always be my friend. That you'll always love me."

Terrin leaned in close and spoke the words of his world to me. I wasn't sure he said exactly what I had said since it took him much longer to say it. When he was through, he rested his head back onto our shared pillow. Just as I was passing into slumber, I heard him whisper, "I will always love you, Mallory."

Destiny

I awoke nearly 18 hours later alone. Terrin had no doubt lost interest in playing nursemaid after his necessity for sleep had been expended. With sore muscles adding to the lack of painkillers in my system, I almost opted to run around the ship in my robe rather than dress myself.

When I opened the door, in a fresh new economy uniform, a barrage of alarms hit me. An occasional rumble of the ship's hull added to the worrisome sounds. The signature sound of a weapon attack made me want to crawl right back into bed. I couldn't do this anymore. I couldn't keep fighting for my life—spending every waking moment looking over my shoulder and peeking around corners.

An announcement came over the intercom system. "Okay, I've temporarily disarmed her weapons," Rey declared, "but she is still threatening to neuter me."

"Well, you did kill one of her generals," Mr. Davis said, adding to the conversation on the speakers. I heard footsteps behind me and discovered he was coming up the hall toward me. Davis saw me and his mouth instantly transformed into a smug smirk. "Hey, the princess is finally awake. You want me to bring her up?" he asked as he pressed the gold pin communicator attached to his all-black suit. In addition to his dark ensemble, he had a matching black eye.

"Oh, good morning, Kit," Rey said so cheerfully over the speakers I nearly laughed. Only he could pause in the middle of a crisis for a polite greeting. "How are you feeling, dear?" he asked with an almost jarring concern. I sensed he wasn't just asking about my injury level. Rey was not a man I considered to be burdened by emotional problems, but he understood he had a particular part to play when someone else was feeling them. I also sensed if it weren't for that particular wound, I might not be freely walking around the ship.

Davis pushed his pin and leaned his shoulder forward for me to speak. "I could go for a few more painkillers," I answered, opting to pass over the condition of my other pain.

"Certainly! Davis, bring her up. Dr. Kessler, meet Kit on the bridge with some happy pills, please."

"Aye," Davis said over the com, before grabbing my arm. "Come on." He pulled me along a few steps before I ripped my arm away. He looked back at me as if I were an errant child refusing to go to bed.

"Pain, remember?"

"Oh, right, sorry," he mumbled, almost sounding sympathetic. He examined me a moment before moving to my bad side and offering his arm to grab onto. Rather than forego a crutch, I accepted his offer, leaning as heavily on him as necessary to avoid pain.

"Speaking of pain, what—"

"Hey, Kit," Edric said as he ran past me down the passageway.

I opened my mouth to respond, but another child whipped past me. "Hi, Kit! Bye, Kit!" Elizandra said. Again, my mouth failed to get a response in, possibly because I was in awe of what I was witnessing. Edric and Elizandra had only just met, and they were already playing together like long-lost friends. Never mind that the ship was being attacked.

"You kids, slow down! This isn't a playground!" Davis yelled after them in an overly deep voice. There was a titter of giggles somewhere in the distance. Despite the scolding, I noticed the corner of Davis's mouth was twitching into an amused smirk. He apparently had a soft side for kids. That was surprising.

Davis caught me looking at him, and a frown overtook the smirk. "What?" he asked defensively.

I wanted to ask him a thousand things—among them was how he found room in his heart for children when it was so terribly consumed by money and ego. "Where did you get that black eye?" I asked, finally deciding on which question was most pertinent. "I thought you missed the action."

"Oh, this, yeah. That was a gift from your boyfriend just before he left."

"Terrin?" I asked, not sure which of my relationships he was referring to.

"Yeah, he said I would know what it was for." Davis glared at me as if there had been some unspoken rule between us about keeping his debauchery a secret.

"Don't look at me like that. You took advantage."

"No, I didn't take advantage."

"Right, you just humiliated me."

"Yeah, whatever, I considered it, but I thought you and Rayne actually had something worthwhile. I didn't want to screw that up."

"Oh, that's touching, you draw the line at—wait. What do you mean before he left? Terrin is gone?"

"Yeah, packed up the shuttle he came in on and skedaddled off to bigger and better things."

"He's not coming back?" I asked.

"I guess not." Davis pulled away from me just as we entered the bridge.

"Where did he go?" I asked after him.

"No, Your Majesty," Rey spoke calmly into his headset at the control panel. "I'm not asking for ransom. I was just trying to give her back when your armada decided to... No. No trick. I would much prefer to give her back. She is treating my ship like her own personal playground. She's going to break something." Rey caught sight of me and handed his headset to Rayne. "You try talking to her."

Rey rushed over to me and gripped my shoulders a moment before wrenching me into a hug. "There, there, you poor girl. I can't even imagine what you are feeling." Despite his behavior feeling slightly scripted, I felt myself relax in the hug. Just as I was getting comfortable with the contact, he pushed me away. With wide eyes, he spoke in earnest. "I want you to know your father was the least reprehensible member of the Coalition. I suspect he really was just a figurehead and had little control over everything that has happened to you."

Although my father's involvement in my laboratory abuses was never a question in my mind, I was certain Rey considered his statement to be a sort of closure for me—giving me permission to mourn my father as the man I perceived him to be and not the man his affiliation had implied him to be.

I nodded and thanked him politely.

Rey stared at me for a long moment. I waited for his kind facade to turn treacherous and the lecturing to begin.

"Rey, now she's threatening to neuter me." Rayne held the headset high over his head.

"Blasted woman," Rey mumbled. He noticed my questioning look and shook his head. "No offense. Your mother has every right to be suspicious of me. This is a rather uncommon act for me. The last 24 hours have been filled with aberrant behavior on my part."

"Would you like me to speak to her?" I offered.

Rey stared at me as if I were overstepping my bounds just by offering. His mouth turned into a smile, clearly a forced smile. "No, don't trouble yourself. I think it's best I keep this situation under control myself."

"Of course." I bowed my head as if to apologize for impeding his authority.

Dr. Kessler called me over as he entered the bridge, and I gratefully escaped the uncomfortable interaction. The doctor grabbed a chair and waved me over to it. Rey returned to his negotiations to rid himself of his unwanted damsel in distress while I sat down so Kessler could examine me.

After a quick temperature check and palpation around my ankles and feet, he gave me the promised hypo-spray injection of "happy pills." Almost instantly, my head felt lighter and shortly after, the throbbing pain in my leg subsided. "I'll need to check the wound once more, but I'm certain you will be immune to infection, anyway."

Kessler continued to stare at me, and I realized he was waiting for a response or acknowledgment. "Okay," I answered, seeing no reason to deny him the right to verify my health. Despite my consent, Kessler didn't resign his gaze. I realized he was trying to formulate a sentiment of condolence for my loss. As awkward as my interaction with Rey had been, I found Kessler's efforts at emotional interaction to be excruciating to watch.

Since meeting him, I had observed his unwarranted draw to me. He really did consider me to be *his* creation. The scientific paternal bond made me extremely uncomfortable. I only hoped he didn't make it worse by offering to take my father's place in some fashion—or something equally uncomfortable.

"I heard that—" Kessler was cut off by Rey yelling about my mother being criminally feminine. The accuracy of the accusation made me snort. When I looked back at Kessler, he continued. "I heard that Terrin left the ship," he said almost as somberly as I expected him to comment on my father's passing.

"So, I've heard."

"I take it things didn't work out."

I dipped my brow, surprised he was so invested in the outcome of my relationship with Terrin. "It's just too difficult to be together without" I glanced around to see if anyone was observing our conversation, but Rey had resorted to banging his head on the console while Rayne and Davis pounded on buttons—no doubt maintaining whatever dampening they needed to defend against the attacking ship. "...well, you know,"

I finished, rather than explain the obvious to a man with extensive biological knowledge.

Kessler was the one dipping his brow at me now. "But he spoke to you before he left, didn't he?"

"Not since yesterday. Why?" I asked.

Two squeals announced the arrival of Elizandra and Edric, zipping into the room. They were still playing tag or whatever game required chasing hand slapping and peels of laughter. I smiled at the unadulterated joy on their faces.

"I just thought he would want to speak with you," Kessler said. "Before he left, I mean."

"Yeah, well, I guess he wanted to avoid a heartbreaking goodbye." I shrugged, trying to pretend like I was indifferent to Terrin's abrupt abandonment. I had no right to be mad about his departure. After all, I was the one who asked him to leave. I was the one breaking his heart... both of our hearts. "Why so interested, doc?" I asked, a little defensively. I wasn't sure if this was the beginning of his paternal reach or just genuine interest, but I decided it might be best to put up a few initial barriers just in case it was the former.

Kessler stared at me, enthusiasm shrinking from his eyes. He must have realized we wouldn't have the type of relationship he wanted. "I assure you, I have no agenda. Terrin and I had a discussion I thought he intended to involve you in."

"Discussion about what?"

"We were—"

"Alright you two, enough of this fun!" Rayne shouted and approached the pair. They squealed and ran from him, but he caught Edric up in his grip and tossed him over his shoulder. Edric objected vociferously and smacked Rayne on the back. Rather than retaliate, he just tickled the boy, making him screech loudly. Davis ran after Elizandra, which bothered me, but rather than catch her, he just trapped her in a corner and jumped side to side like an over-eager puppy. I laughed and shook my head at the sight of two children turning the men on the ship into children themselves.

"I'm sorry, what were you saying, doctor?" I tried to pull my attention away from the unfolding chaos.

"Please, Majesty!" Rey shouted, plugging his ear to hear better. "I just want to give you your daughter. May I please have safe port access!"

"It's nothing," Kessler said, his voice turning indifferent. "I must have inferred more importance to it than there was."

My intention was to ask Kessler what he meant by that, but the question slipped from my mouth when a vision of pure beauty stepped into my path. My dearest companion had always been a sculpture of the finest masculinity. His bronzed, angular features, and silky jet-black hair gave him the ability to look sultry with just a downcast gaze and a slight smile.

Ayil stood before me, his hair intolerably disrupted, his eyes red with dark bags beneath them. His clothing was as far from a fashionable design as possible, but he was the most beautiful sight I had seen in a long time, because there, gently tucked into the security of his arms, was my daughter.

The world around me fell away, and my concerns for Terrin's abandonment evaporated. Even the sorrows of the days passed and the trauma of months gone drifted into the background. My baby was finally out of quarantine—able to be touched, able to be held.

Ayil kneeled before me, offering her to me, but I just stared at her—not wanting to disturb her perfectly pleasant sleep. When I didn't take her, Ayil shifted his arms to display her to me better. I raised a shaking hand to her and touched one of her little hands. Mittens covered her fingers to keep them warm on the cold ship, but even through the cloth, I could feel her strong little digits wrapping around my finger.

I barked out an awful noise that comprised an emotion I couldn't quite qualify as joy or grief. I was crying and laughing, trying to understand how I could be responsible for such an amazing creation.

"Tell me honestly you don't want to have a baby with me now," Ayil said in his smoothest tone. I looked up at him, a little too star-struck to understand what he was saying. "Look how adorable your daughter is in my arms." He brought his face closer to her to show off just how attractive his advertisement for fatherhood should be.

I was entirely certain it was just his usual humor, but I was in the throes of a maternal revelation, heightened by "happy pills" and I was actually considering his offer. Though I had never considered a romantic relationship with my long-time friend, he had been right that we would make beautiful babies. For now, they just belonged to each of us instead of both of us.

Ayil seemed to recognize I was in a kind of stupor and turned serious. "I think it's time you held your daughter, Kit." Irrational panic overwhelmed me—everyone I loved suffered from knowing me. I drew away from him as if not accepting her as mine would somehow protect her from the dangers orbiting around me.

Ayil reached forward and grabbed my retracting hand. He squeezed it tight. "It's okay, Kit. You're going to be great at this. I promise." He winked at me and leaned forward, pushing the bundle of joy into my arms.

As I held her there against my breast, I could feel her weight—not her pounds and ounces, but the pressure she placed on my heart. Since I gave her to Aresties, I lost the very nature of motherhood. But now I could feel her again. The way I had felt her those first months and dreamed of her.

Suddenly everything that mattered so much to me before no longer mattered. Everything important was only important if it was about her, with her, and for her. She was my Destiny.

Quid Pro Quo

As we approached the port on Brahama, Ayil and Edric took Elizandra to get ready for reuniting with her mother. I followed, but Rey landed a heavy hand on my shoulder. "We need to talk." His face was far from the sympathetic man that had hugged me earlier.

I glanced at Rayne and he came to my side. Unfortunately, his only purpose was to take Destiny from my arms. Her vacancy left me feeling cold and empty, but I reminded myself Rayne was a good father and would not harm her. Still, my eyes lingered on her as I followed Rey out of the bridge.

We reached the dining hall, and Rey poured himself a drink. He offered me a drink, but, because of my pain medication, I thought it unwise to accept. Besides that, I wanted to be sober for this conversation.

Following the preparation of a very complex cocktail, Rey sat down at the table across from me and didn't drink it. He simply stared at me, formulating his words. When none came to him, he pulled out a small screen and broadcasted a video onto the white wall ahead of me.

It showed news footage of the chaos on Vagari. The reporter narrated the images of the rebellion and explained the factions behind the riots. Then the biomechanoids arrived to subdue the rioters. Soon after, the soldiers turned violent, killing to maintain order. The reporter tried to rationalize this behavior as a glitch in the programming, but the death toll spoke for itself.

That's when the real chaos began. Everyone, not just the factions, took part in the riots. Fires broke out well beyond the capital. Bombers targeted buildings. It was the close-up view of what I had seen from the sky when I flew overhead.

It was pure bedlam.

Then Rey flipped a switch, and the bios shut down, collapsing in the streets. Hundreds upon hundreds of unkillable machines just laid down and didn't get back up. The reporters declared it a miracle, especially since it followed the announcement of my recovery from death. Some of them even attributed it to me, as if my declaration for peace had programmed them to lie down arms.

The volume lowered on the broadcast, and I looked at Rey's desolate face. He held up his hand, showing me a single digit. "I had a backdoor to an entire army, and I only got to use it once." I swallowed hard, not entirely sure what response would divert his wrath. "And I used it for you," he whispered. I lowered my gaze to the table. "Because you had to make a fucking phone call!" Rey threw his device. It shattered against the wall.

"I was trying to stop the coup."

"I needed that coup!" Rey was so red faced I imagined he might literally blow up.

"People were dying!" I defended.

"That's how a coup works! They needed to die!"

"The people on Vagari are not the enemy! It's the Coalition!"

"And they needed to see that!" Rey slammed his hand on the table. "They needed to witness the biomechanoids slaughtering thousands of people, not dozens, not hundreds—thousands!"

I shook my head. "I couldn't allow that."

"That's not your choice."

"Yes, it is!" I stood up to meet his anger with my own, even though it hurt my leg. "They are my people, my responsibility." Rey didn't respond. "They needed to know the truth about me and about the Coalition's plans."

"And the truth shall set them free, is that right?" I sat back down, realizing I had made zero headway. "Nobody listens to the truth, Kit. Those images will be explained away as a necessary course of action against criminal instigators. The war against the biomechanoids will continue, because I just used my only bargaining chip. I have no leverage."

"Why?" I asked.

"What?"

"Why did you use it?" I asked. Rey glared at me as if my stupidity might splash onto him at any moment. "I know you didn't use your one advantage to save me." His eyes flickered over me.

"Certainly not. That would be an irrational decision made by a man who has no regard for the future."

I waited for him to give me the real reason he saved me, but he didn't offer one. "It wasn't a waste. The lab is gone. The factory is gone. It will take the Coalition months to unravel what you did and bypass it. We have a window to stop this with diplomacy and sanctions. When I get home, I'll speak to my mother about it."

"What do you mean when you get home?"

"We're just about there. I'll talk to my mother as soon as I get off the shuttle."

"And what makes you think you're leaving this ship?" His voice was at a sadistic level of calm and it made me want to crawl under the table. "I negotiated the release of your sister, not you. Your mother doesn't even know I have you. You could have died when that public communicator was blown up. A little scattered DNA should confirm you were obliterated."

"You promised me you would release me."

"On the condition that you stay dead!" Rey threw his finger at me. "You didn't stay dead, did you?"

"Then kill me again. Like you said, scatter my DNA."

"No," he said flatly.

"You can't do this, Rey."

"Why not?"

"Because you can't keep being the hero and the villain! You have to decide on one or the other."

"They aren't so different from a distance."

"No, but they are very different up close." I reached across and touched his hand. "You are a strange and possibly insane man, but I think the only reason I am alive right now is because you want it that way. Not because I am valuable or because it fits into your plans, but because you, Reynard Baloch, have decided I should live."

Rey looked down at my contact with his hand. "Then you should be grateful just to be alive." He stood up and walked toward the exit.

"How did it feel?" I asked.

Rey stopped but didn't turn back. "What?"

"How did it feel to be the hero? To flip a switch and watch those bastards fall. How did it feel to save hundreds, maybe thousands, of people?"

He stayed silent for a long while before turning back to me. "I do that all the time, Kit. It doesn't make the news and no one but the three of us knows about it, but it does save lives. My goal has never been to win. My goal is to balance. You should know better than me that neither your mother's people nor your father's people deserve to be oppressed. The only bad guys are the ones in power who choose to use it to gain more power. Unfortunately, the only way for me to keep them in check is to retain as much power for myself as possible. And yesterday I just squandered a lot of it."

"What about allies?" I asked.

"What about them?"

"You have Rayne—Mr. Turner and Mr. Davis. Don't you think there might be some advantage—some degree of power—with a contact in the palace?"

"A spy?"

"No, a colleague—a friend."

Rey moved back to me and propped his hands on his hips. "Even if I let you go. It wouldn't truly be freedom. There is no place you could run to—"

"I'm done running. Besides, I have a child with Rayne. I'm still going to see you all the time."

Rey nodded. "Oh, right." He paused, contemplating his options. "Well, in that case I will release you, Kit Mallory. But know this..." He returned to me, pointing a finger at me. "I am not doing this to be a hero, or because, deep down, I truly care for you. I am doing it because I know you know, regardless of where you are in the universe, if you become a threat to me, you can be eliminated."

I nodded, more than a little disappointed he still didn't understand the definition of a friend. Satisfied with his threat, he left the room. I took a much-needed breath and rubbed my face.

"Don't let him fool you," Mr. Davis said from the doorway. He was leaning on the frame, not looking smug for a change.

I looked him over, searching for the barbs about to be released. "Fool me about what?"

"Rey may not be a hero in the traditional sense, but he is all about the quid pro quo. Between the Coalition and your mother, they had us running with our tail between our legs. Our shields were overloaded and about to shut down. We barely had enough power to shoot that missile at the factory. If you hadn't disrupted the battle, we would be dead."

"Why are you telling me this?" I shifted out of my seat, wincing as I put pressure on my leg. "This almost sounds like gratitude."

He shrugged and moved to assist me with an outstretched arm. "Well, I know I wasn't the particular face you were thinking about when you asked your mother to stand down, but I was glad to benefit from it." He stopped and turned to me. "I warned him against using the backdoor. I tried to talk him out of it, but he did it anyway."

"There's the pragmatic Mr. Davis I know."

Davis smirked. "I'm just saying, he carefully weighed the risks and still chose in your favor. I'm sure he would say he balanced the future value of his life against the value of the backdoor and determined it was a fair trade."

"And you, what would you say he did?"

"I would say he made his decision very fast for someone who prides themselves on contemplation."

"Maybe he's turning over a new leaf."

"I hope not. Hero work is extremely unprofitable."

I chuckled. "I have no doubt you will find a way to get billable hours for it."

"That's true," Mr. Davis agreed and assisted me to my room.

Welcome

At least forty armed guards met us upon our arrival back on Brahama. As we took our first steps out of the shuttle and into the courtyard, they shifted in perfect coordination, aiming pulse pistols and rifles at our heads.

Since our party was three adults, two children, and one infant, I was more than a little displeased with the threat, but there was nothing I could do besides doing exactly as I was told.

A man stepped forward from the crowd and took particular interest in examining Elizandra before surveying all of us. His eyes paused on me, possibly still unsure if I was a mirage or not. He pulled out a scanner designed to detect metal, heat, and other potential threats. Once it was clear we were unarmed, he allowed us admission into the mansion.

As instructed, we followed him through a maze of outdoor spaces, including the many courtyards and gardens until we reached the "courtyard of the marked." I pressed a hand against Ayil, bidding him to stop. I didn't want him closer to the execution site since he was holding Destiny.

I stared at the gigantic stone in the center of the yard, tinged brown from past victims. It was the only object in the space apart from the nine stone pathways leading to it and the circle of bushes surrounding the area.

I turned back to the break in foliage we had just arrived through, but a guard stepped into place, blocking our exit. I circled around, checking the other eight entrances, but each of them successively filled with an automaton. Although entirely human, the soldiers were only slightly less disturbing than the biomechanoids.

"Elizandra!" My mother's voice was like a crack of thunder in my mind. Both Elizandra and I whipped our heads to look at her. Susan had slipped past one guard and was standing on the other side of the execution block. She snapped her fingers and Elizandra reluctantly moved away from us. She looked back at Edric like she knew she was not likely to see him ever again.

When Elizandra reached Susan, she took her hand and raised her head high, as if taking on the role of princess had transformed her entire body. It was an impressive thing to witness since it was something I was still struggling to learn nearly twenty years her senior.

I watched my mother's face harden as she looked at the remaining five members of our party. Her eyes paused on the baby in Ayil's arms, but she quickly dismissed any sympathy she might have for it and turned away to leave. I looked at my left and right, seeing additional soldiers filing into the area. I wasn't sure what she intended them to do, kick us out, capture us, or kill us, but I knew better than to hope for the best when it came to my mother.

"Mother!" I yelled after her.

Her steps froze, and she turned back to look at me. Her gaze locking onto me like a predator, rather than with any familial acknowledgment. "Impostor," she spat the word at me.

"It's me, Kit."

Susan's head twitched to the one side and hands grabbed me from behind and dragged me forward. "Impersonation of royalty is an offense punishable by death."

"Mother, no!" I yelled as they pushed me down onto the stone block.

"Majesty, she is not lying!" Rayne yelled. I sensed from the tension in his voice he was struggling against someone.

"Let her go, you bitch!" Ayil yelled.

"Daddy, what's going on?" Edric called out.

"Mother, it's me!" I cried out as a sword appeared from out of nowhere.

"Stoooop!" Elizandra yelled the word long and loud. The guard prepared to execute me stopped, glancing at the queen for further instruction. "You will not kill my sister."

"Sweetheart, I know she looks like your sister, but your sister is dead. The man who took you is trying to trick us."

Elizandra looked at me to confirm this with me. I shook my head. "Then why did she save me?" She posed this question to our mother, who didn't have an answer. Elizandra let go of her hand and moved without fear, confronting the man holding the sword. She puffed up her chest, more than compensating for her lacking size and age. "Put your sword down... now!" Despite the order from such a tiny girl, the man looked truly conflicted. He searched the queen for consent to obey the orders of the princess. She nodded, and the man stowed his blade.

The men holding me released me and I stood up. I looked back to check on the others. Ayil, Edric, and Rayne were being held by guards. I turned back and saw my mother staring at me. She wasn't allowing herself to believe I was real yet. She, too, thought I was a mirage.

Very slowly I moved away from the stone and toward her so she could get a better view of me. She noted the limp in my approach and examined the cuts and bruises on my face and arms. "It was a ruse, Mother," I whispered. "A way to get into the capital. To gain access. To save my sister."

Susan was still staring at me. "I saw you get shot. I saw your body. The doctor confirmed it."

"Rey," I answered because that was enough explanation. "He didn't want me to surrender."

"Why didn't you tell me?" Her voice sounded harsh as she pushed her anger forward to hide her real emotions.

"You helped sell the lie." That statement went over like a ton of bricks, judging by the flaring of her nostrils.

"Why are you back, Kit? You could have stayed dead and never had to worry yourself with your old life ever again."

I didn't bother to mention that the option, give or take a few rumors, was still on the table. I nodded back to Ayil. "I wanted to introduce you to your granddaughter."

Susan's anger and grief seemed to pause as she looked between us, baffled. Ayil moved forward with his guard just behind him. When he was close enough, she peeked at the child. Her face seemed to light with some recognition, as if she could see some part of me in the little girl. She looked back at me and then at the child. "How?" she asked, no doubt calculating the baby's age and the unlikelihood that the events of my recent past would have been possible without someone's knowledge of my pregnancy.

"I take it Aresties never reported that aspect of her duty to you." Susan still looked baffled. "It's a long story. If you'd like to hear it, I would like to tell it." I glanced around at the guards. "Unless you would prefer we leave."

My mother blinked at me for a long time and I exchanged a look with Ayil, concerned she might really prefer we leave. Elizandra moved up to Susan and cleared her throat loudly and purposefully. She looked down at her daughter. "Even when a queen is unsure of her actions, she must present as if she is in control," she whispered not so discreetly to Susan as if she were offering her a scripted line for a stage performance.

Susan stroked Elizandra's head and looked back at me. She was calm, but her confusion was gone. "You may stay for a mid-day meal. Then you may go." I didn't bother pointing out I was not the one bidding to leave, but bidding to stay. "Who is the father?" she asked, looking at Destiny.

I stuttered, glancing at Ayil for guidance. "Perhaps we should discuss that when you're seated."

"And when we are not standing in your death chamber," Ayil grumbled.

Susan sighed but accepted that the details of my conception were best absorbed while sitting down.

AMNESTY

Though the meal was just a ruse to put us all at a table and diplomatically discuss the details of my pregnancy, we were, in fact, fed and given enough wine to make us pliable and resistant to lying. One of mother's favorite techniques to gain the upper hand. During the course of the meal, Rayne and I filled in the blanks regarding her grandchild. It took all of about one course before she demanded to hold Destiny and properly survey her next of kin.

When the meal was complete, I asked to speak with her alone—a conversation I dreaded having since it involved far more groveling than I preferred at this point in my life. Rather than take me into a comfortable room to sit as equals, she brought me into the war room. It was the first and likely the last time I would sit in the room, so I considered it an honor even though she took her seat as the Queen instead of my mother at the head of the table.

"Before you begin," I said, almost certainly interrupting her. "I want to apologize for putting you through that. I understand now more than ever how much pain it must have caused you."

Susan lowered her eyes, no doubt wanting to hide her pain while she was acting like my queen.

"I also want you to know I am well aware you will be renouncing me as your heir, officially. My actions, regardless of their success, were without permission and were an outright deception to you and the crown. The empire cannot have a queen or even a princess that is so untrustworthy. I have always put myself and my friendships ahead of my people and that is a quality a leader cannot afford."

Susan sat back, drinking in my obsequious words, but she still wasn't buying them.

"Most of all, I want you to know I love you, and regardless of how you choose to proceed with our relationship, I will continue to love you. Near or far."

That finally broke her, and her lip quivered. She broke into tears, pouring them shakily onto the table. "Goddamn you, Kit!" she yelled. "Every time I think I have you under my thumb, you slip right back out, don't you?"

"I will happily stay under your thumb if you wish it."

"Oh, stop it! Why are you doing this? Why are you groveling to me? I brought you in here to yell and scream at you, not cry."

"I'm sure you can do both."

Susan laughed instead of yelling. "What do you want, Kit?" She pushed down her emotions and looked up proudly.

"As things stand now, I have two options to proceed with my life. I can either stay with Captain Reynard as his captive or I can stay here as a guest of the crown. I'm fairly certain it's the same prison, just with different wardens."

Susan snorted. "Oh, and what makes you think I would allow you to stay?"

"That decision is entirely up to you, but if you should allow me to stay as a guest, I have several conditions."

"Conditions for me?"

"Yes." I paused. "Would you like me to list them now, or have you already made up your mind?"

"Please, allow me all the information so I might make an informed decision."

I cleared my throat and lifted my finger. "There are quite a few. Do you need a break before I start?"

"Your humor has never been an advantage with me, Kit. Perhaps you should just begin."

"Very well. First off, I will require a jetship." Sandra scoffed, but I ignored her. "My previous ship was blown up, so I will require an aircraft for planetary travel."

"Where are you going?"

"Which brings me to number two," I raised my voice, politely reminding her that I was far from done. "As a spurned heir to the throne, I will require employment. Cousin Elder is desperate to get out of her position, so I would like to take up her role as an ambassador. As a skilled pilot with a resume of planetary exploration, I feel I am qualified for work of this nature. There will be much to do on Vagari to repair bonds, so I would like to participate in humanitarian efforts there as well."

"Cousin Elder?"

"Long story. Third, I will be requiring three rooms—potentially four when Destiny gets a little older. I will also need a nanny for when I am working."

"Why four rooms?"

"Ayil and Edric will be joining me."

"Absolutely—"

"Non-negotiable," I said firmly. "Also, as an extension of that requirement, I will need you to start thinking of Ayil as the son you never had."

"Why would I need to do that?"

"Because Edric is going to be the grandson you never had. I will be expecting my queen to provide him with a strict regimen of school and discipline. And I will expect my mother to spoil him rotten when no one is looking."

"I don't even know the boy."

"He's endured more trauma in his short life than either of us can ever claim, and apart from my hopes and dreams for my own child, I will expect nothing short of a happily ever after for that boy."

Susan frowned at me, unfamiliar with the determination that was spilling out of me as both grief and anger. "Was that four or five?"

I looked at the floor for a long moment before looking up. "My last condition is that every last R&D project currently operating to engineer biomechanoids for the empire be stopped and the research destroyed."

"There are no projects for that."

"Don't lie, Mother."

"How dare you? I'm not—"

"You had a Coalition spy at the head of your military, Mother! You are not beyond infiltration. Rey says there are operations and I believe him." Susan didn't argue, but offered no concession. "Agate took me to the factory. They were turning living men and women into automatons. I've seen how far this technology can go and what it does to the people seeking it. I swear on my life, Mother, regardless of where I am or who I associate with, I will make it my life's work to eliminate biomechanoid armies. No matter who they belong to."

Susan stood. "I'll consider your proposal." She moved to walk out, but stopped. "If I agreed to all those things. Would you really stay? Permanently?"

"I imagine I would be traveling a lot as an ambassador, but yes, this would be my home base. Destiny and Edric will need a home and a grandmother."

"You know you can't promise me grandchildren and then just change your mind later. That would be too cruel."

"My mind is made up. I just need your permission."

"You don't need my permission, Kit. This is your home. It always will be."

"And Ayil's."

She seemed to waver but smiled. "I'm sure your friend and I will find a common ground... eventually."

Arrangements

"**S**o, how is this going to work?" Rayne asked as we strolled through the courtyards, him carrying Destiny and me, gazing lovingly at the sight of them. Edric and Elizandra were back to playing. Ayil was doing his best to keep up with them, but even he was wearing out.

"I think we are supposed to bicker about who gets what and how often and then we hire lawyers—"

"I'm serious, Kit. When am I going to see her?" He stopped and looked at me. We both agreed that a starship was not the right place to raise Destiny. Even if Rey wasn't a homicidal madman trying to puppet the entire universe, space was no place for a child to learn or socialize. The problem, of course, was Rayne still had obligations to Rey and regardless of how much he loved Destiny, he wasn't willing to uproot his life for her. Because my life was already disrupted, I decided to make the bigger sacrifice.

"As often as you want," I whispered.

"As often as your mother wants?" he asked.

"I'll bring her to you."

"You say that now, but what about when there are lightyears between us?"

"Then you call and Destiny will see your face and hear your voice. She will know you are her father."

Rayne looked down at his daughter and then at me. "The temptation to steal her and run like hell is overwhelming," he teased.

I chuckled. "You'd bring her back when you realized her diaper was full."

Rayne laughed, but then realized there was indeed an odor coming from Destiny. "Oh, shit."

"Most likely."

Rayne scoffed. "Alright, give me the bag. I might as well hand her off clean and powdered." He grabbed the diaper bag off my shoulder and nodded back to Ayil. "Have you told him yet?"

"No. I was hoping you would stick around until I do. Just in case."

Rayne leaned forward and pressed his lips to mine—a short, albeit meaningful, kiss. "Any man who leaves your side is a fool."

I smiled and meandered over to where Ayil was catching his breath and sat down beside him on the concrete bench.

"Hey." Ayil nodded. "He about ready to go?" he asked, nodding to Rayne changing the baby in a soft patch of grass.

"Just about."

We watched Edric meander in and out of the short bush maze at the center of the garden space. When looking from above, the bushes formed an outdated insignia for the empire, but at ground level, it was just a place for children to run around and get lost in. Elizandra's head also popped above the bushes. She giggled and shrank back down before Edric could turn around to see where she was hiding.

"Man, kids make fast friends," Ayil commented. "He's really gonna miss having someone else to play with."

I smiled at them before turning to Ayil's sympathetic face.

"You, okay?" he asked. I nodded. "Your mother is a real piece of work. I can't believe she almost killed you."

"She's been trained to assume everyone is trying to assassinate her. Combine that with a lot of repressed emotions and you get—"

"Psychotic?" Ayil offered. I stared at him, hoping I wasn't making a horrible mistake. Hoping I wasn't about to lose my last friend. Possibly the only true friend I had ever had. Aresties may have been my friend, but much like my paid entourage when I was young, she didn't have a choice about being with me. Neither did Terrin. And Rayne... Well, he was never a friend.

"Ayil, I'm not going to leave with Rayne. Destiny and I are going to make our own way."

Ayil's questioning look turned a little somber, but then he smiled. "Just the two of you?"

"I was hoping just the four of us." I smiled at him.

"Oh, good, you scared me there for a second. I hope your credits still work. I doubt you'll find a ship like the Starla again."

"That might be a good thing," I said, thinking about how many times the ship's old parts had nearly sunk us. Ayil chuckled and nodded in agreement. "Actually, my mother has agreed to supply me with a ship."

"Really?" Ayil narrowed his eyes at that. I wondered how long it would take him to trust her. Not that he was wrong to be on the defensive. My mother was a complicated person, and her obligations to motherhood and her royal duties made her seem mercurial, but after facing death around every corner, I no longer feared her in the way I did as a child.

"It's an H-class jetship, apparently with a sophisticated defense system. I think I'll have Rey take a peek at it just to be sure, though."

"Jetship?" Ayil frowned. "Kit, a ship that fast would be great, but that's barely enough room for six people to travel, let alone four people to live on. Edric will go stir crazy and me with him."

"We aren't going to be living on it."

"Then where will we be living?"

I looked over the surrounding courtyard. "Here." When I looked back, Ayil was in the midst of turning red. The number of angry and hurtful words perched on his lips scared me more than I could have imagined. Rather than wait for them to spill out and pierce my heart, I spoke again. "What if we did have a baby together?"

The statement did as I intended and shocked Ayil out of his angry thoughts. He stared at me slack-jawed, his lips now vacant. "You told me back on Miorita that you were my number one, but I didn't quite understand what that meant until recently."

"Kit," he whispered. "You know I love you, but... I don't... I mean we..."

I scooted closer to him on the bench and he actually moved back, no doubt afraid I might try to kiss him and intensify our already layered relationship. "Ayil, I'm not asking you to be my husband or my lover." He visibly relaxed. "I grew up bouncing planet to planet—far from neglected and yet all the spoiling in the world did nothing to alleviate the loneliness I felt. And you" I reached up and touched his cheek. "...not alone enough, I suppose." He raised his chin as if denying he should have any emotion connected to his past beyond blind hatred.

I drew away from him, since the subject matter seemed to make my affections intolerable. I leaned over my knees and watched Edric and Elizandra. "I want my daughter to grow up in a stable home with a mother who is affectionate and devoted to her happiness without extraneous obligations. Oddly enough, now that I am effectively fired as an heir, I can do that. My mother and I had a long discussion. We've come to an understanding. I will stay here and raise Destiny. She has provided me with a jetship so I can take on the role of an emissary for the royal court." I swallowed hard and looked back at Ayil. He was looking a little irritated again. I was certain he was viewing this as a betrayal instead of an opportunity. "I negotiated for you and Edric to stay here as well."

Ayil's face contorted, and he could no longer contain his displeasure with my actions. "If you think I am going to stay in the same house as that woman, you are sorely mistaken," he seethed, leaning in close so our argument wasn't obvious to the kids. "I will never forgive her for what she put you through." He stood and walked away.

"This isn't about you, it's about Edric." He stopped in his tracks and turned to face me. I was now stepping on the toes of a single father and about to pay the price. Once again, I jumped up and cut off his words before he could say the awful things his emotions were digging out of the recesses of his mind. "I'm not asking you to forgive my mother or belittle yourself in any way to her. I've made your importance clear to her, and she agreed to treat you as kin—"

"I've seen how she treats her kin, no thank you." He stormed off again.

"I'm asking you to be a father to my child!" I blurted out. Once again, Ayil's stride stopped. He looked back at me with an odd mixture of confusion and worry, like I was going insane. He glanced at where Rayne was doting on his baby girl. "Rayne will always be Destiny's father, but she needs a full-time father figure in her life. I want you to be Uncle Ayil, just like I'm Auntie Kit." I threw my hands up, exasperated. "I don't want to do this on my own. I don't want to do this without you." Ayil still didn't respond. He was being more stubborn than I was expecting. "Please, just say you'll try it. Look how much fun Edric has here." I approached Ayil and twisted my hands into his shirt. "Staying here means he will get a proper education, food, clothing, medical care, and not to mention a staff of nearly 200 to spoil him. If anything, you'll need to spank him just to keep him grounded."

When Ayil still didn't concede and his eyes refused to acknowledge even one benefit, my package had to offer, I began to tear up. I released his shirt and bit my cheek to stop my chin from trembling. I wiped away a few errant tears and cleared my throat. "Rayne said he would wait until you made a decision." I sat back down on the bench and stared out at nothing, pretending to enjoy the view. "I won't make you stay anywhere you don't want to. I just know this is what is right for me and my daughter."

"Edric!" Ayil snapped in his fatherly tone. "Come on out of there." My chest seized, and I wondered how much more breakage my heart could handle. "Head over to Uncle Rayne and say goodbye. We may not see him for a while." Ayil ruffled Edric's hair and shoved him toward Rayne. I stared at Ayil as he slumped down on the bench next to me. He looked at me, slightly perturbed. "Of course I'm staying with you."

Before he could say more, I jumped to him, hugging him and soaking his shoulder with tears and possibly snot. He patted my back and eventually switched into a rhythmic rub. After a minute of tolerated tenderness, he formulated a statement that took several preemptive breaths to actually get out. "Why did you phrase it like that?"

I leaned back and wiped away my remaining tears. "Like what?"

"You said we could have a baby together. Did you just mean raising Destiny together?"

I nodded. "That, yes, but..." I shrugged. "We could have one together." Ayil stared at me. "I mean, we don't have to do it naturally." I laughed. "Sorry, I think I'm just caught up with baby fever."

"Well, we would make beautiful babies together," he said smugly. He stood up and stretched. "But for now, I do like the sound of Uncle Ayil." He reached back and helped me up. He flopped his arm around me and we headed toward Rayne to collect our children. "Maybe Uncle A," he contemplated further.

"Wait for me," Elizandra said, coming out of hiding. "Are you guys leaving now?" She ran up to Ayil and wrapped her arms around his waist. He looked down at the little version of me glued to his waist and smiled introspectively. "Actually, we were thinking about hanging around a bit longer." He wrapped his arm around her, adding her to his entourage of ladies. "What do you think about that?" Elizandra cheered and broke away from Ayil to spin in celebration. Deciding that our pace was too slow, she ran ahead to tell Edric the good news. "Aren't you going to miss it?"

"Miss what?"

"Space travel."

"I'll get to travel, but instead of trafficking questionable merchandise, I'll get paid to go to fancy parties."

"Huh, well, that doesn't sound very exciting. How are we going to get into trouble?"

"I'm sure we'll find a way."

Finale

TROUBLE

"This is by far the most disgusting thing we have ever encountered." Ayil griped as we disembarked my jetship. It was far from the beauty Starla was and it wasn't much larger than a shuttle, but it was fast and that was all that mattered. I could jump from system to system in days rather than weeks. Since my new position as an emissary left me traveling back and forth from planet to planet, getting home after meeting and greeting an endless sea of foreign diplomats was the best part of my week.

"It's your own fault," I grumbled back at Ayil as I pulled my pack up higher on my shoulder. Since he was a newly appointed emissary as well, we were back to traveling the stars together. It may not have been the exact life I had in mind for myself when I left home so many years ago, but it was the best of both worlds. I had a universe full of stars, the luxury of my mother's home, my best friend at my side, and my family within arm's reach. But most importantly, Edric and Destiny were safe. They were being raised in a proper home and they wanted for nothing.

In just a few short months with tutors, Edric had reached a fourth-grade reading level and was turning out to be a bit of a math whiz, too. Ayil was beyond proud of his little genius and discussions about alternative lifestyles had ceased.

If that wasn't already the cherry on top of his new environment, my mother had showered Edric with just as much adoration as Elizandra. I wasn't sure if she felt obligated to include him, or if, like the rest of us, she had just fallen head over heels for the incorrigible boy. At any rate, Ayil had taken notice of her softer side and was, in turn, showing her a good deal more respect than he had at the beginning of our arrangement.

With Edric's life surrounded by a pseudo aunt, sister, and grandmother, he would have plenty of motherly influences in his life. And as for a father figure, I couldn't have asked for a better man than Ayil to guide my daughter through life. As devoted as he was to me, he transferred that same love to her tenfold. I was without a doubt the happiest and most content I had ever been in my life. Who knew all I had to do to achieve all of it was come home?

"How was I supposed to know that wasn't her hand?" Ayil scraped another layer of pink goo off his arm. His effort was fruitless because the pink goo covered him from head to toe. Since I had been standing right next to him during the *incident*, the ejected fluid inundated me as well.

"Rule number one in the diplomat's handbook. Don't make assumptions about the body parts of non-humanoid species."

"She just seemed genuinely happy to meet me."

"I'm sure she was." I bit back a smile.

"I thought she was laughing and then—oh, my god, your mother is going to kill me."

I shook my head and patted Ayil on the back. A mistake since my palm was now covered in sticky slime. "She can't kill you tonight. She's having a party. There will be too many witnesses."

"Another one?" Ayil asked. The frequency of my mother's social events still surprised him. I didn't bother explaining the tactic of control she exerted through obligatory civility. "You go get cleaned up and I'll have a chat with her—take some of the bite out of her bark."

"You don't have to tell me twice." Ayil headed left along the covered path inside the courtyard, while I headed right.

I walked along a wall of endless grape vines and stone columns until I reached one entrance to the mansion. I was about to root out my mother in the ballroom, but I noticed there was light streaming from her office. I peeked inside and saw her sitting at her desk in contemplation. I pushed open the door and dropped my bag on the floor. She jumped and looked up at me.

"Before you hear the rumors," I said, raising my hands in surrender. "We did *not* molest Ambassador Placker's daughter."

Susan looked like she was about to say something, but stopped and looked at me, horrified. "What are you talking about?"

I walked between the two high-back chairs facing her desk. I rested my hands on her prized polished marble top desk and leaned forward so she could get a good view of my slimy condition. "There were some human, non-humanoid interactions that caused—"

She narrowed her eyes. "What did Ayil do?"

I hissed, reluctant to speak, but knowing I had to, so my mother could fix it. "He may have brought a female Darpian to completion in front of an entire room of diplomats."

"What!" My mother stood, ready to lob off Ayil's head with her bare hands.

"It wasn't his fault." I brandished my finger, sending a glob of pink onto her desk calendar. She looked down at it, then back at me, immediately identifying the substance adhered to my clothes. "She clearly placed her tangential prong out as an invitation."

"Are you...? Is that...? Kit! Go wash yourself!"

"I will. I will. I just didn't want you to get the information from another source." I motioned both my hands downward, which propelled more goo onto her desk. "I knew you would want to hear about this as soon as possible."

"Kit, you're getting it everywhere! Stop flailing about!"

"Just tell me we'll be able to handle this like adults—like family. I mean, you wouldn't..." I slowly backed away from her. "Oh, god, you won't..." I moved to sit on one of the cream-colored high-back chairs.

"No! Don't sit!" my mother screamed, arms outstretched, fingers flared, eyes wide.

I paused, hovering dangerously over the seat, and looked at her, confused.

Susan ran around the desk and ushered me, without touching me, to stand again. "Of course, we can handle this like adults. We can do it tomorrow when you and Ayil are properly bathed and have had a good night's sleep."

Susan backed away from me, saving her formal wear from the indignity my blue business suit had endured. As she moved back around the desk, I noticed the man sitting in the other high-back chair. He had been so ensconced in the oversized furniture I hadn't seen him on my way in.

"Terrin?" I asked, even though his identity wasn't in any way hidden. He looked as he usually did—though perhaps with longer horns. The only oddity was that he wore a black suit, as if he were one of my mother's many guests.

"Hello, Mallory." He made the casual greeting sound sexy—or maybe it was just the outfit.

It had been four months since he had left—since I had asked him to leave. The final necessary cut to my heart. I had convinced myself I was never going to see him again. I was certain that time and space were the only thing my heart needed to evict Terrin for good, but apparently it had not been long enough. The blasted muscle was pumping hard just at the sight of him and my brain had shut down in the process, leaving me without an ounce of common sense.

"Are you here to see me?" I asked, sounding slightly hopeful—or perhaps that was desperation.

Terrin's eyes shifted to the floor. "No, I'm afraid I came to see your mother."

"Oh," I said with notable disappointment. I glanced back at my mother, prompting her to explain with my slack jawed gape.

Susan moved back to her chair and sat down. She folded her hands and rested them on her desk. "Terrin and I just had some business to discuss."

"I wasn't aware you two had business."

"I'm actually applying for a new position," Terrin explained. "I just stopped by to discuss the parameters with your mother."

"A job? You mean here?" I took a step back, wondering how that would compromise my current serenity. As much as I stupidly ached for him, I was not eager to sink back into the pathetic pit of Sisyphean love I had spent so many years of my life in.

Terrin noted the movement of my feet and cleared his throat. "The specifics are still being negotiated, but rest assured, I won't accept anything locally without your permission."

"Good." The word came out more contemptuous than I had intended, and I could see the disappointment in his eyes. However, he had to understand how hard this was for me. Just seeing him scored the stitches in my heart—threatening to break them open again. I couldn't and wouldn't allow him—allow me—to do that to myself.

Then again, perhaps he was aware of the impact he had on me. Since accidental coitus had cut my trip short, I had arrived home early. He may have been trying to avoid me and I screwed it up.

"Kit," my mother said after no one had spoken for a while. "We're not quite finished here. Why don't you go clean up. We can deal with the molestation tomorrow."

I looked back at her. "He just got confused, that's all," I whispered. "It was just a mistake. People make mistakes, Mother."

Susan's expression softened. "I know, Kit. There's a class on uncommon anatomy some of our less experienced emissaries take. Maybe we should start with that."

"Yes," I said eagerly. "Thank you," I whispered.

My mother nodded, giving me a small smile. "Okay, we can discuss the details tomorrow. Now, go. Clean up."

"Right." I looked back at Terrin. "Will you be here long?"

"No, I'll leave when I'm through here."

"Oh," I said again with a note of disappointment. My contradictory emotions must have been terribly frustrating for him. It was a wonder he had put up with me as long as he had. The poor man should have fled my presence the first time I refused him. "In that case, it was really good seeing you," I said with fake cheer—hiding the fact that it was more excruciating than enjoyable. I extended my hand for a formal shake.

"Always a pleasure." He looked at my pink hand and smiled. "Perhaps I'll skip the formalities tonight."

"Oh, right, sorry." I pulled my hand away and cleared my throat. I waited a moment longer, staring at him awkwardly. There was nothing else to say or do, but my feet had trouble moving.

His mouth tipped up slightly. "Good night, Mallory."

"Good night." I finally moved my feet—walking away from Terrin for what seemed like the hundredth time in my life.

NANNY

I laughed at Elizandra instructing Edric on how to jump off the side of the pool the right way. She was taking after our mother more and more each day, so there was no hope of correcting her domineering behavior. Instead, I just encouraged Edric to stand up to her. Which was very confusing for the boy, since Ayil was cracking down on anything resembling bullying. He didn't want his son's new privileged lifestyle to make him too presumptuous about his place in the world. Oddly though, I thought Ayil and I had made a good team, keeping him happy and humble at the same time.

While Ayil splashed around the pool with them, I laid out on a chair, sunning myself. Technically, there was no sun since I was under an umbrella with Destiny. Despite my efforts to feed and change her, she was still being fussy. I had hoped a pool side view would entertain her, but no such luck.

"What is wrong with you, baby girl?" I mock scolded her. "Can't you just settle down?"

"Why don't you let me have a try?" Terrin asked from behind me.

I craned my neck to look at him. "What are you doing here?" I asked.

Nearly a month had passed since our last encounter. During which my mother had apparently turned him down flat for a job he had applied for. She hadn't revealed too many details, but Mother implied she was doing it for my benefit rather than her preference of candidates. I felt bad Terrin wasn't getting the position he wanted because of me, but I was also glad my mother understood how much space my parasitic heart required. At another time, I might have considered her behavior meddlesome, but, for once in my life, I was enjoying being protected by her.

"Another visit with your mother, I'm afraid."

"Why do you keep doing this to yourself?" Ayil called over to him, listening to our conversation. "The money can't be that good."

"Oh, it's not about the money," he called back to him. "The benefit package is rather appealing, though." Terrin moved to my side and reached down for Destiny. I reluctantly gave her away. At first, I thought she might bawl since she couldn't possibly remember Terrin from her early infancy, but instead of bawling at the stranger, she instantly stopped crying. Be it the oddity of Terrin's skin, or his horns, but my baby looked at him with fascination—*quiet* fascination. "There, see, she adores me. Just like her mother."

I frowned at the comment and looked away. Yet another little jibe at my expense. Another reminder of my imbecility in love. My uncontrollable heart and my arrogant presumption to aspire beyond my biological restrictions.

"Mallory," Terrin whispered. I looked back. He reached out and brushed his finger along my cheek where a tear had sneaked away—revealing the pain he had caused me. "I'm not trying to make fun of you. I'm honored to be in your heart. I always have been." I nodded and looked away. I didn't want to talk about it or us. "Why don't you jump in the pool? With the kids," he amended when he saw Ayil splashing around.

"I heard that." Ayil aimed an accusing finger at Terrin.

He smiled at Ayil before turning back to me. "You look like you could use a reprieve from mommy duties. I'll watch Destiny for you."

I knew I should refuse out of politeness, but I was exhausted. Plus, if she was going to behave for Terrin, then perhaps I could petition Mother to hire him as a nanny. I also wondered if perhaps Terrin wanted to hold her for a while. He had spent some time with her on Saltu. It wasn't unheard of for him to miss her.

"Okay, maybe for a little bit." I jumped up and gave Destiny a kiss on the cheek. "If she gets fussy, I can take her back."

Terrin smirked at me. "We'll be fine."

I jumped into the pool, much to Elizandra's and Edric's glee. Even Ayil appeared thrilled that he was no longer outnumbered. We played for nearly an hour. It wasn't until after our game of Marco Polo that I noticed Terrin and Destiny were nowhere to be seen.

I hopped out of the pool and went in search of them. When I reached my bedroom, I heard singing. An odd song, to be sure, but only because I had never heard a male gattaw sing.

When I entered, I saw Terrin leaning over Destiny's crib and singing down to her. I approached slowly, not wanting to disrupt him, but at the same time desperate to see my child. When I reached the crib, and saw her fast asleep. I took a much-needed breath.

Terrin finished his last note and looked up at me. His eyes flickered over my body. I was out of breath from running, cold from the cool indoor temperature, and sopping wet since I had neglected to grab my towel on the way from the pool. Add to that my skimpy swimsuit, and I was hardly far from the definition of naked.

"She was starting to fall asleep. I thought a nap might be in order. I hope that's okay."

"Yeah. I didn't know you could sing."

"I'm not sure I can. That's the only song I know. My father sang it to me as a child." Terrin frowned. "You're shivering." He grabbed a blanket from the base of my bed and wrapped it around me. I breathed a sigh of relief as he rubbed my shoulders and back to warm me. "Has Rayne been to see her since he left?"

I shook my head. "No. We've been doing video calls just to get her used to his voice, but she's young. It's not like she'll remember that he visited once a year or twice."

"That must be a little disappointing for you." Terrin moved away from me and took a seat on my bed. I ignored the part of me that rejoiced at seeing him taking up space in my private area.

I shrugged. "I knew this wouldn't be a traditional child-rearing experience for either of us."

"Still, a child needs a father."

"That's why Ayil is here. We're even thinking about having a child together."

Terrin's eyes glazed as he stared at me. "You and Ayil are"

"Hmm?" I frowned at his shocked expression. "Oh, no! Sorry! Um, nothing intimate, just IVF. We haven't decided for sure yet. I think I just want the whole pregnancy experience. I kinda got gypped on the last half of mine, you know?"

"But you two aren't together?" he asked, still not entirely relaxed.

"No." I laughed. "Why would that have suddenly changed?"

"It wouldn't be unheard of. Both of you in this domestication situation might change how you look at each other."

"No. Ayil is wonderful, and I'd be lucky to have him, but he has a long way to go before he can be anybody's significant other. And truthfully, he's like a brother to me now. I could never be with him in that way."

"What about Rayne? Any regrets about saying goodbye to him?"

I cleared my throat, not wanting to admit to anyone—even Terrin—that I thought so little about Rayne these days. I doubted I had ever truly loved him the way I thought I had. My draw to him was turning out to be truly circumstantial. "Why so many questions about my love life?"

"I want you to be happy, Mallory. I always have."

I pulled the blanket around me as I peered in at Destiny. "I am happy."

"I'm pleased to hear that."

"How is the job hunt going? Surely, you've been applying for other jobs."

Terrin shook his head. "I feel a debt is owed to me and I expect in time your mother will agree to pay it."

"You know my mother isn't one to argue with successfully?"

Terrin closed his eyes and fluttered them as he took in a controlled, soothing breath. "It's been a very long and trying process, and I have prostrated myself more than I prefer, but I believe I may be making a little progress. She didn't outright refuse me this time. I'm going to come back next week for her official answer."

"Why is she making you come all the way back here? Couldn't you just call?"

Terrin stood. "I find communicating with your mother is easier when she doesn't have a disconnect button available to her."

I laughed. "I don't doubt that."

Terrin moved to the door. "Mallory, I know it's difficult to see each other after... everything, but do you mind if I visit with you again when I come back?"

I frowned. "Of course, I don't mind."

Terrin stood in the door's frame for a moment, staring at me. "I want you to know I have spent a great deal of time thinking about what you said to me. The reasons you asked me to leave." I took a stuttered breath, feeling a new coldness wrap around me. "You were right to make me consider my options. It's one thing for us to attempt a non-traditional union, but it's another thing to give up my option to have a child." He glanced back at the crib behind me. "You were looking out for me and my best interests when I was too blinded by my attraction to you to think clearly about my future. I want to thank you for that."

I felt an ease come over me. I hadn't expected from his words. He forgave and vindicated me all at once. "I want you to be happy too, Terrin."

Terrin bowed his head slightly. "Until next time." He winked and left. I smiled after him, feeling for once in my life like I was finally at peace with a part of my past that had been haunting me since the day I met Terrin. Finally, we could be friends—just friends.

Two Steps Back

A week later, I heard a knock at my bedroom door. "Come in," I yelled over the comb in my mouth as tried to make myself presentable. My hair was a disaster—I wasn't used to my new layered style—and my dress looked like it had come directly from my mother's closet, but I was at least dressed and made up. I could always abandon my hair and don a stylish hat before meeting my mother's guests.

I had always hated her endless balls and masquerades as a child, but now, as an adult, I loathed them. She strategically coordinated every major business conversation and political play under the guise of cocktails and cheese puffs. The reality was my mother drank non-alcoholic champagne all night and waited for her colleagues to be just drunk enough to agree to whatever changes she wanted to make. Since there wasn't a breathalyzer for signing documents, my mother could expedite negotiations left and right. I had thought my revoked royal title would eliminate my need to be presented at any more parties, but where there was a will, there was my mother.

Just as with my ambassadorial duties, I had to present myself as a representative of the crown. Though my almost death and planetary plea for an armistice had made me a household name, people still had trouble recognizing me. Sadly, my face was not altogether very unusual. All it took was a new hair color and layers of makeup and I could blend into the sparsest gatherings. Also, the woman people expected to see no longer existed.

"I'm almost ready," I called out to whoever arrived to fetch me. I was nearly an hour late to the festivities, no doubt making my mother furious. Being late was not something she considered fashionable—especially since it meant missing my introductions to delegates and councilmen while they were still sober.

"Don't hurry on my account," Terrin said from my bathroom doorway. I looked over at the tuxedo he was wearing—even more strapping than the suit from the other night. Instead of the traditional penguin style, he was wearing an exquisitely textured champagne dinner jacket over a silky black shirt and vest. There was no tie or bow tie, just a high open collar that left his broad neck and the beginning of his chest exposed.

"Oh." My mouth gaped at his beauty, and the comb dropped to the floor. "What are you doing here?" I said, forgetting my manners.

"I told you I was coming back."

"I know, but why tonight? There's a party tonight. I can't be with you tonight—I mean, I have to be with them—to socialize. I—I have duties." I couldn't believe how much I was babbling. I resented the fact that even after his perfectly lovely visit last week I was back to being this inarticulate blob of a woman.

Terrin smirked and glanced down at his suit. "Well, I rarely dress up this much for job interviews. I'm afraid it was the only time she was willing to speak with me, but don't worry, I'll stay out of your way." Despite that statement, he moved out of the doorway and took a long appraisal of my state. "What are you wearing?" He frowned at my bulky beige dress, particularly the tulle flower on my right shoulder. "And what have you done with your hair?"

I looked at my frazzled brown hair in the mirror. Part of it was sticking up in an incurable rat's nest. "I just need to get the snarls out. Destiny rolled a car through it this afternoon. I was part of her race track. I think a wheel is stuck in there, but I can't get it out."

Terrin leaned down and picked up the comb from the floor. "Allow me," he said and turned my head to face the mirror so he could tackle the tangle.

"I'm surprised you're not pulling your sword to cut it out," I said after a moment of silence.

Terrin said nothing at first—he was concentrating too hard, but then a smile crept up on his lips. "Is this your real color?" He tugged on a lock of my boring brunette hair color.

I shrugged. "The greatest beauticians in the galaxy couldn't answer that."

"You seriously don't remember your hair color. When did you start dying it?"

I cleared my throat. "Um, there was an incident when I was quite young. My mother had my hair made up into little ringlets so we could take a family photo. It was back when they still tolerated each other enough to play family for me. I hated the curls so much. I thought they looked like snakes and once I got that in my head, I had a fit. Anyway, I got hold of the shaver when the hairdresser had gone to fetch my mother and I shaved off all my hair." Terrin halted and stared at me in the mirror. He didn't laugh as I expected him to. He seemed to understand this wasn't a pleasant memory for me.

"What did she do to you?"

"To me nothing. She just about killed the hairdresser for leaving the shaver plugged in. She and my father had an all-out fight about his lack of discipline and her overly strict parenting. That was the day they officially decided to get *divorced*—aka stop pretending for me."

"And in your young mind, you blamed your actions for causing it."

"I know it was bound to happen eventually, but it still hurts to know I might have had a few more months or possibly years of placation if I had been a better-behaved child."

"Nonsense," Terrin said firmly. "As a mother, you know a child cannot be held responsible for the ramifications of becoming socialized." Terrin pulled a tiny rubber circle away from my scalp and showed it to me. "You can no more blame yourself for your innate fear of snakes, as you can blame Destiny for tangling your hair."

I took the wheel from his hand and turned to gaze directly into his eyes. "Thank you," I whispered.

He stared down at me, eyes glinting with something more than the friendship we purported to have for each other. "Always," he responded in an equally soft whisper.

"Anyway," I said, drawing back suddenly to smooth down my hair and dismiss the heat rising between us. "Bald as a baby, I started wearing wigs. Since my mother was trying to soften the blow of the divorce, I got to choose any wig I wanted in any color. So began my love affair with color. After my hair was long enough, I had a standing appointment for cut and color."

Terrin rested his hip against the counter. "Why haven't you told me that story before?"

I chuckled. "I don't know. Not my favorite story, I guess."

"Hmm," Terrin murmured as he watched me strategically place my hair into a bun which showed off the pure black layers that were hiding beneath the bland brown ones. "You missed a bit." He grabbed a bobby pin from my container and moved to lift the remaining black strands I had intentionally left out of my bun.

I whipped around, straining my back against the sink as I took the pin from him. "Oh, it's okay, I always leave that part down," I lied.

Terrin narrowed his eyes at me, and after a beat, his curiosity turned a little sour. "Turn around. Let me see it."

"See what?" I batted away his attempt to reach for my hair.

"You know what." His shoulders and chest raised with a deep breath and he stiffened. "Please, don't make me force you to show me. I deserve to see the damage I have done to you."

"It's not" My eyes fluttered over his. He was determined to see the back of my neck and, as embarrassed as I was by it, I turned to let him look.

His hand crept up the base of my spine until it reached my neck, lifting my hair. He pushed my head forward and gripped my hair out of the way as he inspected what remained of the scar. I peeked in the mirror and saw the baffled look on his face. "What is this?" he asked. "This isn't my bite." he sounded downright offended—as if some other man had bitten me.

"It's a white ink tattoo," I said.

"What?" His face cringed.

"I had them create a design to blend in with the teeth marks. Technically, the bite is still there. It's just under and in between the lines."

He shook his head at me and released his grip on me. "Why didn't you just get it dermabraded off?"

I almost shrugged, but stopped myself. "I didn't want it off. I thought it was all I had left of you—of us, I guess."

Terrin did a short pace across the bathroom before turning his scolding gaze back to me. "That isn't the gattaw way, you know? The bite is never meant to scar a woman. I am not proud of doing that to you."

On any other day in my life, I might have recoiled from him and apologized, but today I just laughed at him and shook my head. "Do you seriously think I dyed my hair for years because I was afraid of snakes or felt bad for my parents' divorce? I did it because it meant something to me." I thumped my chest for emphasis. "Terrin, contrary to the massive impact you have had on my life, my experiences with you don't belong to you." I pointed to the back of my neck. "This doesn't represent to me what it does to you." I pointed to the tattoo and the underlying scar. "I didn't want to get rid of the scar because of why you gave it to me."

"I gave it to you because I was hormone-crazed," Terrin snarled.

"No, you gave it to me because you thought you were losing me and you wanted to hang on to that part of me that adored you, regardless of our differences. When I considered removing the scar, it felt like I was erasing that connection, but not removing it felt like I was admitting to some kind of defeat—like I would always be under your thumb or crushed by my own heart."

"So, I did what comes naturally to the mind and heart. I put it under something new. Instead of new memories and new loves, I buried it in a new design. That way, I would still have a reminder of you, but not one that evoked an image of ownership or control." I scoffed. "If anything, tangling your bite mark up in this new design proves to me that you belong to me." Terrin's face went blank. "Well, at least the Terrin inside of my head."

I watched him debate this explanation. Regardless of my reasoning for keeping the scar, I knew he was still unhappy about the behavior that caused it. In his eyes, it still represented his lack of control, as well as his selfish desires. "Very well," he said, sounding like a sullen teenager. "If I can't change that scar, I can at least change the other atrocity you're wearing." Terrin ripped his short sword from his hip and came at me.

I jumped back, banging into the sink. "Oh, hell no! You are not cutting my hair," I said through gritted teeth, brandishing a manicured fingernail at him.

Terrin's mouth twisted into a wry smile. "It's for your own good, Mallory. I can't allow you to leave this room with that ridiculous mop on you." He moved forward, pressing into my space. "Turn around," he ordered.

"Don't you dare," I seethed.

He bit his lip, no doubt trying to contain his smirk. He failed miserably. "Turn around," he whispered. "Trust me, Mallory."

I swallowed hard, feeling as if I was taking some kind of test. Despite having a little metaphorical PTSD from my first hair incident with Terrin, I turned to face the mirror. He reached around me and pulled me back against his chest. I let out a huff first from his forcefulness, but also because he made no effort in propriety. Terrin's forearm pressed against one breast as his hand fully engulfed my other breast. I looked at him through the mirror, wide-eyed with shock that he was being so familiar. Not that he was unfamiliar with this contact, but still...

He leaned in close to my ear, even as he held my gaze in the mirror. "Hold still," he whispered. "I don't want to hurt you."

Terrin lifted his short sword over my shoulder and, for one slightly irrational moment, I thought he intended to slit my throat. "Terrin," I whimpered. Shushing me gently, he dragged his hand across my breast. He pinched the oversized flower attached to my right shoulder strap and descended the blade. He deftly severed the connecting threads, and the flower fell to the floor. "You're an asshole," I blurted out.

He laughed. "Did you really think I was going to cut your hair?" Terrin plucked out the remaining fibers of the cloth before sheathing his sword. He looked at me in the mirror suspiciously. "Or did you think I might do something worse?" Terrin leaned in and kissed my neck. He very—very—gently nipped at the flesh as he moved up to my ear and sucked the lobe. My mouth fell open as I watched him through the mirror.

His hand still braced around my body, now brazenly dipped beneath the fabric to gain access to real flesh. I let out a hobbled moan as he pinched my hardened nipple. Terrin's lips shifted to the back of my neck as his other hand slipped through the bias cut of my dress. Barely keeping track of the multiple contact points on my body, his hand was suddenly slipping down the back of my panties. His fingers simultaneously entered me even as he bit the back of my neck. Though it was a gentle bite, the pleasurable feeling matched with my fear made me cry out. The perceived pain dissipated as he massaged his fingers in and out of me, giving me internal and external gratification.

I couldn't resist what I was feeling. The pure, unadulterated joy of having Terrin touching me again was beyond a dream.

Memories of our previous encounters flooded back and the overlapping experiences drown out my common sense. I released a mournful cry at my end, nearly ready to drop to my knees and praise the heavens for giving me some release from my current anguish.

Terrin's hands relinquished their contact, and I felt bereft. The pressure that had partially been holding me up released and I had to steady myself to keep from falling over. Then I heard the jingle of a belt buckle and the unzipping of a fly. I turned around and saw Terrin reaching in to release himself.

"What do you think you're doing?" I asked him as I backed away.

He looked up at me, his face elated. "It's alright, Mallory."

"It's not alright." I shook my head. "Goddamn it, Terrin. What are we doing? We're going in fucking circles, getting closer and closer to the drain. Don't you think I want to let you have me?" I asked, motioning to his hand, still in the process of releasing himself.

"You can," he assured me.

"No, I can't, and I feel like shit right now. I shouldn't have let you do that. I'm sorry."

"I wanted to do that."

"Why?" I yelled with unnecessary volume.

Terrin furrowed his brow. "Because I love you."

I shook my head. "No, that's not why." I scoffed and rubbed my face. "It's just the bite all over again, isn't it?"

"What?"

"This isn't about sex anymore."

"Excuse me?" Terrin began putting himself back together again, pants and belt.

"I can't tell if you're doing this to control me or torture me. Which is it?"

Terrin's mouth gaped, and for a moment he just stared at me. It reminded me of when I asked him to leave the first time. "I'm sorry. I wasn't aware my touch was torturous to you. I thought that final crescendo was an indication of your pleasure."

"You know what I mean, Terrin. I can't do this anymore. I can't keep pretending. No more fairytales. I kissed the frog, Terrin, and he's still a frog."

"Yes, I'm still a frog, but you are no longer a princess."

"No, I'm an emissary. What was your plan with all this, Terrin? Get a job on my mother's security detail so you could be close to me." Terrin propped his hands on his hips, silently giving me permission to continue my rant. "How did you think that was going to work for me? I can barely concentrate when you're around Terrin. How am I supposed to focus on remembering names and conversing intelligently when you're near me? I can't do my job when I'm making doe eyes at the gat in the back of the room!"

I gasped even as I finished the sentence. Those weren't even my words—they were my mother's. I covered my mouth, pleading with time to rewind so I could shove the statement back behind my lips.

Terrin's entire body went slack, and he stared at my shaking head. "There's a first," he said calmly.

"You know I didn't mean that."

"You may not have meant to say it like that, but you did mean to say it." Terrin adjusted his jacket and moved to the entrance.

"Terrin, please, I'm sorry."

"You're right, Mallory." He motioned between us. "This isn't working. I have inadvertently been torturing you by coming here and I do apologize. I am going to remedy this once and for all." Terrin walked out of the bathroom and a moment later, I heard my bedroom door slam. As much as I wanted to curl up into a ball and cry about yet another tumultuous goodbye to my relationship with Terrin. I had to preserve my make up and make an appearance at mother's party. After all, it was my job to represent the crown. And the crown was not in love with a gattaw.

Dance Partners

Ayil grabbed me the minute I got into the ballroom. "Where have you been?" He shook me slightly. "I tried to kiss the delegate from Ontrei, and fist bump Councilman Garp."

"Oh." I grimaced at his social faux pas.

"Your mother is going to put me to the nines. Why are we even here? We are outgoing representatives."

"Because my mother loves an entourage of loyalists around her at all times."

"Since when did I become a loyalist?"

I shushed him quietly and smiled at a passing couple. "Seriously," I warned Ayil, "don't joke about that. The political climate is too hazardous for sarcasm."

"I just don't get the constant parties. I mean, it's never just a meeting or just a dinner."

"She likes to mix business and pleasure whenever she can."

"If that's true, how does she maintain such a huge stick up her ass?" Ayil said between the clenched teeth of a fake smile. "This isn't even pleasure, you know? It's just another job. If your mother unclenched for even a second, that stick would fall out."

"Doubtful," I said. "It's most likely integrated with her spine by now. Losing it could leave her paralyzed."

"Hmm." Ayil nodded introspectively. "Let's try it. We'll switch her champagne out for the real stuff. Ahhh, she's coming." With a quick cowardly departure, Ayil was gone, disappearing into the crowd of fine suits and sophisticated dresses.

"Kit!" My mother came up behind me and spun me on my heel to face her. "Where have you been—and what are you wearing? Where is the dress I picked out for you?"

"There was a minor incident with a blade. I barely made it out with my nipples intact."

"Don't say nipples in public," my mother scolded me. I looked around to see if anyone was listening to my anatomically correct language. "What's wrong with you?" Susan scanned my face.

"Apart from the dress?" I resisted the urge to touch my hair and mess up the effort I had put into it.

"You look flushed. What have you been doing?"

"Nothing," I answered much too quickly. She narrowed her eyes at me, demanding an answer. "I had an argument with Terrin," I admitted. I didn't mention the argument had spawned out of the incredible orgasm he had just given me.

"Terrin?" My mother's eyes widened into saucers. "He's here?" She started looking around the ballroom for his green head.

"Yes," I answered. "Or he was. He may have left. Weren't you expecting him?"

"No."

"He said he was coming back to get your answer about his job application."

Susan's face contorted, and she let out a most uncharacteristic growl of frustration. "That man is relentless. I've told him 'no' a thousand times."

"Why, is he unqualified?" I asked, not imagining he would persist to demand a position he didn't think he could adequately fill.

"It's about the..." Her eyes landed on me and she lost patience for the conversation. "Oh, never mind. I'll take care of this once and for all. Just stay here and" Susan trailed off, unable to find the right instruction for me before leaving.

"Mother? What's the big deal?" I went after her. I wanted to know what job she was so reluctant to give out. I assumed it was a security detail, like all the others. Surely, he didn't want to be placed back in charge of me. Given the trouble, Ayil and I got into, the subject of a bodyguard had come up, but Terrin was the last person I needed watching over me. That would only get me into a different type of trouble.

"Kit!" a woman called over to me. I looked over and saw my cousin Elder weaving through the crowd to get to me. She stopped before me wide-eyed and stuck out her hand to shake. "So nice to see you again." Elder hugged me. While strapped in her tight embrace, she whispered in my ear. "I'm so sorry about everything that happened to you, but I am so glad you decided to become an emissary."

"I actually kind of like it," I said as she pulled away from me.

"I have had time to myself for a change. Yesterday, I went to a play." Elder's eyes started to tear up. "Do you know how long it has been since I've seen a play?"

I didn't know. Nor did I realize my becoming an emissary was allowing her to languish in useless luxury, but I nodded and shrugged. "You're welcome."

She hugged me again and offered her eternal gratitude by gifting me a debt. I wasn't sure I would ever require such a thing, but one never could tell who they would need a favor from in the future. She drew back just as Ayil arrived with a drink for me. He saw Elder, and they exchanged the scowl of former enemies meeting in neutral territory. "Ayil," she said, acknowledging him with only the barest of civilities.

"Elder," he responded. She walked away, and he stared after her. "I think I hate her," he said, as if it had taken a tremendous evaluation of his feelings to make that determination. He handed me a champagne flute and ushered me to the nearest snack table, where he grabbed a handful of radishes. "Did you know Terrin's here?"

"Yeah, he stopped by to see me, but then he left."

"No, he's here now." Ayil motioned lazily over to the bar he had just come from, but I couldn't see him. "I don't know what's going on, but your mother is hella bent on getting him out of her mansion. He just refused to leave, and she threatened to have him escorted out. That's when he said he would break the arms of any man attempting to remove him. When I left, your mother was turning bright red. I was sure she was going to start shooting lasers out of her eyes."

"Shit," I hissed. "Okay, umm, let's just meander over like cool cucumbers and break this up before she brings in the pulse pistols."

I looped my arm through Ayil's and we proceeded with our choreographed speed walk to the bar. With plenty of fake smiles and nods, no one noticed we were rushing toward a ticking time bomb. As we arrived at the bar, I took up position next to my mother, who had her lips pinched back so tightly she no longer had a mouth. She noticed my arrival and mumbled, "We'll talk about this later."

Ayil took up a spot across from me, more between the two than taking sides. Mostly, he was just there to drink champagne and eat while the carnage unfolded before him. Terrin didn't take any interest in either of us and kept his stubbornly stoic gaze on my mother.

"I'm running out of patience for later, Susan," Terrin said. I glanced across to Ayil, who had a radish poised at his lips, paused out of shock for Terrin's blatant disregard for the queen's customary title of reverence. It was unlike Terrin to disrespect her in such a way, but to my surprise, my mother didn't even flinch at this intimate use of her name. "Perhaps it's time we involve Mallory in our negotiations." I looked at Terrin, curious now if he was applying to be my bodyguard again. He had to know I would never take his side in that plead. Tonight was just more proof that we needed to keep our distance from each other.

"There are no negotiations. The answer was no the moment I met you." Mother's words sounded vengeful instead of diplomatic. I worried now she was being unfair to Terrin.

"Please tell me you aren't holding a decade-old grudge against me."

"Not at all. I just have certain expectations for my—" my mother glanced at me. "—employees and I don't intend to hire—"

"A gat?" Terrin asked.

Susan clammed up, not quite denying the accusation.

I couldn't stay quiet any longer. "Mother? Please tell him that isn't true. You reign over hundreds of different races, species, and subspecies. You're the most impartial leader we've had in two hundred years. I know you would never hold anyone's origin against them."

My mother looked at me, her eyes not reflecting any pride at my statement. "It's not that simple, sweetheart."

I felt a slight stab to my heart and for the first time in my life, I felt like my mother wasn't being the best queen she could be. "It is that simple. Terrin has more than earned the right to a position with the crown. Give him what he wants."

Susan glanced at Terrin, who was not gloating at the support I was offering him. Once again, her face bunched up, and she looked as if she might throw a punch at the Gattaw before her. Ayil must have sensed the ensuing bloodbath, because his eyes lit with delight as he washed down his last radish.

Instead of blowing up, however, the vigor drained from her face and, with a defeated tone, she said, "Terrin isn't applying for a job, Kit. The reason he has been visiting me is because he has been asking for your hand in marriage."

Ayil spat his champagne out, spraying my mother with the bulk of it. She turned her glower to him, catching sight of new prey to be angry with. He looked back at her, mortified.

"I'm so sorry, Majesty," he mumbled. He pulled his tuxedo handkerchief out of his pocket and began dabbing at her dress.

Meanwhile, I stared at Terrin, though he was still not looking at me. He was finally wearing a smug look of achievement. One that few people ever earned from my mother. Though Terrin had always been one of them.

A tingling sensation was setting into my limbs, demanding I seek a fainting couch, but I forced myself to keep control of my unnecessary damsel's response to Terrin's romantic gesture. "Is that true?" I asked, even though I knew my mother wouldn't lie about anything so serious.

Terrin finally turned to me. His expression softened, and he nodded. "Yes, it's true. I knew as long as you were living here, I would need your mother's approval to be with you. Unfortunately, she has been denying my request repeatedly and delaying my proposal to you."

Again, I closeted off my feelings, not allowing myself to even imagine a partial happily ever after. "How many times have you asked?"

"I've asked many times." Terrin glared at my mother. "I had hoped to win her over in time, convince her I am worthy, but she seems intent on keeping us apart."

Swallowing hard, I bolstered myself for another rendition of my tired old speech. I didn't want to keep hurting Terrin, but I had to hold my ground. "I'm sure she is just looking out for us both." I looked at my mother, hoping she might at least pretend to agree with this, but she wouldn't add anything. "Much as we have discussed, the longevity of a marriage between two incompatible species is... uncertain."

Instead of looking at me with the same tortured gaze that usually transpired between us during these conversations, Terrin's lip tipped up into an even smugger smile. He turned his condescension to my mother, and she scoffed. She mumbled something in Gattaw, which surprised me since I wasn't aware it was one of her known languages—however, there were many. Terrin raised his brow at her, but didn't respond in any language.

Susan rolled her jaw and narrowed her eyes on Terrin, before begrudgingly speaking the last words I expected to hear from anyone's mouth... ever. "You are compatible."

Ayil spit yet another mouthful of champagne at my mother. She growled and grabbed the champagne flute from his hand. "Will you stop drinking if you can't contain your astonishment!"

Once again, my limbs disappeared, and I took a step away from everyone. There was a ringing in my ears that made me feel outside of myself. "I don't understand," I heard myself ask.

"I'll explain," Terrin assured me, but I remained unconvinced. I felt like someone had just put me in a dream and at any moment, I was going to wake up. The fear seeping into my body wasn't for the statement I had just heard, but for the anxiety of waking up and losing it all again. This was no longer the burden of Sisyphus; this was pure hell with devils and pitchforks.

I looked at my mother, pleading for her to say something to steady me. She was unhappy, to say the least, but she didn't seem to have any thoughts of wisdom to tie me back to my body. Ayil was blindly dabbing her with his handkerchief and he had officially reached her cleavage. "Stop it," she hissed at him and batted his hand away.

"I can't," I mumbled and backed away. "I don't"

"Come with me, Mallory." Terrin extended his hand to me. When I didn't take it, he moved a little closer and shook his outstretched hand at me. "Mallory, please!" His plea was only a hissed whisper, but the look on his face was life or death. He must have thought I was still rejecting him—even with the revelation.

I could hardly do that. It was all I had ever wanted. He was the man I had always wanted for myself. I still didn't understand, though, and I wasn't sure I believed it. How could we be compatible and how did he know that?

I placed my hand tentatively in his and just when I thought I might float clear out of my body and never return, Terrin wrapped his arm around my back and ushered me onto the dance floor. He pulled me in close and I felt myself touch ground again. I leaned into his shoulder, refusing to look at him or even think while we danced.

I didn't dare think.

He was saying something to me, but I wasn't listening.

I took in the feel of his hand around my waist and the way I felt pressed up against him. We had never danced before. Of all the things we had done together, we had never had cause to dance. As strange as that was, it was the way his hand felt against mine that intrigued me the most. I looked over at his fingers wrapping around mine, cupping my hand.

"Mallory." He moved his bracing hand to tip my chin up. "Please say something. I beg you." He was so desperate to have me acknowledge what I had just been told. I had never seen him reveal this much fear before. "I'm sorry about what happened earlier. I got carried away. I was going to explain, but you obviously didn't understand my intentions were... well, certainly not honorable, but you weren't in any danger."

"How?" I uttered. The word sparked an inkling of joy in him.

"I—" Terrin's eyes turned to the face that belonged to the finger thumping on his shoulder. Ayil and mother were taking a turn on the dance floor next to us. They were an odd pairing, but I knew they were trying to reach us without drawing attention to themselves.

"I'm cutting in," Ayil said. Since we still had a lot to talk about, Terrin and I both objected, but Ayil's face morphed into something sinister. "Now," he demanded, staring hard at Terrin. My normally high-spirited friend looked incensed. I glanced at my mother, wondering if she had revealed something to him that was missing in my explanation.

Terrin reluctantly released me from my dance obligation. Ayil relinquished his grip on Susan and slipped between me and Terrin. With his back to me, Ayil took up his newly coveted position as Terrin's partner. The gattaw hardly blinked at the transition and began his dance again with his new partner.

Feeling a little ousted, I moved to mother to take her as my new partner. We both shifted our hands up and down, not sure which position each of us was to take in this impromptu coupling. Just as we figured it out, she raised her hands in disgust and waved me away. She scoffed and disappeared into the dancing couples around us. "Majesty," I called after her, trying to maintain the decorum of this official event.

For a moment, I stood there, wondering how the biggest revelation in my life had resulted in me without a single dance partner. I was certain there must have been some deeper meaning to construe from all this, but for the life of me, I just felt a little abandoned.

I looked back to see where Terrin had danced Ayil off to, but they were no longer spinning on the floor. They were off in a far corner, hiding among the pillars at the far end of the room. By the look on Ayil's face and the finger he was brandishing at Terrin, there was a pretty hefty discussion happening. Terrin pointed to his chest, but Ayil outright slapped his hand away before vehemently gesturing to his own chest. Despite the assault, Terrin didn't retaliate. If anything, he was relaxing. His head bowed slightly. Whatever lecture Ayil was giving, Terrin was dutifully listening to it.

Family

Since Ayil and Terrin were in the midst of a crucial conversation, I made my way out of the ballroom to get some fresh air. When I realized my mother had retreated to her office instead of socializing with her guests, I exchanged my fresh air for the smell of leather and wood.

I plopped down in one of the high-back chairs in my mother's office. She was sitting behind her desk doing paperwork. I never understood what it was my mother actually did—outside of parties. I had skipped the planet before I had begun the real training of becoming royalty. Now I would never know. One day, I would have to ask my sister.

Susan finished her scribbled sentence and looked at me. Her expression was truly heartbreaking. So much anger was fighting to get past her frown, and yet she was near tears.

"Do you truly hate him that much?" I asked, feeling my own eyes sting with fresh moisture.

"Does it matter?" she asked.

"Of course it matters. I'm staying in the household of my queen. I can't be with a man she doesn't approve of."

Mother stared at me a long moment, as if I were a stranger to her. "I didn't say 'no' to his request as your queen. I said 'no' as your mother."

I nodded, understanding now that this was a far more serious problem. I could at least negotiate with my queen. With my mother, there was no room for such things as diplomacy.

"Okay," I nodded, as tears spilled down my cheeks.

"Okay?" she asked.

"Yeah." I stood from the chair, my arms shaking and my heart officially on the verge of emotional death. "I'll tell him I can't be with him and send him on his way."

"Kit, spare me the reverse psychology."

"Yes, Mother," I mumbled, not really listening to her. I reached the door, ready to go deliver the worst news I had ever had to deliver to Terrin—a refusal that had nothing to do with incompatibility.

"But you love him," Susan said behind me. "You always have."

I turned back and watched her struggling with the conundrum before her. She wasn't seeing me as I was, just as I used to be, or how I thought I should be. "No. There are only two people in my life whom I have *always* loved. And since one of them is gone, I won't risk the other." I moved away from the door and motioned to the out there that was my home. "I won't give up all of this. I came here for Destiny and Ayil and Edric. I want this to be their home. I want them to feel safe and to never go hungry. You're right, I do love Terrin—I think since the moment I laid eyes on him. But I won't disrupt the livelihood of three other people to have him." I shifted to leave again; my strength of heart renewed by my loyalty to my family.

"Sit down," mother commanded.

I looked back and saw her coming around the desk. She stopped at her roll cart of liquor and poured two rather large drinks. I sat back down, and she handed me one of them. Then she sat across from me in the other high-back chair.

One long sip and a pregnant pause later, she spoke. "Terrin called me for the first time a few months ago. Not terribly long after... everything. He inquired after your health and generally about what was going on. I asked him why he didn't call you and he explained he was giving you some space. He hinted at what had been going on between the two of you—but it was far from news to me." Susan gazed off into nothingness for a moment. "He very casually asked about your relationships. He wanted to know if there was any chance Rayne would be returning to your life or if any new suitors had entered the picture."

"What did you tell him?" I asked, curious if she might have lied to keep Terrin away.

"I told him the truth," Susan defended, anticipating my suspicious nature. "I told him Rayne was no longer in your life beyond his fatherly obligations and you were far too preoccupied with motherhood to be thinking about anything as frivolous as dating."

"And then he asked for my hand?"

"Oh, no, no." Susan chuckled. "Terrin is far smoother than that. He was seducing me, you see. I got a call a week later. He inquired after Destiny and told me about the time he spent with her on Saltu. He said he had come to feel a particular connection to her and that he would enjoy seeing her, but he didn't want to intrude. So, being the proud grandmother I am, I sent him photos."

"He saved her life," I said. "She was literally just born. He devised a carrier using—"

"I know," Susan interrupted my bragging. "I didn't disbelieve his claims. I know Terrin is a very capable man. His ability to care for small children is enlightening, but not surprising."

"I just mean, I don't think he was using his request to manipulate you. I think he legitimately cares for her."

"Yes, I think so too. Truthfully, I wonder if any of those first conversations were truly about you or me." Susan sipped her drink. "After that, we had periodic conversations about Destiny, and he would inevitably ask after you. I would share a little bit about the trouble you and Ayil had most recently gotten yourselves into, and he would share a tale or two about your time in space. It was an odd interaction, I thought—for us, I mean. But I enjoyed the stories he shared with me. Such tales of your bravery and determination... and stupidity," she added, in case I might get too big of a head. "He was far more translucent about your activities than you ever were."

I shrugged. "I didn't want you to worry," I mumbled. "If I had told you the whole truth, you would have sent an armada after me."

"Rightly so," she said. She sat for a moment, swirling her drink and staring off into her own thoughts. I sipped on my drink, which was much too strong for my tastes, but I covered my cough as a throat clearing.

"I always knew you had feelings for Terrin," Susan continued. "The way you looked at him... Even in the beginning, it was more ardor than any young woman should possess for a man—let alone one so inappropriate. Later, it was also obvious that your childhood crush was consuming you. I feared so much for your heart. I thought Terrin was above it. He took your crush in stride. I think initially he was amused by you. To him, you were just a cute little human girl begging for attention like a puppy."

I scoffed. "Really?"

"Oh, yes, if you saw what I had seen in him in those early days, you would not be so in love with him now. Gattaw are raised with a presumption of superiority to all species, and Terrin was no exception." She looked at me and I wondered if I looked a little green. "That changed, of course. I'm not sure when. It may have started while you were still here, but the transformation was completed after you left." Susan downed the rest of her drink. "Then both of you were idiots."

"I started to suspect Terrin had an agenda," she continued, "but I was still enamored with his stories, so I was patient and listened. At some point, he outright admitted his feelings for you had gotten ahead of him. He said he was embarrassed to admit he was having a difficult time being separated from you. He said he wanted to be your mate, regardless of the impact on his family line." Susan turned to me. "I told him I understood what love could do to a person—how it could delude them into thinking they were capable of more than they truly were. I reminded him of the biological limitations of human and gattaw relationships. That's when he told me you were not as incompatible as he once thought."

She paused for a moment, remembering—or perhaps she was just getting tipsy. "Then he formally and respectfully asked for your hand in marriage."

Susan stood and circled around to sit in her usual chair. She was getting back into her queen mode, sloughing off her mother costume entirely. "I told him 'no.' Then there were some declarations of love that I'm certain would embarrass him if I repeated. I told him 'no' again and again. That's when he started coming to see me. He was past the point of seduction and had decided to approach me as a businessman." Susan dropped her empty glass on her desk with a thud. "Tonight, it seems, he's well past all forms of decorum and is ready to throw you over his shoulder and carry you away like property if necessary."

I leaned over my knees and bit back my emotions so I could speak rationally. "Why did you refuse him?" Susan scoffed as if it was a stupid question, but I didn't think it was. "No, I'm serious, Mother. I've relinquished my right to the crown, so there would be no scandal. There are very few social implications to our union—beyond general contempt for anything unusual. And if what he's saying is true about the compatibility, then there are no physical ramifications either. You have a grandchild. If you want another, I'll have one with Ayil."

"What?"

"Never mind. My point is, what else is left to object to?" I scooted to the edge of my seat and cleared my throat. "Do you really despise having a gattaw as a son-in-law?"

"No, Kit, my general dislike for the gattaw culture has never extended to Terrin. I actually like him quite a bit, if I'm being honest." I nearly fell over at hearing that, but refrained from giving the declaration too much attention.

"So, if I like him, and you like him" My heart was thumping, dreading the answer to my next question. "Why can't we be together?" I hadn't expected the tremble in my voice, but this was, after all, the final piece of the longest relationship puzzle ever.

Susan's lips turned into a tight pout, and tears filled her eyes. "Because I didn't want him to take you away again. I missed so much of your life. Every other year and then seven years stripped away. He knows more about you than I do, Kit. My own daughter and I have to hang on his every word to get to know you."

My mouth gaped, and I shook my head. "Mother, I'm not going anywhere. I told you I want to raise my child here."

"For now!" she snapped. "What happens when you get bored with this system and want to see something new?"

"Then I'll take a proper vacation and return to my home. Mother, you have made my life so much easier. I don't need to run, because I'm no longer being forced to be someone I'm not. If Terrin wants me, then he will need to integrate into my life—our life." I chuckled at this rare moment of insecurity from her. "Why do you think he was wooing you? He wasn't manipulating you. He wasn't asking for my hand in marriage. He was trying to form a bond with you because he was asking for permission to join our family."

"You would really stay?" she asked, her brow knitted with disbelief.

"Yes." I stared at her, watching the last piece of my puzzling life fall into place.

After a long moment, she eased back into her chair and whispered, "Okay."

"Okay?" I asked.

"Tell Terrin he has my blessing."

I smiled and nearly burst out of my skin. I stood and reached across the desk to squeeze her hand. "Thank you," I said before leaving her office.

Together

As I left my mother's office, reality, as I knew it, came together into one magical cohesive image. Standing there, thinking about all potential futures—all of which finally involved Terrin—I was beyond happy. I had been content with my life and my odd family, but now, having the intimacy I craved was beyond all expectations. Terrin was the cherry on top. And what a delightfully handsome cherry he was.

Standing there like a smitten teenager, I wanted nothing more than to bask in the moment. I should have been running to announce my mother's lifted sanctions, but I could hardly do more than smile. My brain wasn't even really thinking anymore. There was just a slow love song droning on in the background, like it had always been there, but I hadn't noticed until now.

I meandered away from the office and into the courtyard beyond. I sat down on a bench and imagined my life with Terrin by my side. The chill in the air forced me to pull my feet up and huddle with my legs to keep warm, but I didn't go back inside. I wasn't ready for reality—my dreams were just as satisfying to me at the moment.

Eventually, though, reality found me.

"May I join you?" Terrin asked.

Startled by the real man, not just the imaginary one in my head, I bolted my head up and stared at him. He was looking at me with that same smugness he had earlier. Something was different about him. He wasn't just Terrin, my friend, or former bodyguard. For once and finally, he was behaving as a man, equal to me as other men.

Since I was too dumbfounded to answer, he didn't wait for permission and sat down on the bench with me. His arm fell over the back of it as he leaned into the wood. Though he wasn't touching me, I was keenly aware that his fingers were just a needle's width from my bare skin.

I realized then what was so different about Terrin. It was me. I was different.

I had spent my entire life fixated on a man who couldn't be with me. Now, it seemed, he could. I hadn't realized how much safety there was in knowing what could and could not happen between us. I was feeling exposed by this potential approaching consummation. Just as exposed as I felt standing naked at the end of Rayne's bed that first time. As ridiculous as it sounded, the thought of proper intercourse with Terrin was making me feel *re-virgin-ified*.

Terrin seemed to sense something was wrong, but didn't ask me about it. He shifted slightly, drawing his hand away from me and sitting a little more upright. "I saw you were speaking with your mother."

"Yes. She's given us her blessing."

Terrin's eyes shot to me and he strained to keep his smile at a less than gleeful height. "That's wonderful to hear." He blinked at me, no doubt discomforted by my silence. "That is wonderful, isn't it?"

"Yes," I blurted out. "It's" I searched for the right word. "...everything." Terrin put his arm back out and dragged his finger along my arm. It tickled and made me shiver. "I saw Ayil giving you hell. What was that about?"

Terrin closed his eyes and let out a rumbling groan with his next exhale. "He was under the impression my knowledge of our compatibility was of long standing—which I explained it was not," he said pointedly, in case that might have been my assumption as well. "After that, I got *the lecture*." Terrin stared out at the beautiful courtyard now lit by moonlight. "I underestimated Ayil—how much he cares for you." Terrin dragged his gaze back to me, now admiring my appearance in the moonlight. "He reminded me of your father tonight. He also gave me *the lecture.*"

"What is *the lecture*?" I said, mimicking his accentuation.

"It wasn't long after our first major blow out. The one where I spent the better part of an hour explaining my rules." Terrin rolled his eyes, no doubt realizing how ridiculous they all were and perhaps a little mad at himself for not recognizing the signs of an underlying conspiracy. "He came to visit me and said the strangest thing." Terrin looked at the ground as if trying to recall the exact phrasing. "A man can never truly defend that which he does not love." Terrin chuckled. "I thought he was rambling, so I barely paid him any attention. He started explaining that hired soldiers would never be as good as countrymen because they didn't love the land they were fighting for. There were several other examples, but at one point, he put his hand on my shoulder and when I looked at him, he said, 'For all your strength and dedication, not one drop of your blood oath will ever compare to what I would do or risk for my daughter.' That was when I realized he was threatening me."

Terrin turned to me, a certain somberness in his expression since the man he was speaking of was gone. "I didn't say anything. At the time, I think I may have considered him foolish. He just patted my shoulder and said, 'When you love her as much as I do, you won't need a blood oath to do your duty.' It was by far the most civil condescension I'd ever experienced. He had a way of maintaining his leadership without flaunting his position. I respected him for that." I wiped away a tear, and Terrin frowned. "I'm sorry, Mallory. It was not my intent to upset you."

"You didn't. It's a good memory."

"Indeed, it is. I'm a better man for having known him."

For a long moment, neither of us spoke, almost as if we were offering the silence as a tribute to my father. Despite the elephant just sitting right there on the bench with us, Terrin didn't try to close the distance between us or instigate the act that was now causing me as much anxiety as a school test.

"I want to apologize again for earlier." Terrin sat up a little straighter and focused back on the view. "I don't know what I was thinking—obviously I wasn't. I didn't want to tell you like…" Terrin motioned back to the ballroom. "…that. I had a much more romantic scene in mind back when I had hopes of gaining your mother's affection." Terrin rubbed his temples. "I'm thoroughly embarrassed and I'm sorry I had to put you through that—through all of this. I should have just told you the minute—the second I knew."

"How long have you known?"

"I noticed something odd about Kessler's data on Inferno—I recognized one enzyme in your system. I hadn't thought much of it since you had a lot of abnormalities, but then on the battlerunner—when you cut yourself on my spurs, the blood caused some of them to retract. I wanted to experiment more, but you sent me away. Since I didn't want to get your hopes up, I opted not to explain. After the coup, I consulted with Dr. Kessler. He ran some tests and determined that you do indeed carry the enzyme."

I set aside my questions about the enzyme; I moved on to more pressing issues. "Why did you leave then?" Terrin's face flashed with guilt. "I was hurting in more ways than one, and you were gone when I woke up. I know I told you to leave, but if we were compatible, then every demurral and dismissal would have been forgotten."

Terrin took in a deep breath. "Tell me how you feel right now. Be honest, what's going through your mind now that you know I can be with you?"

"Happy," I said immediately.

"And?"

I frowned, not wanting to give him my full honesty, but knowing he was trying to make his argument for leaving. "Terrified and a little sick to my stomach," I whispered.

Terrin nodded, showing no offense to the result of my raw emotions. "I left because I was overwhelmed. And because I still wasn't sure if Rayne was out of the picture. And I wanted to give some thought to what you had said. I had to think about the consequences of being with you. I had to determine if I was okay with never fathering a child."

"Are you?" I asked, trying not to place any hope in his answer.

"I was, but then you said you and Ayil were considering having a child and I realized if I joined this family maybe I could have a similar arrangement, should I change my mind. Assuming you would approve of being an adoptive mother."

I nodded and laughed. "I think it would be nice to have a little green devil running around here."

Terrin chuckled. "What a strange group we would be?"

"So, you've considered what life would be like here: my mother, Ayil, two rambunctious preteens, and a screaming baby."

Terrin leaned in to whisper to me, "You forgot to mention the beautiful wife I would get to wake up next to."

My face bloomed with heat, and I clutched my knees even tighter. "I thought gattaw didn't marry."

Terrin rocked his hand as he groaned. "We have a blood ceremony designed to constitute mutual commitment. I think it would be considered an equivalent to marriage."

"Oh, goody, more bloodletting. Count me out."

Terrin tipped his head back and let out a bass laugh. "Actually, you've already participated in it."

"What?"

"The day my father died. You took my knife and cut yourself with it. Our blood was shed together by the same blade and on sacred ground. That was the blood ceremony."

"But we didn't... I didn't... Does that mean...?"

"Yes, it means by the standards of my culture we are married and have been since we left Miorita." I stared blankly at him and he held my gaze, a brazen smirk on his face as he watched me come to terms with once again unknowingly being attached to a man I hadn't intended to marry. My anxiety rose, and I looked away to calm myself with some deep breaths.

"I have questions."

"Okay."

"Lots of questions."

"Why don't we walk a little? You look chilled." He stood and offered me a hand up, after which he shimmied out of his dinner jacket and offered it to me. I slid my arms into it, feeling Terrin's residual heat like a warm embrace. I noted the familiar scent that appealed to me like cologne and a welcoming home fire. "Better?" he asked.

"Much."

He extended the crook of his elbow and I clung to him as we walked. "I really am so happy we aren't incompatible, but there's a small part of me that doesn't believe—doesn't trust. Not that you would lie, but maybe you just got some misinformation."

"I understand, and that is perhaps why I didn't outright tell you, but any doubt I had was laid to rest earlier. I am now one hundred percent confident in your body's ability to accept me."

I gave him a crooked smile, not entirely sure if that statement sounded romantic or clinical.

"Do you remember our discussion about the bite? Why I was inclined to bite you?"

"Yes."

"It's true the gattaw bite their mates as a symbol of love and I would be lying if some men, myself included, didn't view it a little more like..." He trailed off, not wanting to finish his sentence.

"Ownership?" I asked, but withheld any judgment.

His head sagged, and he sighed. "I wish there was another word for what it feels like—obligation, devotion…" He shook his head. "No, I'm afraid I do want to possess you, Mallory." He looked at me, begging for forgiveness even as he confessed his avarice. "I want more than ever to keep you all to myself."

"Do I have to call you master?" I said rather mirthlessly. "You will have to share me with Destiny and Ayil and—"

Terrin pulled me close, not allowing me to continue making light of his admission. "You know what I'm talking about, Mallory," he said earnestly, commanding my attention. "Tell me once and for all that Rayne is out of your life. Tell me you choose me."

"I choose you," I said without hesitation, and he relaxed. "You don't have to bite me to possess me, Terrin. I was yours long before I knew what that actually meant."

Terrin reached forward and caressed my cheek. He let his fingers drag down my neck and onto my chest. His descent stopped, and he suddenly pulled away. "Let's see, where was I? Oh, yes, the bite." He patted my fingers, as if to check my attachment to him, before walking on through the colonnade surrounding the courtyard. "The tradition of biting was never meant to represent possession. That was just a byproduct. It was actually meant as a sign of protection."

"How much do you know about gattaw reproduction?" He looked at me and I instantly went red, I didn't want to admit how many times I had looked up the details of penal spurs and cervical abrasion impregnation, trying to find a loophole—as if I was the only woman trying to grow a bullet-proof vagina. Terrin seemed to glean the reason for my sudden shyness and coughed away a chuckle. "I mean, have you explored the pregnancy aspect of it?"

"No, I stopped taking interest in gattaw anatomy after penal spurs."

Terrin let out a quiet harrumph. "If only." He pinched my side, making me squirm. "Had you bothered to read any farther than penal sheaths, you might have found that the female gattaw, during pregnancy, begins shedding an enzyme that we call lorathin. Very loosely translated, it means the blood of life." I nodded, not surprised that blood was once again symbolic, even in reproduction. "It's a temporary protection mechanism for the fetus. Since penal spurs could damage it or break the mucous plug, it's necessary to abate or prevent their extension."

I stopped and released his arm so we could speak face to face. "The lora..."

"Lorathin."

"The lorathin is an enzyme that prevents the spurs from coming out?"

"It's a lot like goosebumps on humans." Terrin lifted my hand and pushed the jacket sleeve up to reveal my arm. He trailed his finger gently along the skin, tickling the little hairs. Between that and the chill in the air, I quickly broke out in gooseflesh. "The stimulation of intercourse causes the penal follicles to activate. The arrector muscles contract and the spurs discharge like claws." Terrin flared his hand like a claw before gently dragging his hard nails along my forearm. "This abrasive treatment is exceptionally stimulating for a gattaw female, but as you know, such an intercourse is much too painful for the delicate flesh of the human woman." He leaned down and kissed one of the very slight scratch marks he had left on my arm. "So, we must calm the muscle contraction of the follicles and keep them at bay." Terrin rubbed my arm, warming it and calming my bumpy flesh. "That way, the receiving female, whomever she might be, can enjoy the unrestricted momentum of her partner's thrusts."

Terrin barely got the last word out before I leaped on him. I smothered his lips with a demanding kiss. He fell back slightly, possibly even defensively, since my advance was more attack than embrace. He growled under my lips as he pulled me closer. I pushed my tongue into his mouth and he grunted—as if surprised by it. I felt a column press to my back, and I released his lips. "Take me now, Terrin," I rasped, now panting from my racing heart. "I can't wait, please."

"We are completely exposed here, Mallory."

"I don't care," I whispered and reached down, fondling the length that was pressing against my leg. I couldn't feel any spurs yet, so I boldly massaged his girth.

He growled and captured my wrist. He pushed my hand tight against my hip. He lassoed my other wrist even as I tried to take over where I had left off. With my hands no longer functional, I took over with my mouth. I leaned into his neck, kissing, licking, and nibbling along his throat. "Do female gattaw ever bite their males?"

I felt his laugh against my lips. I dragged my tongue down his sternum as far as I could while in my confinement. When I reached the end of my leash, I retracted and looked into his hooded eyes. "Release me," I whispered as seductively as I had ever said two words in my life. "Let me give you what you want. What we both want." I leaned in slowly to kiss him, but instead of a kiss, I slid my tongue across his lower lip.

Terrin exhaled and shoved me back, pushing me firmly against the column behind me. "No," he said between clenched teeth. "I will not do this. Even if I didn't fear your mother's wrath for such untoward behavior, I will not claim you out here like an animal unable to control myself. I've waited this long. The least I can do is take you in a proper bed. Or at least behind a closed door."

I melted against the pillar, feeling defeated. I resented being scolded, but he was right. I was being extremely inappropriate. Our love did not need to be on display like a pornographic play. "I'm sorry. I didn't mean to make you angry."

Terrin's eyes widened, and then he released my wrists, shifting his grip to my waist. "Oh, Mallory, this is not anger. I am flattered by your passion and I would never deny you your pleasure, but..." He stepped back and looked around. "I must be careful."

"Careful?" I asked, unsure he was still speaking about my mother.

"I need to finish my explanation about the bite. That is assuming you can control yourself," he mocked.

I gave him a sour glare. "Then stop talking about thrusts and erections."

"Arrectors."

"Whatever."

Terrin offered his arm again, and I took it even though I still wanted to nibble my way down his chest. "Who knew a biology lesson would get you in the mood?"

"That was not a biology lesson and you know it. If you don't want to get eaten, don't poke the bear."

Terrin smiled. "Indeed."

We walked through a darkened alley that opened into yet another courtyard. This one had a fountain that sounded like a babbling brook. I broke away from Terrin and moved to sit on the edge of the koi pond beneath it. The large stone flat and cold was very familiar to me. As I stared down at the same fish I had looked at when I was a child, I considered more than a few things about my future with Terrin. At first, it was just little things, like how I might fit his clothing into my closet. Should I move Destiny into a private nursery rather than continue to use the sound dampener? But then my thoughts turned to more serious matters—the cultural differences and how people might see our interspecies relationship. Then my thoughts turned to something Sicily said.

"What if I'm not enough?" I blurted out.

When I looked at Terrin for the answer, I found him standing on the edge of the pond, watching me. I was almost sure he hadn't taken his eyes off me since I sat down. I was certainly used to him monitoring me, but this was different. He was watching me, admiring me, and longing for me. It was almost disconcerting. "Pardon?" he asked, his head tilting as if he might not have heard me over the trickling water.

I felt bile rise in my throat as I tried to phrase my question in a way that wasn't layered with ethnocentric judgment. "Will you be taking multiple wives?" I pushed the words out as fast as I could, trying to keep them from catching on the lump in my throat.

Terrin's face blanked and his body went slack. He stumbled back a step before catching himself. His concerned eyes showed another potential scolding, but he restrained himself, undoubtedly seeing my anxiety. He sat down on the rock across from me. "Why would you ask me that?" He spoke gently, notably not answering my question.

I swallowed hard. "Sicily said some gattaw males take several mates to keep them satisfied."

"Ah." Terrin's head tipped back with realization. His mouth turned up into an odd smirk as he scratched his neck. "And you thought listening to my ex-girlfriend would be a reliable source for information on gattaw mating."

"So, they aren't polygynists?" I asked.

"Some are—as are some humans," he added, reminding me that gattaw were far from the first to value resources over monogamy. "In all my years, you are the only woman I have ever bitten," he pointed out. "You are the only one I have ever risked my life for and broken a blood oath for." He stared at me, trying to impress upon me the sacrifices he had already made to prove his love to me.

"I know. I don't doubt your devotion, but I'm not designed for you. What if suppressing your spurs makes our love making less pleasurable for you? What if I can't... satisfy you?"

Terrin sat for a moment staring into the fountain, his fist resting against his mouth, his teeth latched onto the knuckle of his index finger. Eventually, he turned back to me and spoke. "I understand why you would be concerned, but you are woefully mistaken." He smiled at me as if I was so very naïve. He must have realized he was pissing me off, because he straightened his mouth and started speaking in a more edifying tone.

"As we just discussed, females of my species are very much stimulated by the penal spurs. It's frequently why you don't see male humans and female gattaw together. Even when you do, I seriously doubt they don't utilize some prosthesis to accomplish the task. During times of pregnancy, a female gattaw endures a less than satisfactory sex life, but for the males it becomes more enjoyable." Terrin looked at me, as if checking to see if I was listening.

"It's better?"

"Not that a male doesn't derive a great deal of pleasure during normal sexual intercourse, but according to every gattaw I know, the stimulation of an unfettered intercourse is..." Terrin looked away from me as if unable to focus on his words. "I have not had the pleasure myself, but it is a well-known fact." Terrin sighed and shook his head. "So much so that the gattaw have a very nasty history of rape." He looked at me, as if taking full responsibility for the shame of this history.

"Pregnant intercourse is so sought after that men will risk life and limb to get access to a woman with child. That is the origin of the bite. That is why a man walks in front of his wife instead of with her. The blooming belly of pregnancy must be shielded from other men. It also gives the male a chance to eyeball the approaching men, so he sees who might be taking an interest in his mate. And the bite on the back of the neck signals to any man glancing from behind that she is not without protection. That any attempt to molest her would be met with significant opposition."

"In the case of a single mother—where her mate has died or abandoned her—the female's father will actually bite her. I've even seen a widowed mother bite her widowed, pregnant daughter. And in the same tradition, she would walk behind her mother in the marketplace to hide her belly." Terrin looked at me, pride brimming in his eyes. "You would be hard pressed to find any man willing to combat a mother protecting her daughter. That is not a battle most gattaw males could win. So, you see, it was never meant to be about control or ownership. It is about love and loyalty." Terrin shifted from his rock and kneeled before me, cupping my hands in his.

"Mallory, the enzyme your body produces cannot be synthesized. You are producing it at high levels—meaning my follicle response will be completely nullified. You'll be in no danger of a single cut. It's also permanently in your system. And also aberrant to female gattaw, you have the enzyme in your blood, sweat, and... saliva." Terrin glanced away as he said saliva as if embarrassed by what potential pleasure that might offer him. "Although I am unfamiliar with the benefits of this enzyme, I think I can safely say I will be a slave to the pleasures you provide me."

Seeing the ardor in Terrin's eyes rallied my ego. He looked at me as if I were the greatest gift he had ever received. Perhaps I was. "Are you saying I've had this enzyme in me the whole time?"

Terrin nodded. "It was a byproduct of Kessler adding gattaw DNA into your genome. Just as you are resistant to sickness, you are also resistant to... me."

"All this time, we've been fighting our desires, and I didn't have to worry."

"It would have been a very different trip back to Brahama after I collected your bounty had I known." He slid his thumb across my hand. "But, all for the best. Since, without our lengthy wait, you would not have become a mother."

I nodded, agreeing that the minor deviation was worth it. "Still, what are the chances of you meeting a human with gattaw DNA? Maybe I'm your frog princess, after all."

Terrin smirked and closed his eyes as if to relish the thought of his very own happily ever after. "As much as I would like to look at this from the perspective of a love story, I'm afraid I can't." He moved from his kneeling position in front of me and sat next to me on my rock. "The truth is, Mallory, you were not magically created to provide this green man with a mate. You have this ability independent of my participation. You could provide this pleasure to any gattaw."

I scoffed, just as stunned by this statement as he must have been by my suggestion of polygyny. I shifted to look at him, my knees banging into his. "I would never! You're the one I love. I've never even considered another gattaw for a mate," I assured him.

"I know you haven't, but that doesn't mean they might not take you from me."

"I could never love another the way I do you. Nothing another man could do could woo me away from you."

Terrin reached up and pressed a finger to my lips, not to shush me, but to trace his finger along my lip. "Those words are music to my ears, and I loathe to ruin this romantic moment. I would much rather kiss these lips than darken your mood." He retracted and stood. He reached back, offering me his hand. "You are still looking at this like a fairytale and I need you to stop." I huffed and slapped my hand into his, not liking the sound of this part of his lesson.

He wrapped my arm in his, and we walked again. "When I say another might wish to take you from me, I do not mean he will entice you. If he would risk life and limb to have a pregnant gattaw who—by no small stretch—is much stronger than a human woman, then you, my love, would be no match to stop him." I frowned and huddled against his arm, suddenly feeling very cold. "I don't want to scare you, Mallory, but I do need you to understand something. You would be very valuable to a gattaw. There is not a one I think that wouldn't kill to have you. I know you are used to being coveted for your DNA, but this would be a much different type of predator."

I nodded. "I understand," I said, hoping he would stop talking, but, like most of Terrin's lessons, they weren't finished until he beat them into my memory.

He guided me inside and we headed up the nearest set of stairs. "As your mate, I accept the responsibility of caring for you. That includes defending you against other men. Should a gattaw discover your... condition, I will kill him." I glanced at him, surprised he was just outright telling me of his plans to murder. This conversation was sounding more like I was speaking with Rayne.

"However, I don't relish that thought. That's why I am going to ask you to do a few things to assist my efforts in protecting you." I nodded, more or less giving him permission to outline his rules. "You will *never* return to Miorita." The emphasis on never was undeniable and since I had no reason or desire to go there again, I nodded. "Because of the improbability of a satisfactory union between us, our relationship cannot be made public." I frowned, not liking the prospect of denying my love. However, I understood why he wouldn't want to draw attention to us being together. "And finally, while outside of these walls, I will not act as your mate, but as your bodyguard. I think it would also be wise to allow people to believe you and Ayil are a couple." I especially didn't like the idea of going back to having Terrin as my bodyguard, but again, I understood his purpose. "Okay," I mumbled, acquiescing to whatever Terrin wanted.

Having finally made it to my bedroom, I pushed inside and immediately sat down on the edge of my bed to take my heels off. Feeling deflated and once again without control of my love life, I pouted, not even deigning to look at Terrin.

He shut the door, being sure to lock it before joining me on the bed. He pulled his dinner jacket off my shoulders and began rubbing my back. His fingers dragged across my bare skin above the dress's fabric. "You know I wouldn't ask this of you if I didn't believe there was a significant danger."

"Yes," I grumbled. I sounded like a spoiled child who was complaining about not being allowed to have sprinkles. Never mind that I already had ice cream and chocolate syrup, I still wanted the sprinkles.

His fingers stopped at the midway point in my back. "Is there anything I can do to make up for ruining your night?" He pinched the zipper on my dress and slid it down to reveal my lower back. His warm hands caressed my exposed skin. I closed my eyes and embraced the moment. It was the calm before the storm. The wind was stirring and the sound of distant thunder warned that there was trouble coming.

I turned to him, our faces just inches apart. I reached out and touched his face, letting my fingers glide along the scaled skin of his jaw. The skin along his neck was softer like leather. "I've wanted to do this for so long."

"As have I," he whispered.

I shook my head. "No, this. Touching you. I've longed to just... feel you."

The corner of Terrin's mouth tipped up at my transfixed state. He reached up and undid the buttons on his black shirt and vest before slipping them off. He dropped them on the floor next to my high heels. "I am yours to explore, my love."

My eyes roved over his broad shoulders, strong biceps, and sinewy chest. Even in this seated position, he was a pinnacle of strength.

As I dragged my fingers down his sternum and across his pectoral muscles, I could feel his heat. A core temperature that could tolerate the mercurial temperatures of the desert.

I shifted my hand to his stomach to feel the silken texture of his small scales. His chest rose higher now, vigilant of my proximity to his velvet skin.

I looked at him as I tickled the skin just above his belt. "Lie back," I whispered.

He swallowed hard, but did as I instructed, leaning against his elbows so he could still monitor me. I unbuckled his belt, and he cleared his throat. "Mallory," he whispered to me.

I hushed him and slowly—very slowly—lowered his zipper. I trailed my hand down the last of his silky skin until I reached the smoothest skin on his body. Terrin grunted as I took him in hand, rubbing his hardening length. He panted heavily as his desire awakened.

"Careful." He raised a trembling hand to stop my manipulation just before his full arousal pushed his spurs to the surface.

More fascinated than afraid of the incompatible portion of his erection, I examined the design a little closer. It was not Terrin's insertion that would cause me pain, but his withdrawal. Each keratin spine would lift, dragging against the tender lining of my anatomy.

Still not entirely convinced that my kiss could cure my frog prince, I dragged my tongue across his shaft. His stomach tensed as I did, but I remained focused on the outcome of my experiment. His spurs retracted almost immediately, quelled by the magical enzyme that I alone permanently possessed.

I finally looked at him, noting the look of pride and subdued joy on his face. I returned those sentiments tenfold, feeling emboldened by the one truly superhuman trait I possessed.

I had been a disappointment through most of my life in one form or another. I had hurt Terrin—leading him on and then denying him more than once. Our tumultuous relationship had been inappropriate, inadequate, and indecorous. But now, looking back, I could see that it was enduring, unbreakable, and uncompromising.

Terrin may not have believed this was a fairytale, but I knew in my heart that we were meant for each other. And I was about to prove it to him.

A threat nestled itself in my ardent gaze. He noticed my change of demeanor and his brow dipped, questioning my sudden shift in mood. I reached forward and grabbed the base of his girth. He reached out and touched my hand as if to stop me, but I wasn't asking for his permission. I was demanding his attention. I wanted him to see me strike this match. I wanted to set him afire just to watch him burn.

With little to no warning, I descended my mouth on him, enveloping the head of his erection. He gasped and sat upright. "Mallory," he scolded me. "Don't!" He grasped my head as if he might rip me away, but as my mouth descended onto his length, his breathing became ragged and his objections became stuttered and incomprehensible.

I held him in my mouth for a beat, allowing my saliva to subdue his spurs. Then I slid my lips back up his phallus. He shuddered and cussed in Gattish as I began to languidly, but rhythmically, suckle his tip.

The grip he had on my head shifted to my neck. He cleared the hair from his view and rubbed his thumb across the scar and tattoo covering it. He started whispering something in Gattish. I didn't understand a word of it, but it sounded like he was... praying.

I chose that moment to take him in again, forcing a lamented groan to push from his lips. "I want to be with you, Mallory. I've spent far too much time imagining your legs wrapped around me to deny myself or you that pleasure." When I didn't stop and instead increased my pressure, he squeezed my shoulder, his claw-like nails digging into my skin. "Insolent woman," he said through clenched teeth. "Why must you always defy me?"

He squirmed beneath me, one hand twisting in my comforter and the other gripping the back of my neck. "Mallory, you must stop," he said in a more beseeching tone. "I can't endure this. I won't be able to pleasure you if you don't stop."

Much as I ignored his demands, I had no interest in his pleas for mercy. He had already given me a glimpse of the pleasures he could provide. I planned to do the same for him.

"Mallory," he tried one last time to dispute my disobedience, but he lost the argument shortly after. His breathing hastened and his thighs tensed. He let out a roaring groan as his body spasmed, bucking against my mouth and flooding it with his surprisingly hot discharge.

I made quick work of cleaning myself off before toppling onto the bed with Terrin. As proud as I was of my achievement, he seemed positively distraught—panting and shaking.

"Are you okay?" I asked, legitimately concerned that I had somehow hurt him.

He turned a worried expression on me. "That was the most exquisite experience. Thank you."

I smirked and stroked his face, which was a good deal cooler—most likely because of his panting breaths.

"You shouldn't have wasted my vigor, my love. It may be some time before I can properly bed you."

"That's okay. There's always tomorrow."

He let out a low rumbling chuckle, then kicked off his shoes and scooted himself further onto my bed. I assisted with the removal of his pants, leaving him naked on my bed. "Your turn." He indicated my dress, which I hadn't yet removed. I slipped off the bed and did my best to slither out of the fabric sexily.

"All of it," Terrin commanded when I tried to climb back onto the bed with my underthings still on. I rolled my eyes, but removed my bra and panties as ordered.

"Turn around." Terrin swirled his finger.

I scoffed. "What? Why?"

"Because I want to gaze upon the woman I love."

I blinked at his earnest declaration and slowly turned around so he could admire my body as freely as I had his. When I turned back, I saw hunger in his gaze. "What were you saying before? Not the cuss words, but the prayers?"

"Prayers?" Terrin's brow lifted with surprise. "You give me too much credit, Mallory. The words I was speaking were far from godly."

"What did you say?" I asked as I crawled back onto the bed.

He raised his chin, sucking in a deep breath. "I don't think you are ready to hear the ramblings of a gattaw male on the verge of ecstasy."

"That bad?" I crawled up alongside of him and settled into the crook of his welcoming arm. I rested my head on his chest and listened to the steady beat of his heart as his body warmed me.

"Gattaw are not known for being gentle lovers. Since our partners are usually as aggressive, it isn't a problem."

"Does that mean you prefer rough sex?" I asked, suddenly concerned that I was still not going to live up to the standards of a gattaw female.

Terrin reached down and tugged my face to look at him. "I prefer whatever you prefer. If there is one thing that is universal between gattaw and human males, it is that we will do whatever it takes to please our mates." Terrin leaned downed and kissed me softly—demonstrating his capacity for gentleness.

I lay against Terrin's chest for some time. As I listened to his beating heart, I felt at ease. My life—such as it could ever be—was tranquil. Everything finally made sense—the destinies that were forced upon me had finally abated and the futures I had imagined for myself were solidifying around me. I was where I wanted to be. I was with the people I wanted to be with. But most importantly, I had become the woman I wanted to be—undefined by prophecies or titles. I was free.

Terrin's chest rumbled with quiet laughter. "You're not falling asleep, are you?"

"Hmm," I said, clearly not awake.

He shifted beneath me and rolled me over onto my back. He looked down at me and made a clicking noise with his tongue. "In my culture, it's tradition for a first mating to last several hours."

"Hours? I thought you were spent."

Terrin smirked at me. "Sorry to disappoint, but I'm not even near done with you tonight." He leaned down and kissed my neck as he centered himself between my legs. He moved his kisses down to my breasts and I arched to receive him. When

I could hardly wait any longer, he placed himself against my entrance and gazed at me.

This was the penultimate step in our relationship and, much like me, he was not stopping to gain my permission. He was warning me that it was his turn to light the fire, but this time we would both burn. With his eyes locked on mine, he pushed forward, and I discovered my frog had been a prince all along.

Want More Spice?

Craving a little more romance?
Check out **After Dark** on my website to read additional love scenes between Terrin and Mallory.

Thank you for reading.

THE WARDEN

SUCCESSO

FELICIA JEDLICKA

THE WARDEN
Successors

Somewhere in depths of the arctic circle lies a prison that holds as many secrets as it does monsters.

Thrust into the secret world of supernatural criminal containment, Ethan and Cori do their best to serve the prison's warden and acclimate to life as they now know it. While Ethan thrives under Danato's effort to mold him into the next warden, Cori's independent nature rebels against the intemperate man at every turn.

As the plus one in the warden's effort to expand his personnel, Cori finds that the honor of her servitude to this enigmatic man will involve a lot of shit-shoveling. And that's not a metaphor. Benefiting from the freedom of her janitorial duties, she recruits a lovestruck werewolf to escape her captivity. Though a death sentence according to the prison rules, Danato is reluctant to be responsible for the death of yet another woman he has grown to care for.

After another of life's poetic misfortunes brings Cori back to the prison, she finds herself at square one. Newly motivated by despair, she is determined to make the best of her situation, just like Ethan. Unfortunately, her lofty pursuit to steal the wardenship steps on more than a few toes. While Cori has been living a normal life, Ethan has blossomed into a man worthy of leading the prison. His resentment of Cori's twice-over betrayal leaves him vulnerable to the many creatures in the prison that can't be contained behind bars. Cori and Ethan will soon learn how lesser demons deal with broken hearts.

Thank you so much for reading. I hope you
enjoyed the ride and if you aren't getting off here,
I encourage you to sign up for my newsletter
so I can return your generosity with new release
updates and special offers.

Sign-Up

You can also find me on Facebook or visit my
website. Keep reading!

Website

Facebook

About the Author

As a Nebraska native, and a small-town girl at that, I have very little to occupy my time beyond imagining a world outside of my reality. By the grace of God and the seat of my pants, I have kept my waning attention span on the task of becoming an author.

So here I am, an indie author, peddling my words in cyberspace and enduring my comeuppances with an unwavering determination. I may not be a professional, and I certainly am not perfect, but if you've made it this far, you have to admit, this smartass yokel spins quite a yarn.

From the self-inflicted sweatshop conditions of my unairconditioned childhood home, to the arthritis reaping positions of a sedentary lifestyle, I bring to you: my sarcasm, my oddity, and my heart. Take it with a grain of salt or a teaspoon of sugar, but take it for what it is: a story born of the mind, translated to paper, and gifted to you.

I thank you for your readership and even more for your support. Please recommend this book to your friends and family via any social media that you use. Word of mouth is still the best advertising and is greatly appreciated.

Most importantly, keep reading. I'll keep writing.

www.ingramcontent.com/pod-product-compliance
Lightning Source LLC
Chambersburg PA
CBHW011437200726
48289CB00009BA/2790